REAVER™

CREATED BY JUSTIN JORDAN & REBEKAH ISAACS

JUSTIN JORDAN
Writer, Creator

NIKO HENRICHON
Artist

CLAYTON COWLES
Letterer

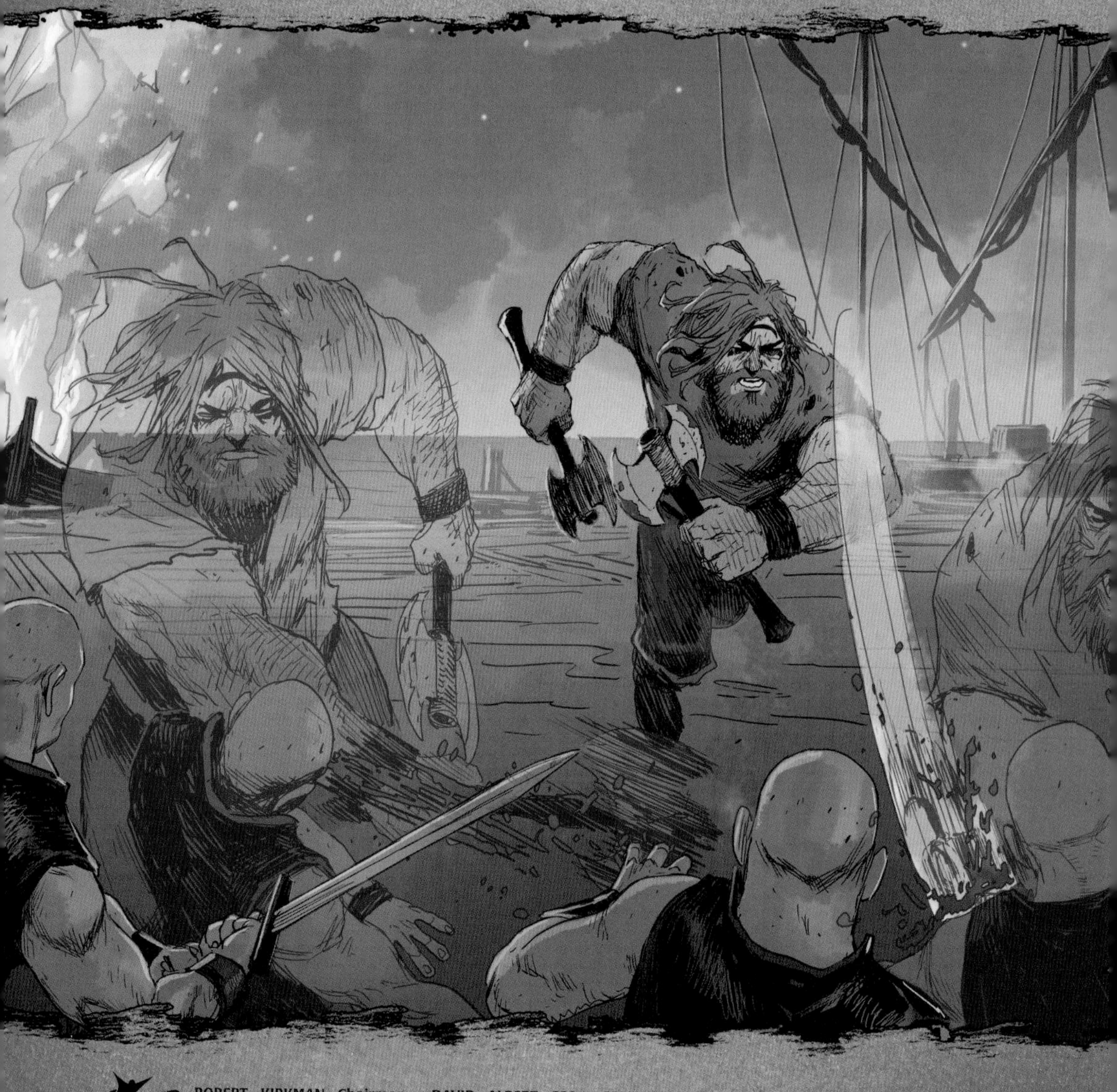

ROBERT KIRKMAN Chairman DAVID ALPERT CEO SEAN MACKIEWICZ SVP, Editor-in-Chief SHAWN KIRKHAM SVP, Business Development BRIAN HUNTINGTON VP, Online Content SHAUNA WYNNE Publicity Director ANDRES JUAREZ Art Director ALEX ANTONE Senior Editor JON MOISAN Editor ARIELLE BASICH Associate Editor CARINA TAYLOR Graphic Designer PAUL SHIN Business Development Manager JOHNNY O'DELL Social Media Manager DAN PETERSEN Sr. Director of Operations & Events Foreign Rights Inquiries ag@sequentialrights.com Other Licensing Inquiries contact@skybound.com www.skybound.com

IMAGE COMICS, INC. TODD MCFARLANE President JIM VALENTINO Vice President MARC SILVESTRI Chief Executive Officer ERIK LARSEN Chief Financial Officer ROBERT KIRKMAN Chief Operating Officer ERIC STEPHENSON Publisher / Chief Creative Officer SHANNA MATUSZAK Editorial Coordinator MARLA EIZIK Talent Liaison NICOLE LAPALME Controller LEANNA CAUNTER Accounting Analyst SUE KORPELA Accounting & HR Manager JEFF BOISON Director of Sales & Publishing Planning DIRK WOOD Director of International Sales & Licensing ALEX COX Director of Direct Market & Speciality Sales CHLOE RAMOS-PETERSON Book Market & Library Sales Manager EMILIO BAUTISTA Digital Sales Coordinator KAT SALAZAR Director of PR & Marketing DREW FITZGERALD Marketing Content Associate HEATHER DOORNINK Production Director DREW GILL Art Director HILARY DILORETO Print Manager TRICIA RAMOS Traffic Manager ERIKA SCHNATZ Senior Production Artist RYAN BREWER Production Artist DEANNA PHELPS Production Artist www.imagecomics.com

JON MOISAN
Editor

BECKY CLOONAN
Cover Artist

ANDRES JUAREZ
Logo Design

CARINA TAYLOR
Production Design

REAVER VOLUME 2. FIRST PRINTING. November 2020. Published by Image Comics, Inc. Office of publication: 2701 NW Vaughn St., Ste. 780, Portland, OR 97210. Copyright © 2020 Skybound, LLC. Originally published in single magazine form as REAVER™ #7-11. REAVER™ (including all prominent characters featured herein), its logo and all character likenesses are trademarks of Skybound, LLC, unless otherwise noted. Image Comics® and its logos are

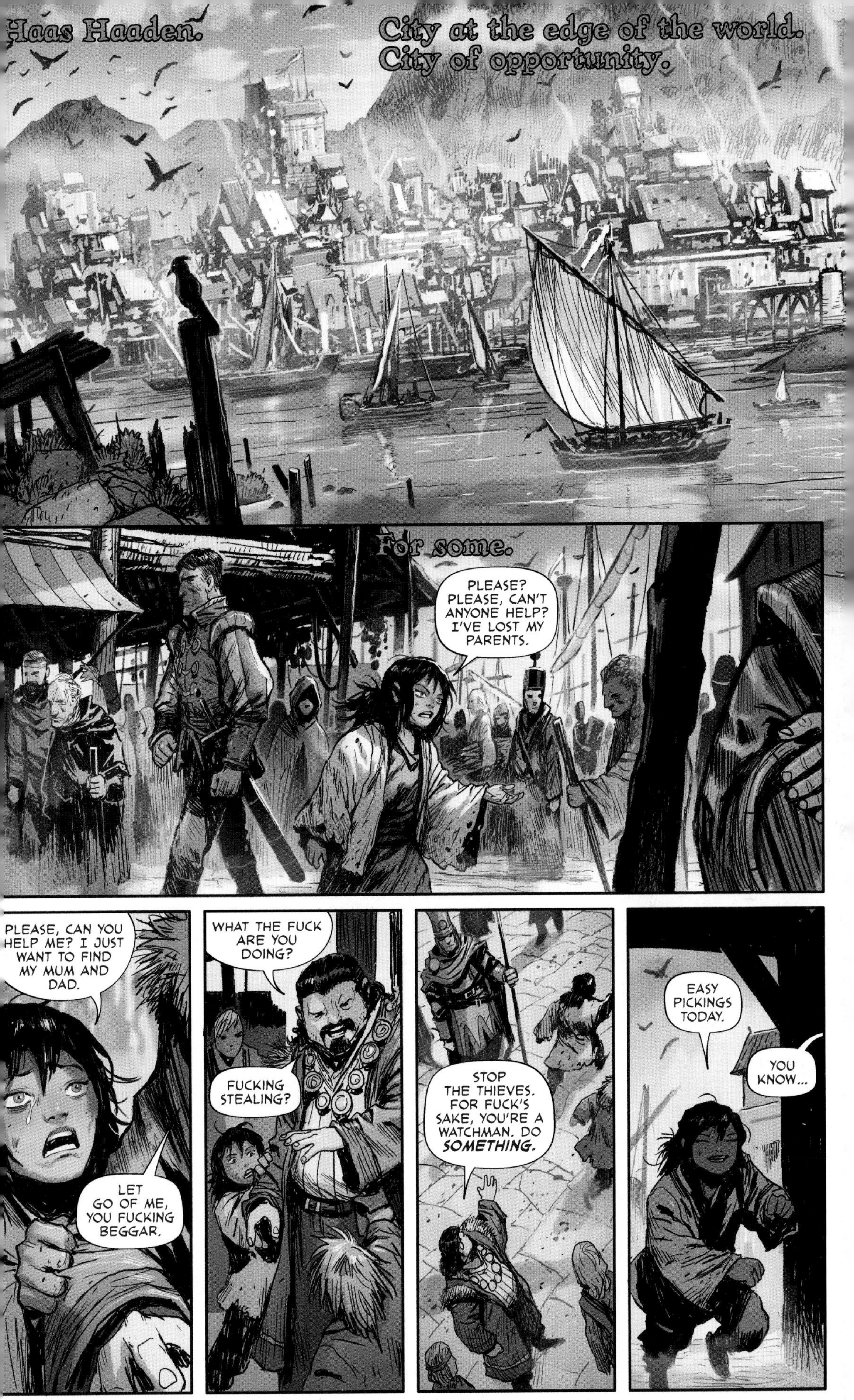
Haas Haaden.
City at the edge of the world. City of opportunity.
For some.
PLEASE? PLEASE, CAN'T ANYONE HELP? I'VE LOST MY PARENTS.
PLEASE, CAN YOU HELP ME? I JUST WANT TO FIND MY MUM AND DAD.
LET GO OF ME, YOU FUCKING BEGGAR.
WHAT THE FUCK ARE YOU DOING?
FUCKING STEALING?
STOP THE THIEVES. FOR FUCK'S SAKE, YOU'RE A WATCHMAN. DO *SOMETHING.*
EASY PICKINGS TODAY.
YOU KNOW...

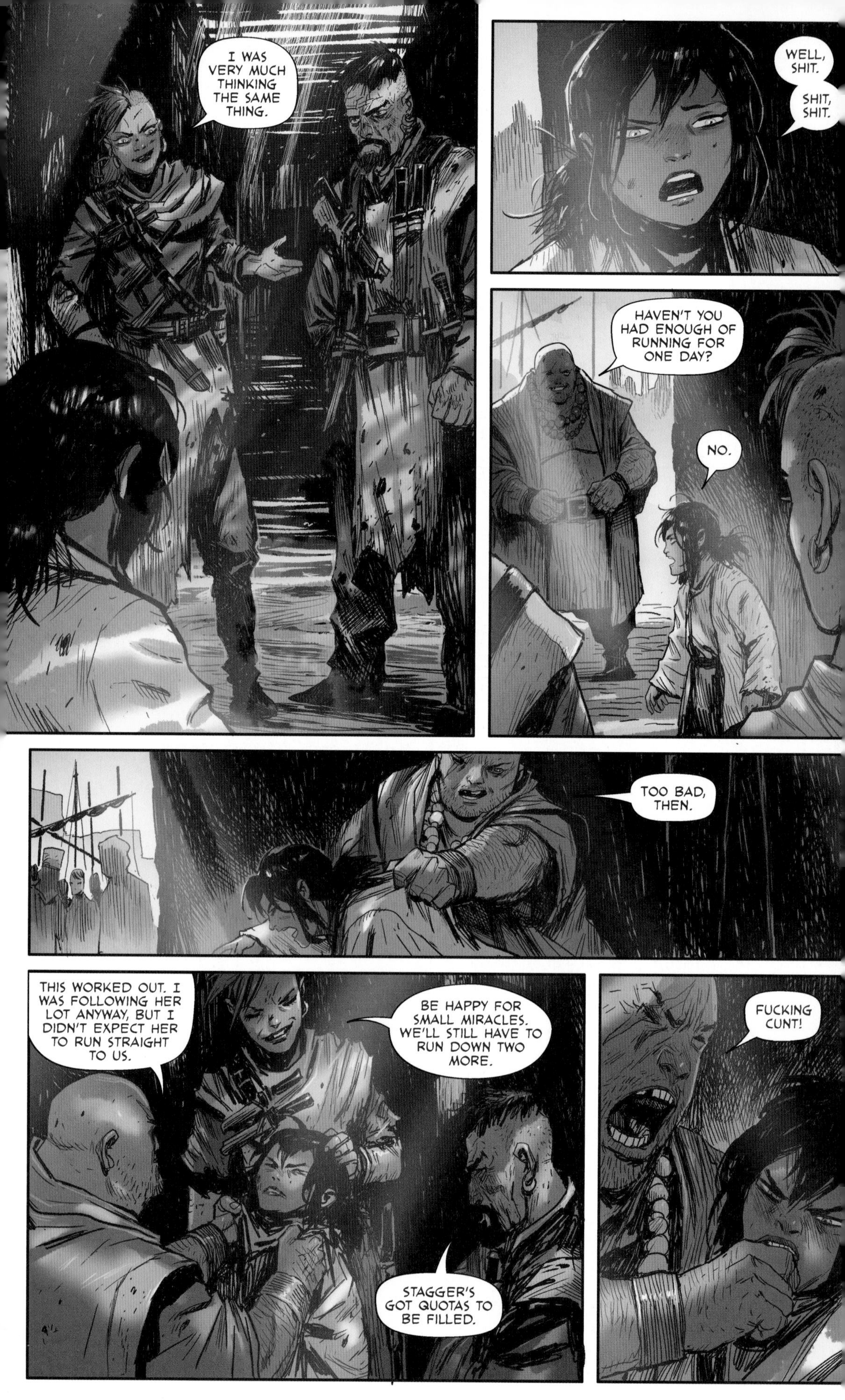
I WAS VERY MUCH THINKING THE SAME THING.
WELL, SHIT.
SHIT, SHIT.
HAVEN'T YOU HAD ENOUGH OF RUNNING FOR ONE DAY?
NO.
TOO BAD, THEN.
THIS WORKED OUT. I WAS FOLLOWING HER LOT ANYWAY, BUT I DIDN'T EXPECT HER TO RUN STRAIGHT TO US.
BE HAPPY FOR SMALL MIRACLES. WE'LL STILL HAVE TO RUN DOWN TWO MORE.
STAGGER'S GOT QUOTAS TO BE FILLED.
FUCKING CUNT!

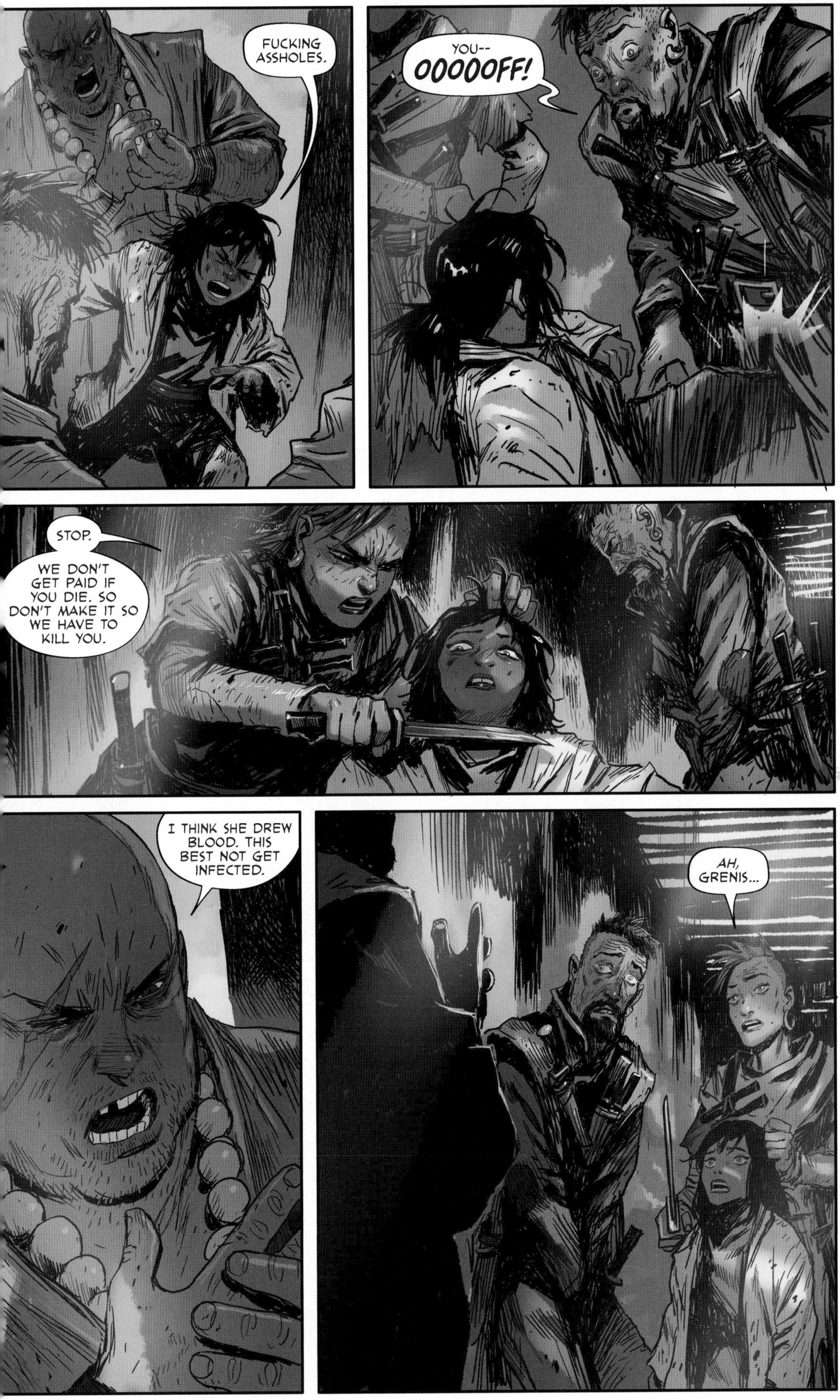
FUCKING ASSHOLES.
YOU-- OOOOOFF!
STOP.
WE DON'T GET PAID IF YOU DIE. SO DON'T MAKE IT SO WE HAVE TO KILL YOU.
I THINK SHE DREW BLOOD. THIS BEST NOT GET INFECTED.
AH, GRENIS...

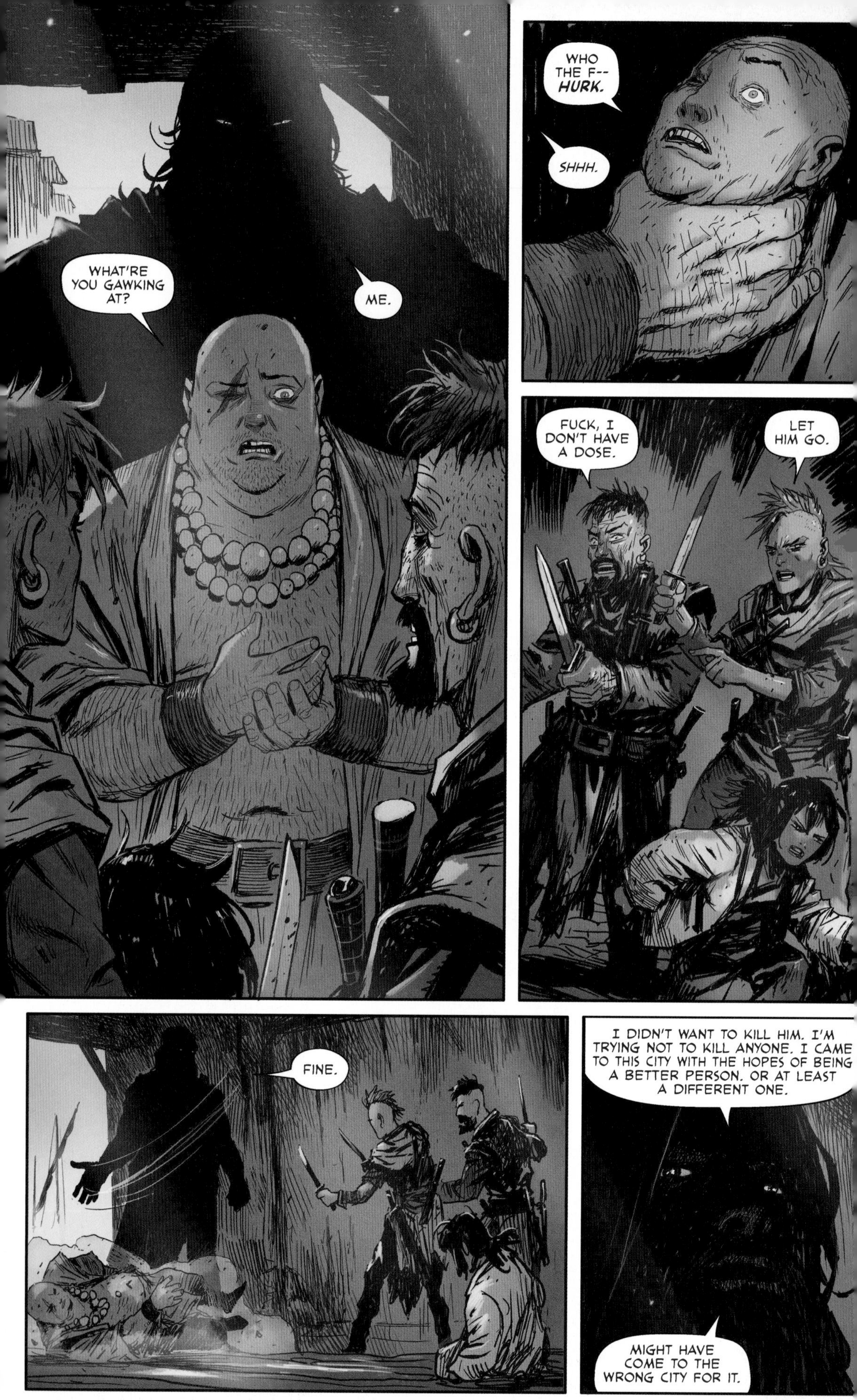

WHAT'RE YOU GAWKING AT?
ME.
WHO THE F-- HURK.
SHHH.
FUCK, I DON'T HAVE A DOSE.
LET HIM GO.
FINE.
I DIDN'T WANT TO KILL HIM. I'M TRYING NOT TO KILL ANYONE. I CAME TO THIS CITY WITH THE HOPES OF BEING A BETTER PERSON. OR AT LEAST A DIFFERENT ONE.
MIGHT HAVE COME TO THE WRONG CITY FOR IT.

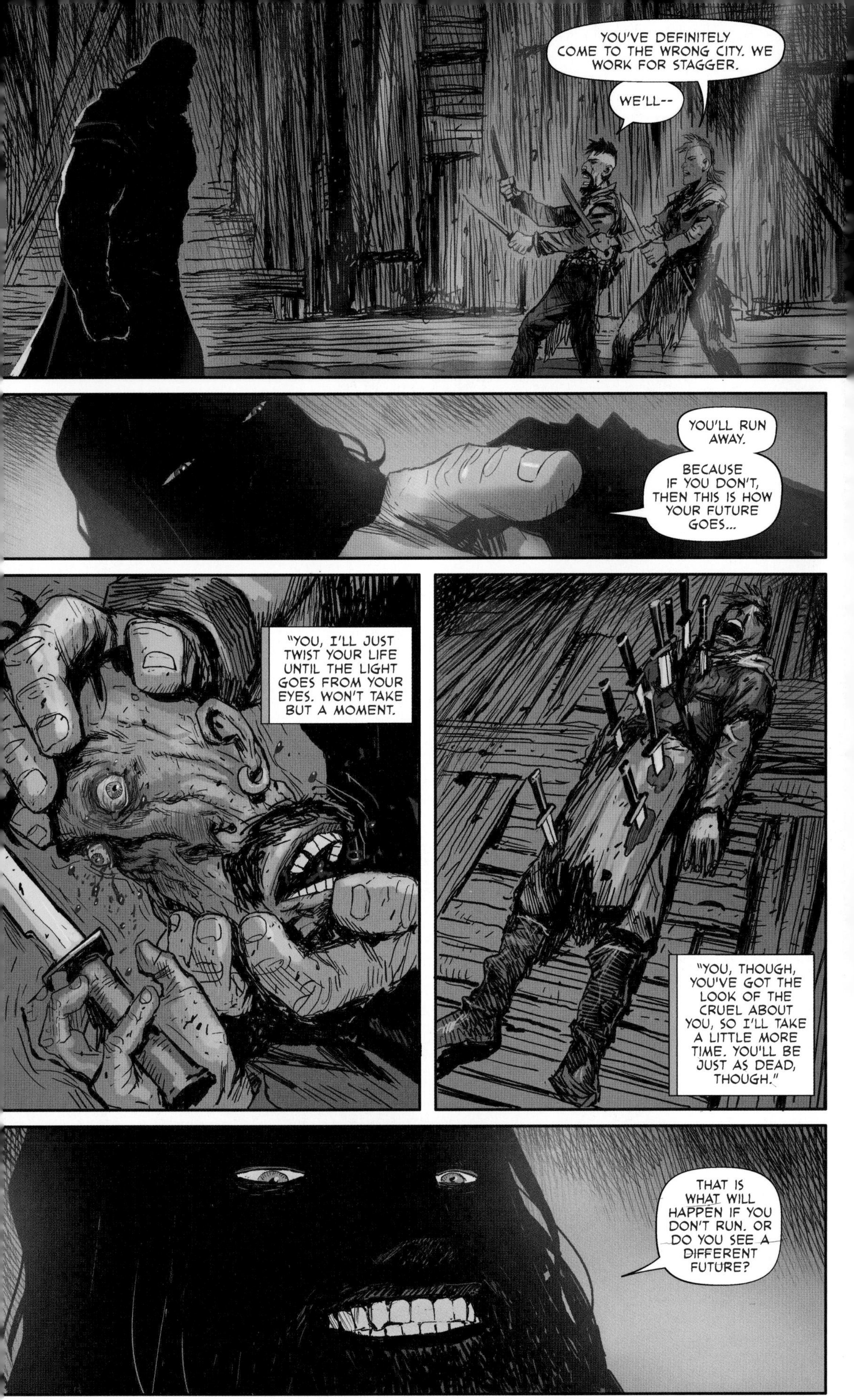
YOU'VE DEFINITELY COME TO THE WRONG CITY. WE WORK FOR STAGGER.
WE'LL--
YOU'LL RUN AWAY.
BECAUSE IF YOU DON'T, THEN THIS IS HOW YOUR FUTURE GOES...
"YOU, I'LL JUST TWIST YOUR LIFE UNTIL THE LIGHT GOES FROM YOUR EYES. WON'T TAKE BUT A MOMENT.
"YOU, THOUGH, YOU'VE GOT THE LOOK OF THE CRUEL ABOUT YOU, SO I'LL TAKE A LITTLE MORE TIME. YOU'LL BE JUST AS DEAD, THOUGH."
THAT IS WHAT WILL HAPPEN IF YOU DON'T RUN. OR DO YOU SEE A DIFFERENT FUTURE?

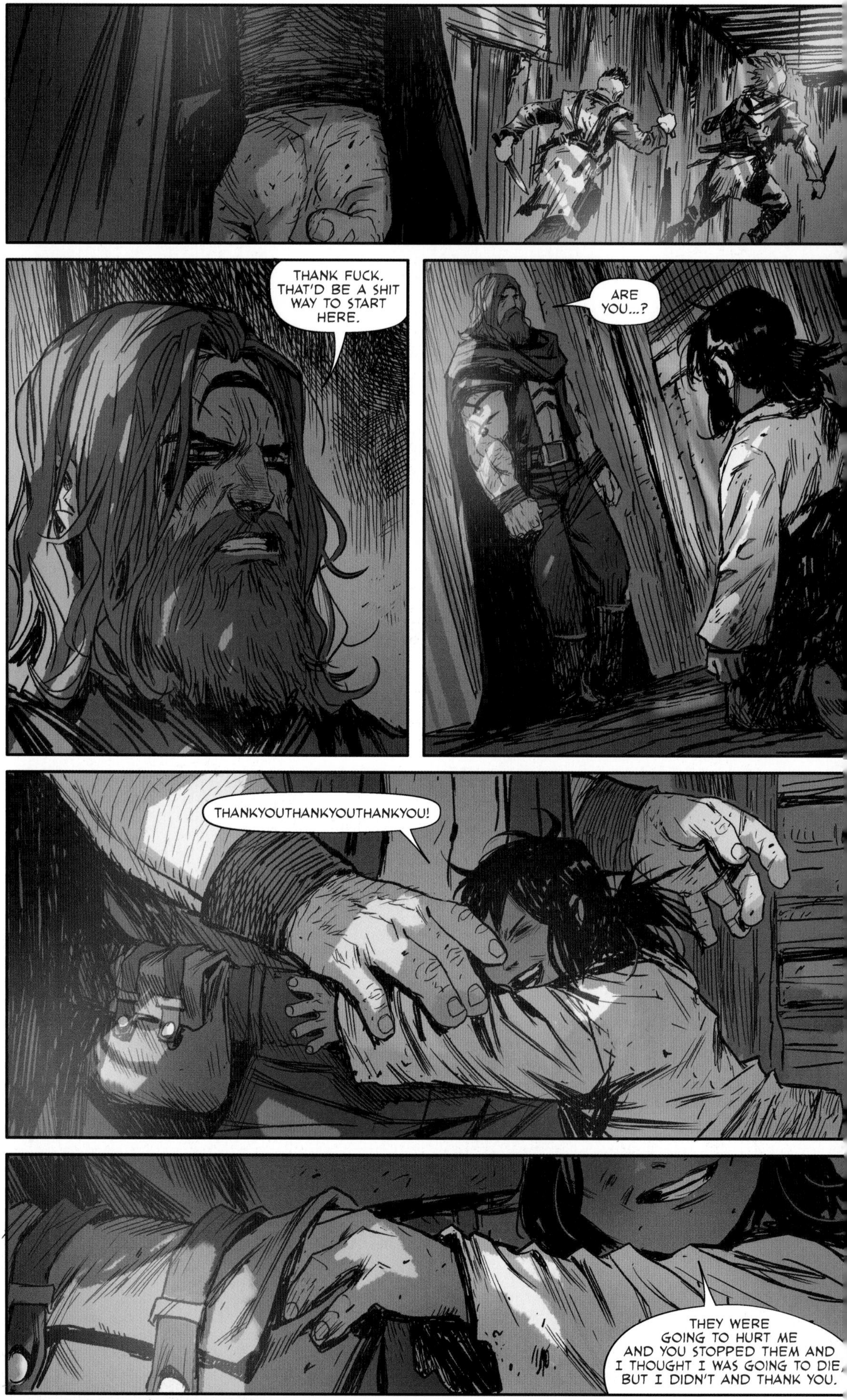
THANK FUCK. THAT'D BE A SHIT WAY TO START HERE.
ARE YOU...?
THANKYOUTHANKYOUTHANKYOU!
THEY WERE GOING TO HURT ME AND YOU STOPPED THEM AND I THOUGHT I WAS GOING TO DIE, BUT I DIDN'T AND THANK YOU.

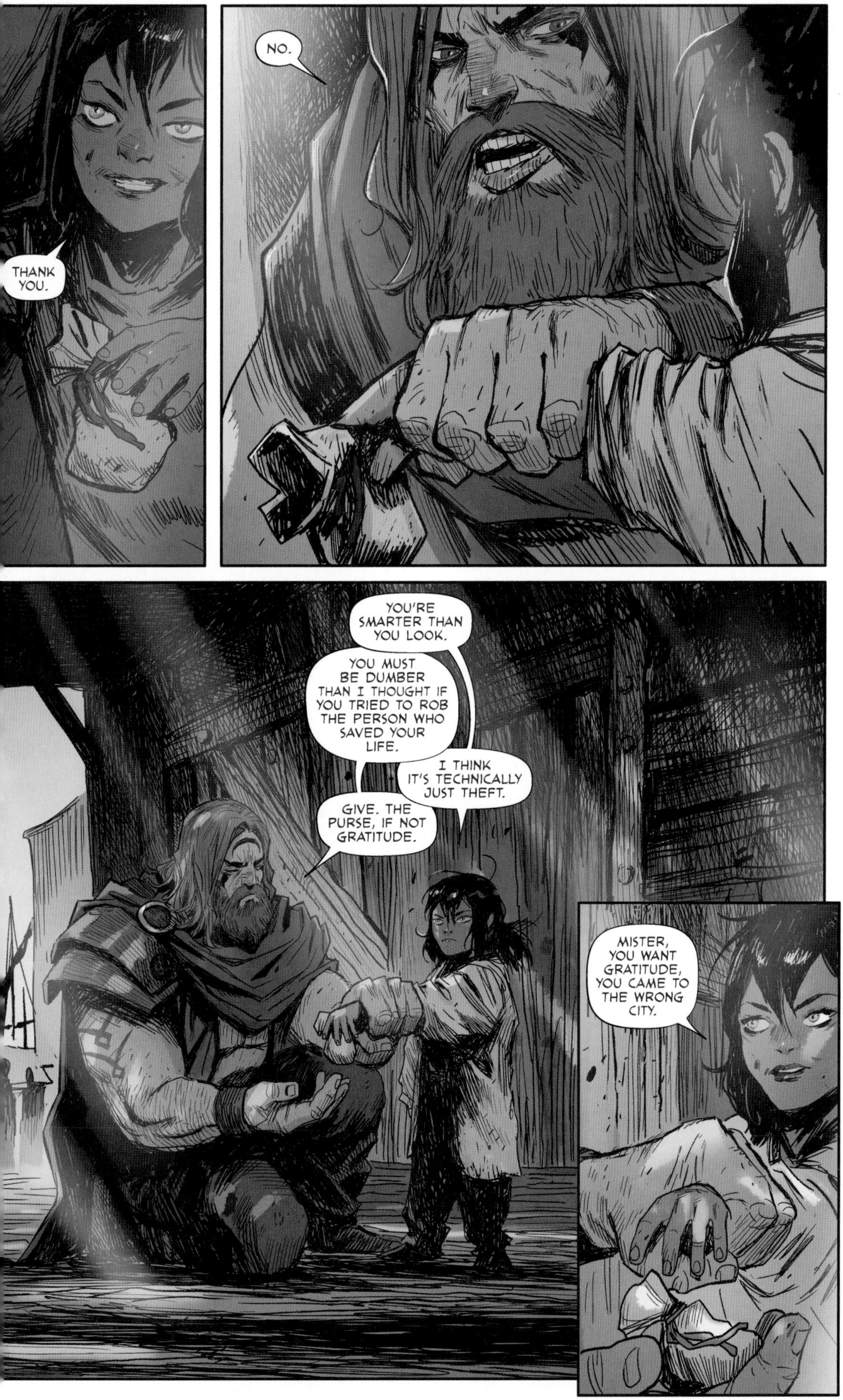
THANK YOU.
NO.
YOU'RE SMARTER THAN YOU LOOK.
YOU MUST BE DUMBER THAN I THOUGHT IF YOU TRIED TO ROB THE PERSON WHO SAVED YOUR LIFE.
I THINK IT'S TECHNICALLY JUST THEFT.
GIVE. THE PURSE, IF NOT GRATITUDE.
MISTER, YOU WANT GRATITUDE, YOU CAME TO THE WRONG CITY.

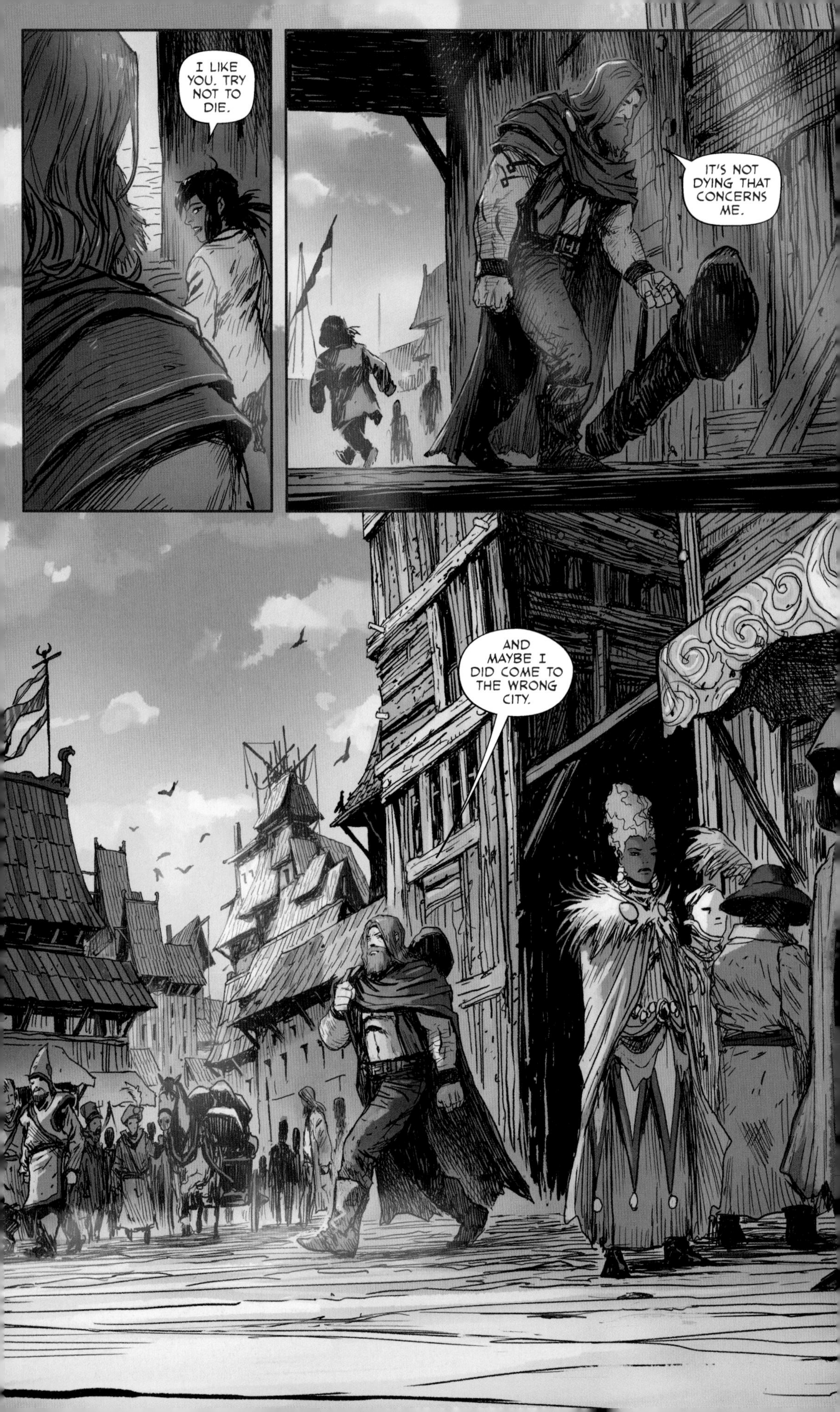
I LIKE YOU. TRY NOT TO DIE.
IT'S NOT DYING THAT CONCERNS ME.
AND MAYBE I DID COME TO THE WRONG CITY.

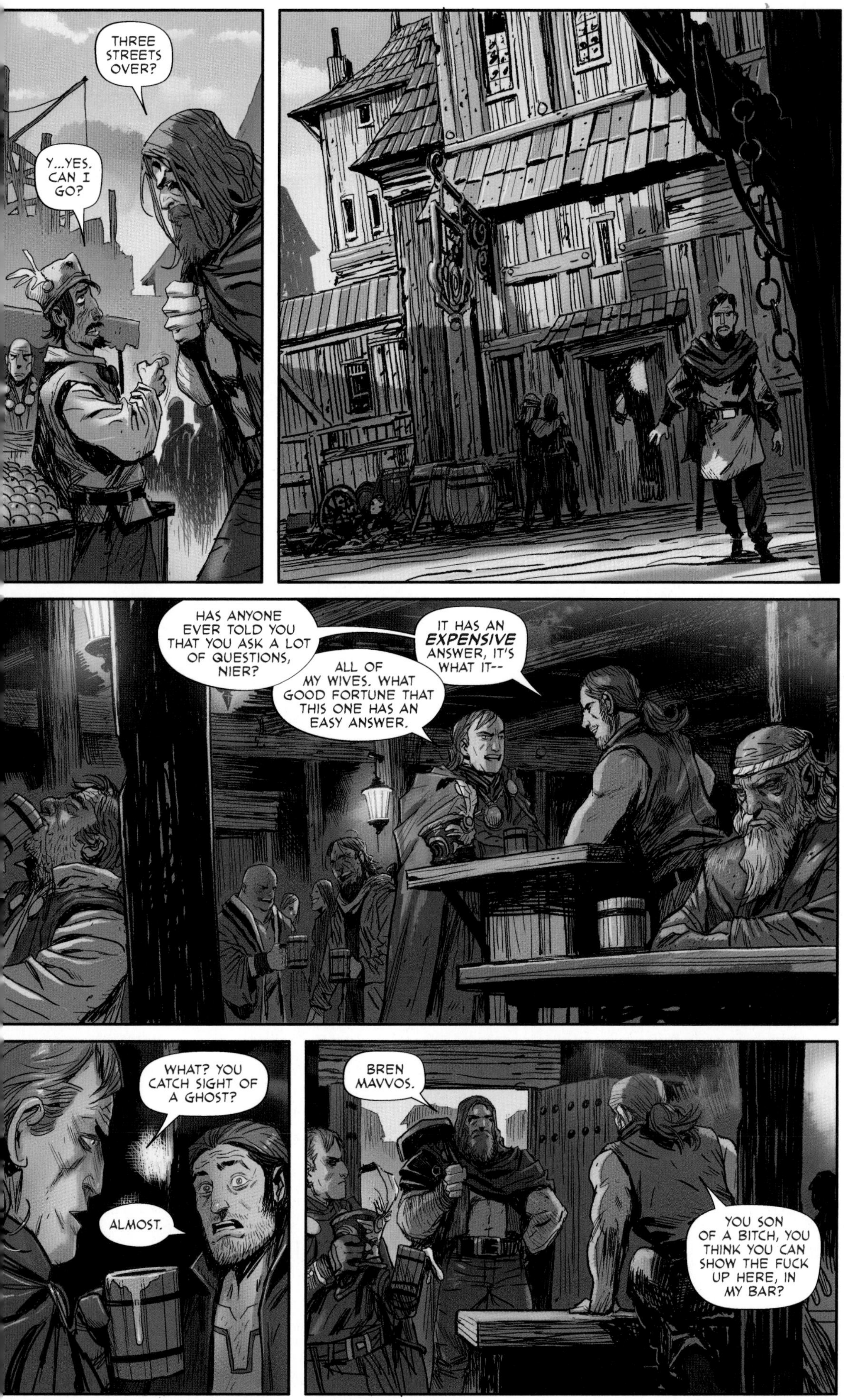
THREE STREETS OVER?
Y...YES. CAN I GO?
HAS ANYONE EVER TOLD YOU THAT YOU ASK A LOT OF QUESTIONS, NIER?
ALL OF MY WIVES. WHAT GOOD FORTUNE THAT THIS ONE HAS AN EASY ANSWER.
IT HAS AN *EXPENSIVE* ANSWER, IT'S WHAT IT--
WHAT? YOU CATCH SIGHT OF A GHOST?
ALMOST.
BREN MAVVOS.
YOU SON OF A BITCH, YOU THINK YOU CAN SHOW THE FUCK UP HERE, IN MY BAR?

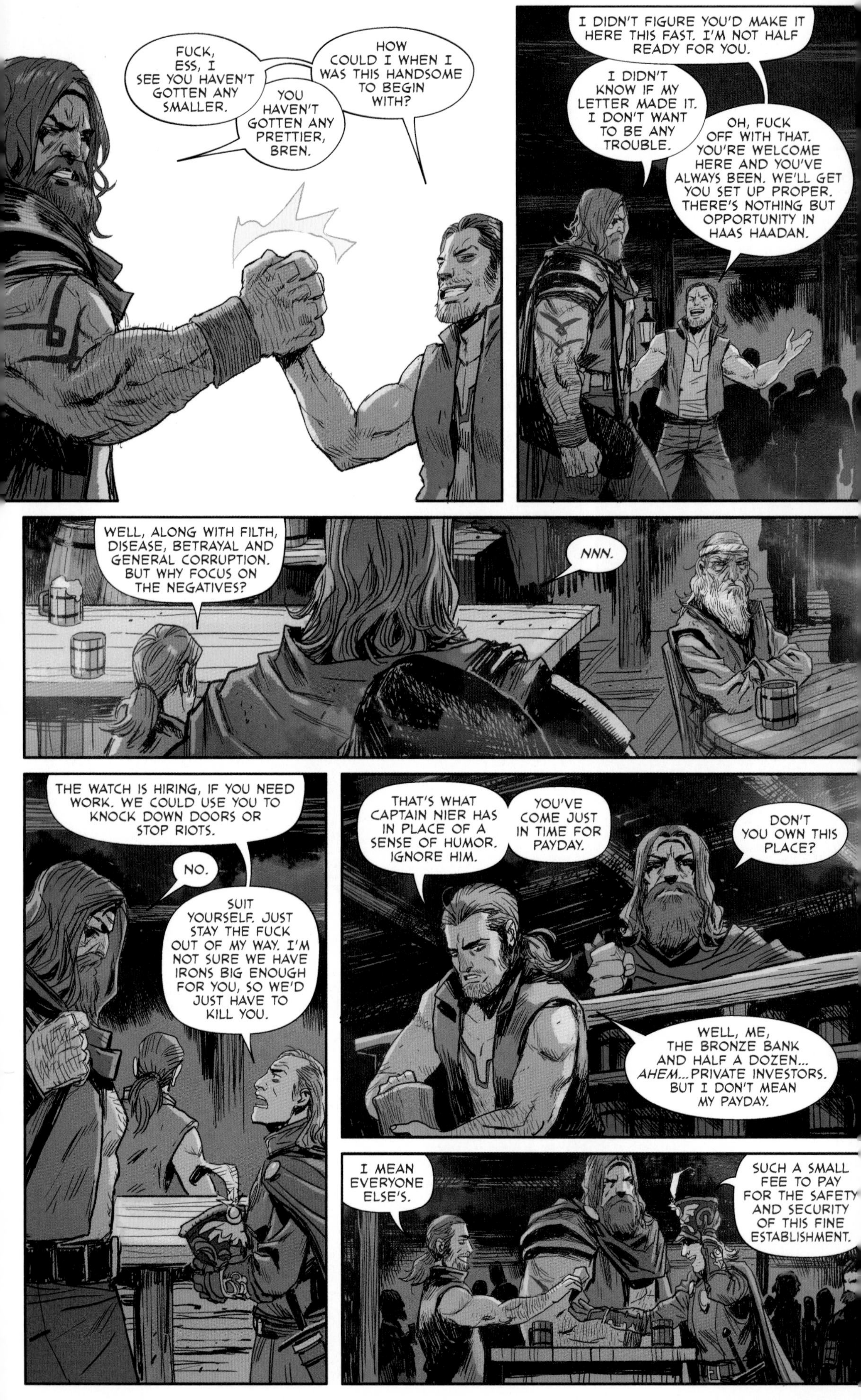
FUCK, ESS, I SEE YOU HAVEN'T GOTTEN ANY SMALLER.
YOU HAVEN'T GOTTEN ANY PRETTIER, BREN.
HOW COULD I WHEN I WAS THIS HANDSOME TO BEGIN WITH?
I DIDN'T FIGURE YOU'D MAKE IT HERE THIS FAST. I'M NOT HALF READY FOR YOU.
I DIDN'T KNOW IF MY LETTER MADE IT. I DON'T WANT TO BE ANY TROUBLE.
OH, FUCK OFF WITH THAT. YOU'RE WELCOME HERE AND YOU'VE ALWAYS BEEN. WE'LL GET YOU SET UP PROPER. THERE'S NOTHING BUT OPPORTUNITY IN HAAS HAADAN.
WELL, ALONG WITH FILTH, DISEASE, BETRAYAL AND GENERAL CORRUPTION. BUT WHY FOCUS ON THE NEGATIVES?
NNN.
THE WATCH IS HIRING, IF YOU NEED WORK. WE COULD USE YOU TO KNOCK DOWN DOORS OR STOP RIOTS.
NO.
SUIT YOURSELF. JUST STAY THE FUCK OUT OF MY WAY. I'M NOT SURE WE HAVE IRONS BIG ENOUGH FOR YOU, SO WE'D JUST HAVE TO KILL YOU.
THAT'S WHAT CAPTAIN NIER HAS IN PLACE OF A SENSE OF HUMOR. IGNORE HIM.
YOU'VE COME JUST IN TIME FOR PAYDAY.
DON'T YOU OWN THIS PLACE?
WELL, ME, THE BRONZE BANK AND HALF A DOZEN... AHEM... PRIVATE INVESTORS. BUT I DON'T MEAN MY PAYDAY.
I MEAN EVERYONE ELSE'S.
SUCH A SMALL FEE TO PAY FOR THE SAFETY AND SECURITY OF THIS FINE ESTABLISHMENT.

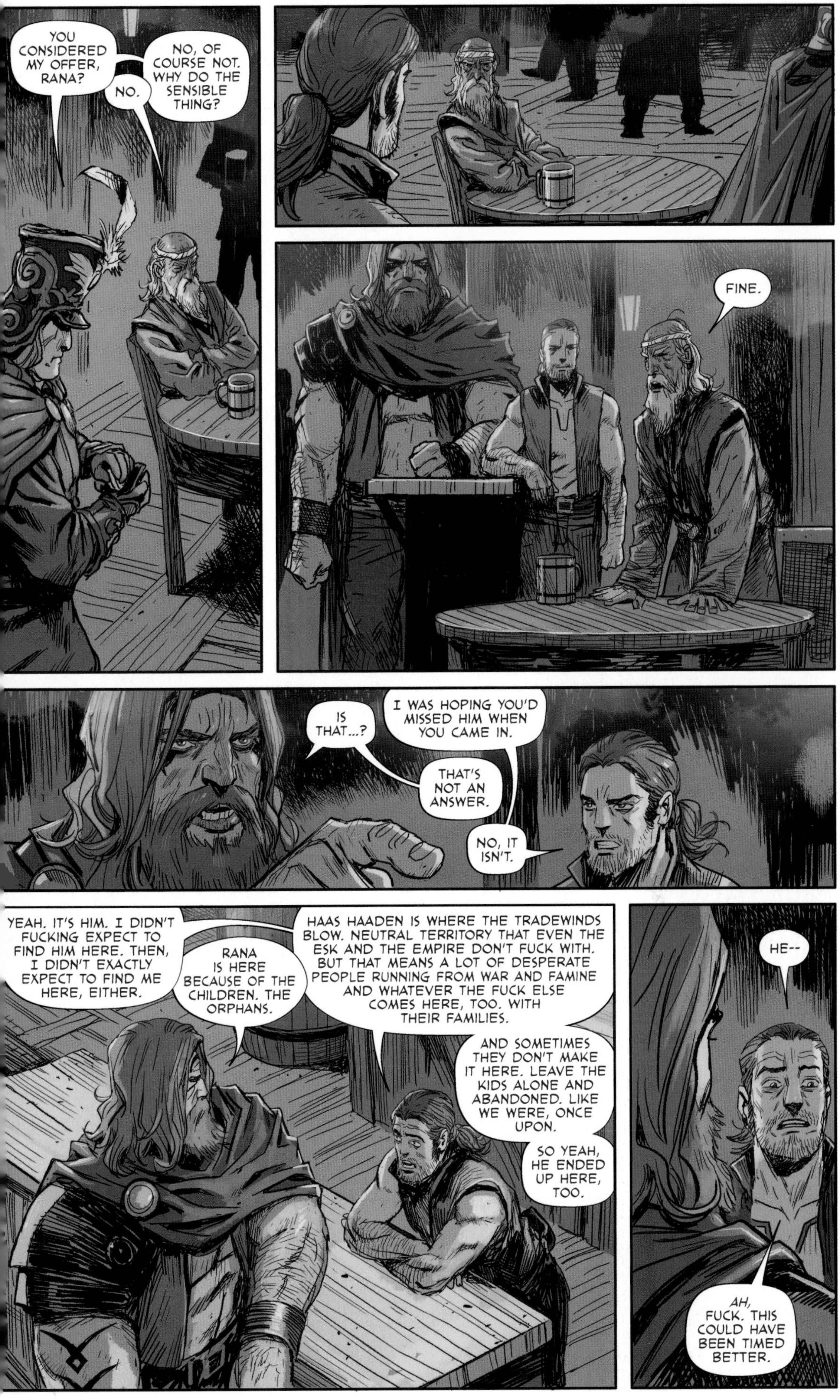
YOU CONSIDERED MY OFFER, RANA?
NO.
NO, OF COURSE NOT. WHY DO THE SENSIBLE THING?
FINE.
IS THAT...?
I WAS HOPING YOU'D MISSED HIM WHEN YOU CAME IN.
THAT'S NOT AN ANSWER.
NO, IT ISN'T.
YEAH. IT'S HIM. I DIDN'T FUCKING EXPECT TO FIND HIM HERE. THEN, I DIDN'T EXACTLY EXPECT TO FIND ME HERE, EITHER.
RANA IS HERE BECAUSE OF THE CHILDREN. THE ORPHANS.
HAAS HAADEN IS WHERE THE TRADEWINDS BLOW. NEUTRAL TERRITORY THAT EVEN THE ESK AND THE EMPIRE DON'T FUCK WITH. BUT THAT MEANS A LOT OF DESPERATE PEOPLE RUNNING FROM WAR AND FAMINE AND WHATEVER THE FUCK ELSE COMES HERE, TOO. WITH THEIR FAMILIES.
AND SOMETIMES THEY DON'T MAKE IT HERE. LEAVE THE KIDS ALONE AND ABANDONED. LIKE WE WERE, ONCE UPON.
SO YEAH, HE ENDED UP HERE, TOO.
HE--
AH, FUCK. THIS COULD HAVE BEEN TIMED BETTER.

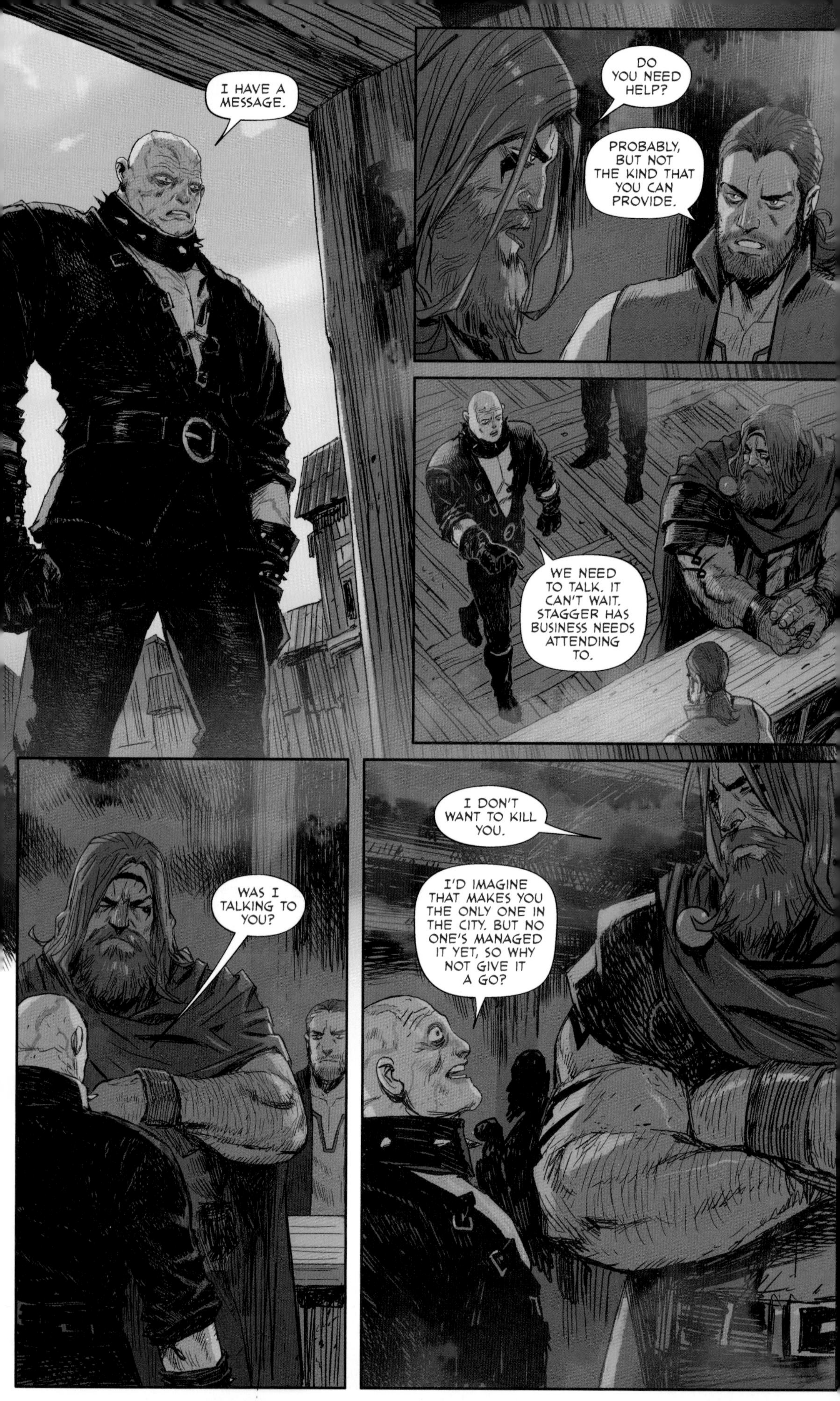
I HAVE A MESSAGE.
DO YOU NEED HELP?
PROBABLY, BUT NOT THE KIND THAT YOU CAN PROVIDE.
WE NEED TO TALK. IT CAN'T WAIT. STAGGER HAS BUSINESS NEEDS ATTENDING TO.
WAS I TALKING TO YOU?
I DON'T WANT TO KILL YOU.
I'D IMAGINE THAT MAKES YOU THE ONLY ONE IN THE CITY. BUT NO ONE'S MANAGED IT YET, SO WHY NOT GIVE IT A GO?

I DO APPRECIATE A GOOD DISPLAY OF MANLY POSTURING, BUT NEITHER OF YOU NEEDS TO DO THIS.

THE MAMMOTH YOURS?

HE'S NOBODY, BUT HIS OWN.

IT'S FINE. THIS IS JUST WHAT DOING BUSINESS IS LIKE HERE. STAGGER RUNS WHAT I SUPPOSE COULD CHARITABLY BE CALLED THE CRIMINAL ELEMENT HERE, SO WHEN IT HAS TO DO WITH HIM, I HAVE TO LISTEN.

I COULD--

YEAH, YOU PROBABLY COULD. BUT YOU DON'T WANT TO AND I DON'T NEED YOU TO. YOU CAME HERE FOR A DIFFERENT LIFE. SO BE DIFFERENT, ESS. BUT THERE IS SOMETHING YOU CAN DO FOR ME. FOR US, ACTUALLY.

US?

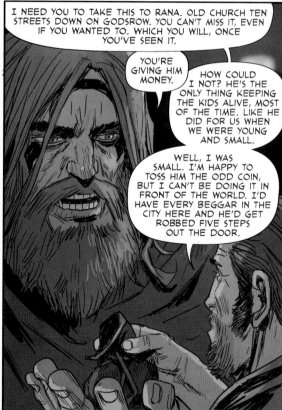

I NEED YOU TO TAKE THIS TO RANA. OLD CHURCH TEN STREETS DOWN ON GODSROW. YOU CAN'T MISS IT, EVEN IF YOU WANTED TO. WHICH YOU WILL, ONCE YOU'VE SEEN IT.

YOU'RE GIVING HIM MONEY.

HOW COULD I NOT? HE'S THE ONLY THING KEEPING THE KIDS ALIVE, MOST OF THE TIME. LIKE HE DID FOR US WHEN WE WERE YOUNG AND SMALL.

WELL, I WAS SMALL. I'M HAPPY TO TOSS HIM THE ODD COIN, BUT I CAN'T BE DOING IT IN FRONT OF THE WORLD. I'D HAVE EVERY BEGGAR IN THE CITY HERE AND HE'D GET ROBBED FIVE STEPS OUT THE DOOR.

BE SEEING YOU.

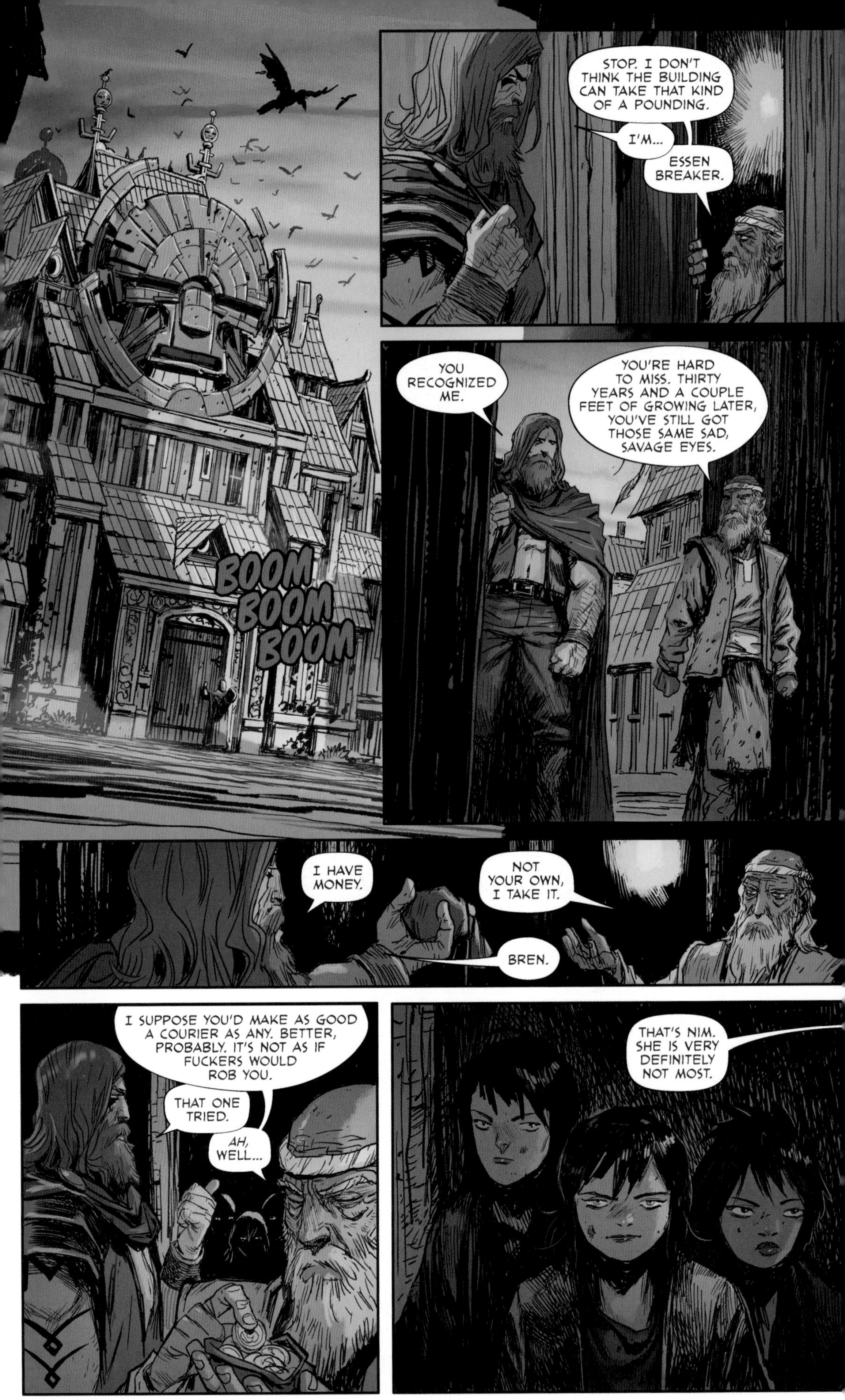
BOOM BOOM BOOM
STOP. I DON'T THINK THE BUILDING CAN TAKE THAT KIND OF A POUNDING.
I'M...
ESSEN BREAKER.
YOU RECOGNIZED ME.
YOU'RE HARD TO MISS. THIRTY YEARS AND A COUPLE FEET OF GROWING LATER, YOU'VE STILL GOT THOSE SAME SAD, SAVAGE EYES.
I HAVE MONEY.
NOT YOUR OWN, I TAKE IT.
BREN.
I SUPPOSE YOU'D MAKE AS GOOD A COURIER AS ANY. BETTER, PROBABLY. IT'S NOT AS IF FUCKERS WOULD ROB YOU.
THAT ONE TRIED.
AH, WELL...
THAT'S NIM. SHE IS VERY DEFINITELY NOT MOST.

"IT'S NOT ANY DIFFERENT THAN WHEN I FOUND YOU. DIFFERENT PLACE, DIFFERENT YEAR, BUT THE SAME BASTARD WORLD. THE EMPIRE, THE ESCALENE, SOMEONE ALWAYS HAD A WAR. AND WAR MAKES ORPHANS, EVENTUALLY."

THIS HELPS. BUT THERE'S ALWAYS MORE MOUTHS THAN MONEY.

YOU DO GOOD WORK.

I DO NECESSARY WORK. DO YOU KNOW WHAT IT'S LIKE TO LOSE YOUR PARENTS? IN A CITY LIKE THIS? IN A WORLD LIKE THIS?

YES. I SUPPOSE YOU DO.

I CAN'T STOP THE WORLD FROM BEING A SHITHOLE, BUT I MAYBE CAN MAKE IT HURT A LITTLE LESS FOR THEM.

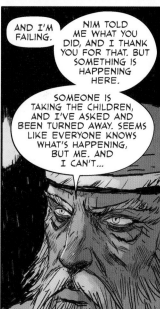

AND I'M FAILING.

NIM TOLD ME WHAT YOU DID, AND I THANK YOU FOR THAT. BUT SOMETHING IS HAPPENING HERE.

SOMEONE IS TAKING THE CHILDREN, AND I'VE ASKED AND BEEN TURNED AWAY. SEEMS LIKE EVERYONE KNOWS WHAT'S HAPPENING, BUT ME. AND I CAN'T...

I CAN'T STOP IT. CAN I?

I HEARD ABOUT YOU, ESSEN BREAKER. THE DEVIL'S SON. I DON'T KNOW WHAT THEY DID TO YOU AFTER THEY TOOK YOU BOYS AWAY FROM ME. BREN WON'T SAY AND I WON'T ASK. BUT I'VE HEARD ABOUT YOU. WHERE YOU GO, DEATH FOLLOWS.

I CAN'T LET IT FOLLOW YOU HERE.

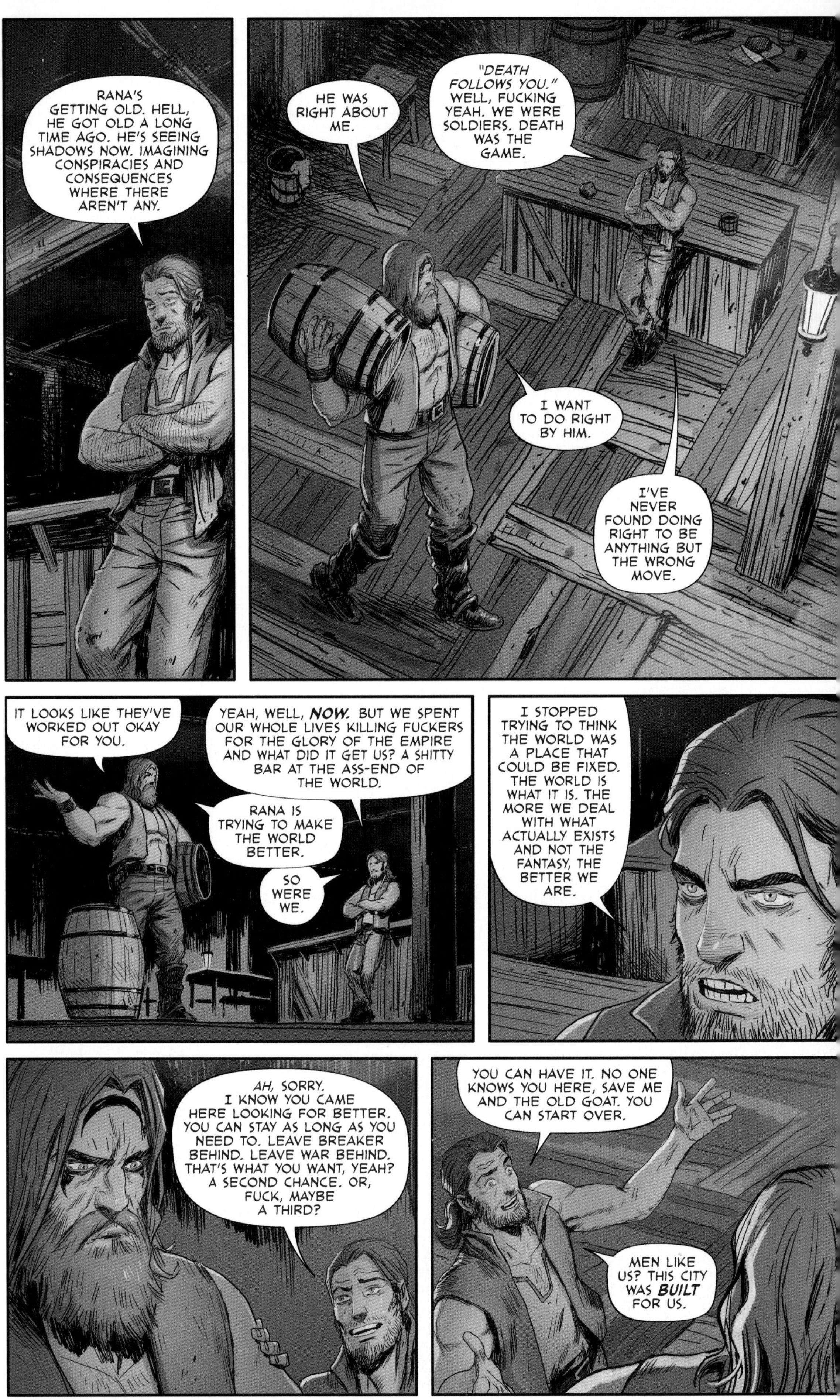
RANA'S GETTING OLD. HELL, HE GOT OLD A LONG TIME AGO. HE'S SEEING SHADOWS NOW. IMAGINING CONSPIRACIES AND CONSEQUENCES WHERE THERE AREN'T ANY.
HE WAS RIGHT ABOUT ME.
"DEATH FOLLOWS YOU." WELL, FUCKING YEAH. WE WERE SOLDIERS. DEATH WAS THE GAME.
I WANT TO DO RIGHT BY HIM.
I'VE NEVER FOUND DOING RIGHT TO BE ANYTHING BUT THE WRONG MOVE.
IT LOOKS LIKE THEY'VE WORKED OUT OKAY FOR YOU.
YEAH, WELL, NOW. BUT WE SPENT OUR WHOLE LIVES KILLING FUCKERS FOR THE GLORY OF THE EMPIRE AND WHAT DID IT GET US? A SHITTY BAR AT THE ASS-END OF THE WORLD.
RANA IS TRYING TO MAKE THE WORLD BETTER.
SO WERE WE.
I STOPPED TRYING TO THINK THE WORLD WAS A PLACE THAT COULD BE FIXED. THE WORLD IS WHAT IT IS. THE MORE WE DEAL WITH WHAT ACTUALLY EXISTS AND NOT THE FANTASY, THE BETTER WE ARE.
AH, SORRY. I KNOW YOU CAME HERE LOOKING FOR BETTER. YOU CAN STAY AS LONG AS YOU NEED TO. LEAVE BREAKER BEHIND. LEAVE WAR BEHIND. THAT'S WHAT YOU WANT, YEAH? A SECOND CHANCE. OR, FUCK, MAYBE A THIRD?
YOU CAN HAVE IT. NO ONE KNOWS YOU HERE, SAVE ME AND THE OLD GOAT. YOU CAN START OVER.
MEN LIKE US? THIS CITY WAS BUILT FOR US.

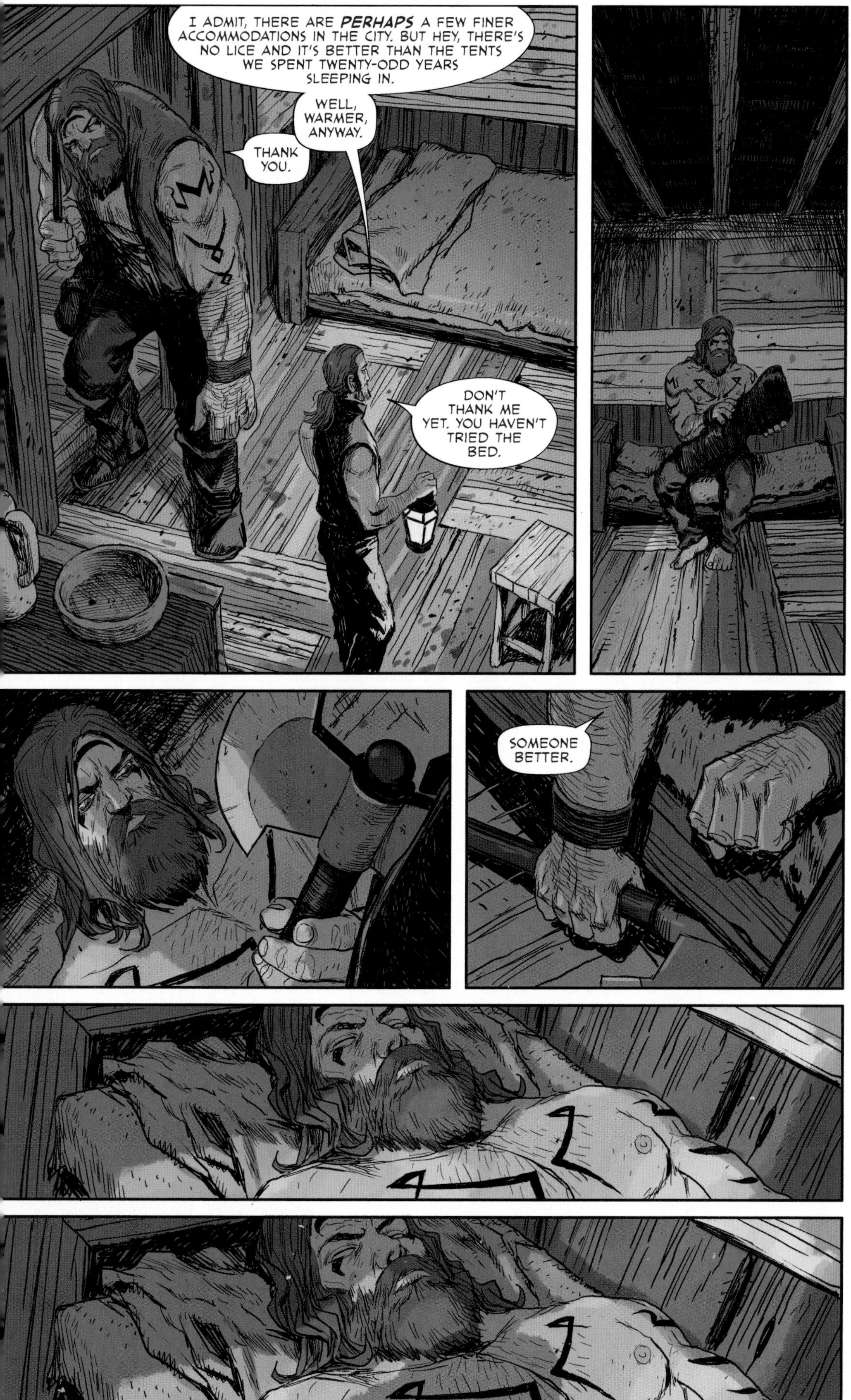
I ADMIT, THERE ARE *PERHAPS* A FEW FINER ACCOMMODATIONS IN THE CITY. BUT HEY, THERE'S NO LICE AND IT'S BETTER THAN THE TENTS WE SPENT TWENTY-ODD YEARS SLEEPING IN.
WELL, WARMER, ANYWAY.
THANK YOU.
DON'T THANK ME YET. YOU HAVEN'T TRIED THE BED.
SOMEONE BETTER.

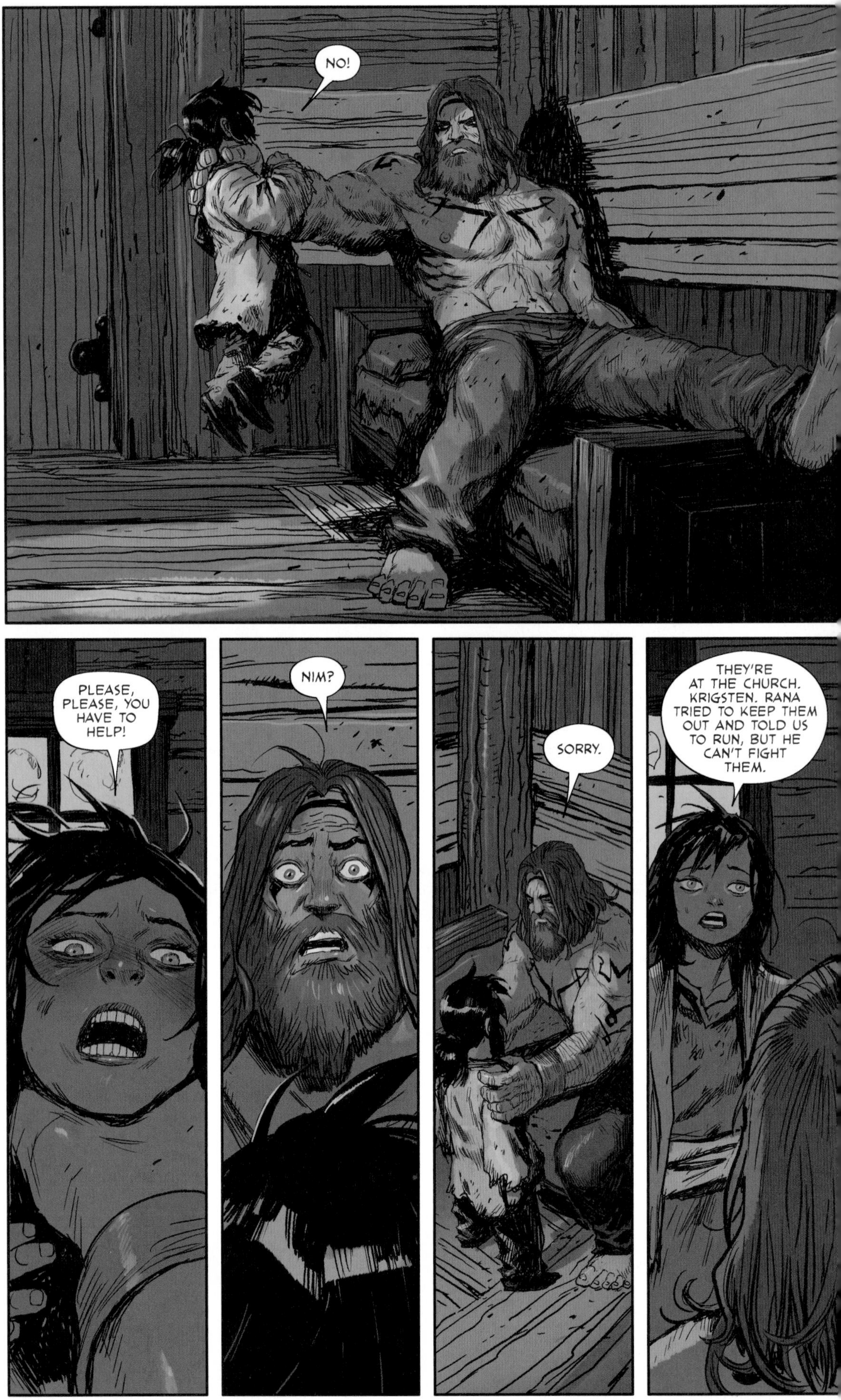
NO!
PLEASE, PLEASE, YOU HAVE TO HELP!
NIM?
SORRY.
THEY'RE AT THE CHURCH. KRIGSTEN. RANA TRIED TO KEEP THEM OUT AND TOLD US TO RUN, BUT HE CAN'T FIGHT THEM.

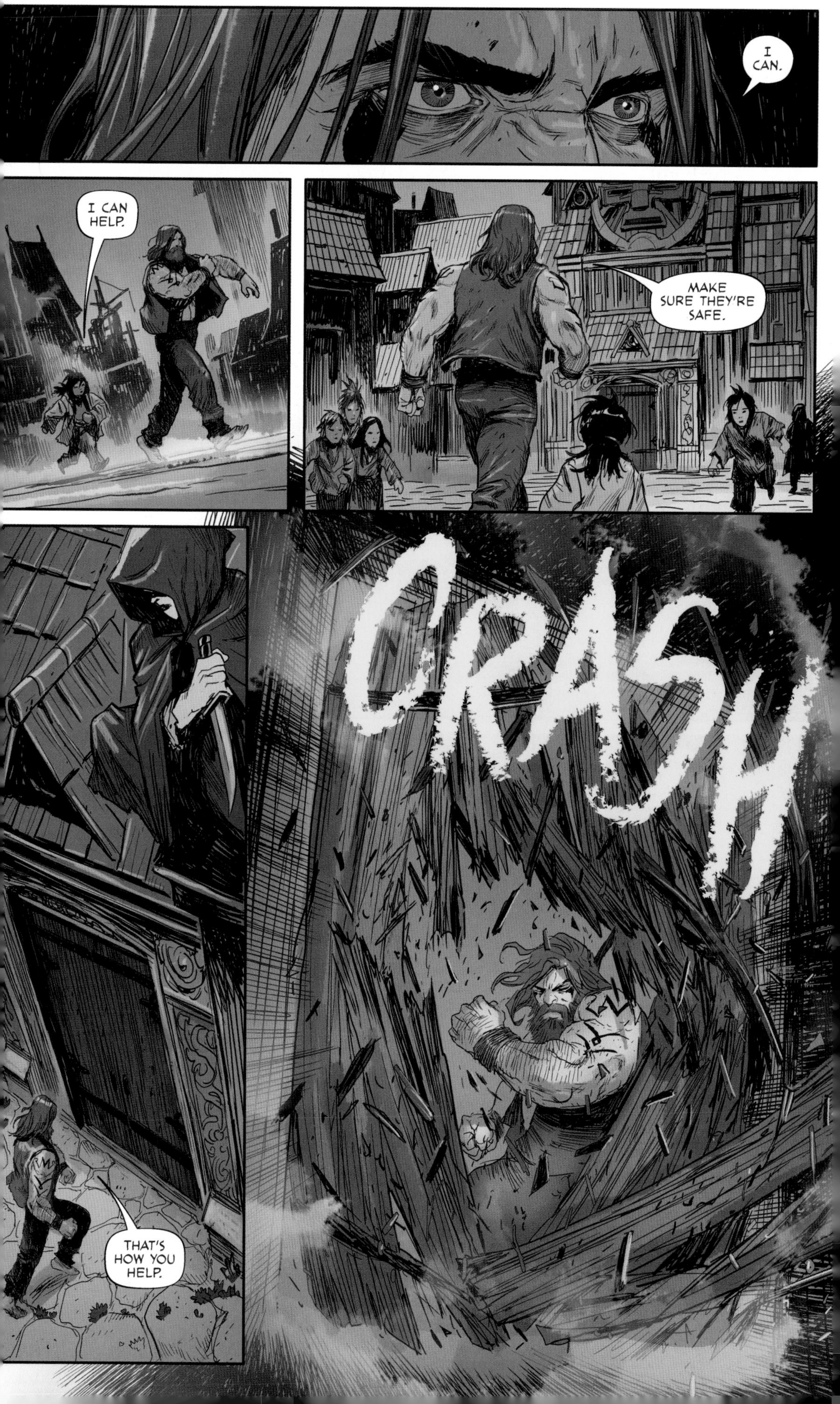
I CAN.
I CAN HELP.
MAKE SURE THEY'RE SAFE.
THAT'S HOW YOU HELP.
CRASH

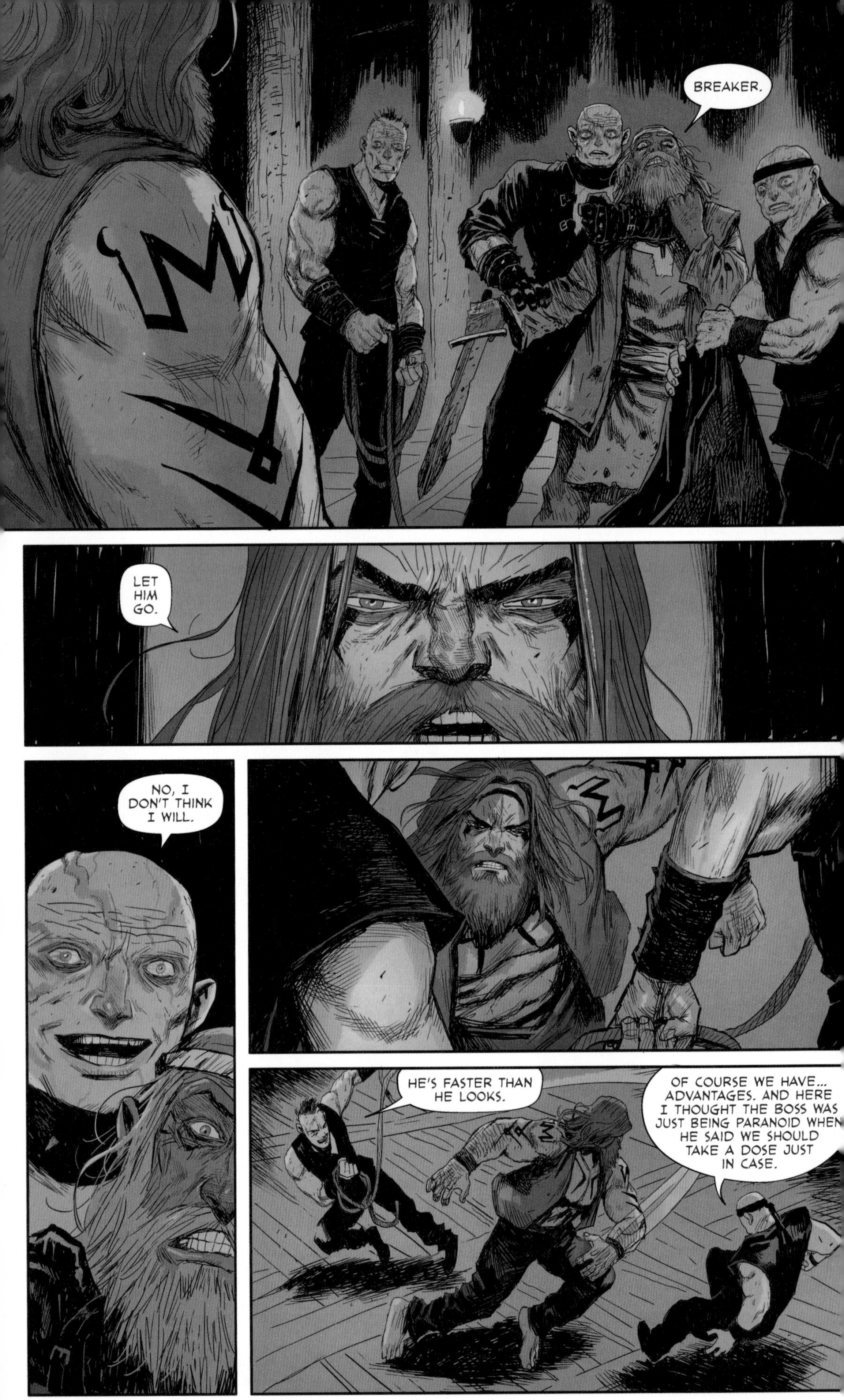
BREAKER.
LET HIM GO.
NO, I DON'T THINK I WILL.
HE'S FASTER THAN HE LOOKS.
OF COURSE WE HAVE... ADVANTAGES. AND HERE I THOUGHT THE BOSS WAS JUST BEING PARANOID WHEN HE SAID WE SHOULD TAKE A DOSE JUST IN CASE.

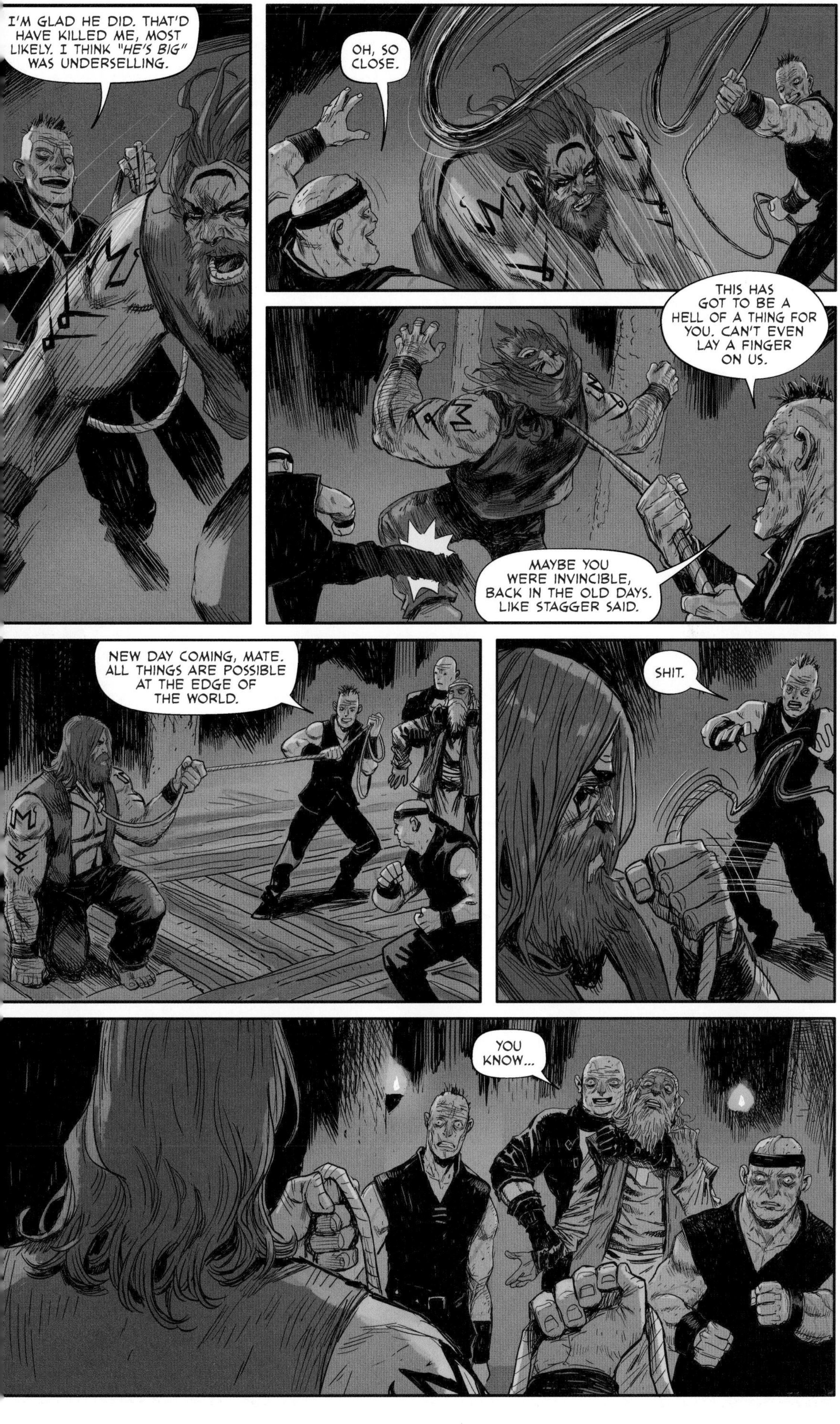
I'M GLAD HE DID. THAT'D HAVE KILLED ME, MOST LIKELY. I THINK *"HE'S BIG"* WAS UNDERSELLING.
OH, SO CLOSE.
THIS HAS GOT TO BE A HELL OF A THING FOR YOU. CAN'T EVEN LAY A FINGER ON US.
MAYBE YOU WERE INVINCIBLE, BACK IN THE OLD DAYS. LIKE STAGGER SAID.
NEW DAY COMING, MATE. ALL THINGS ARE POSSIBLE AT THE EDGE OF THE WORLD.
SHIT.
YOU KNOW...

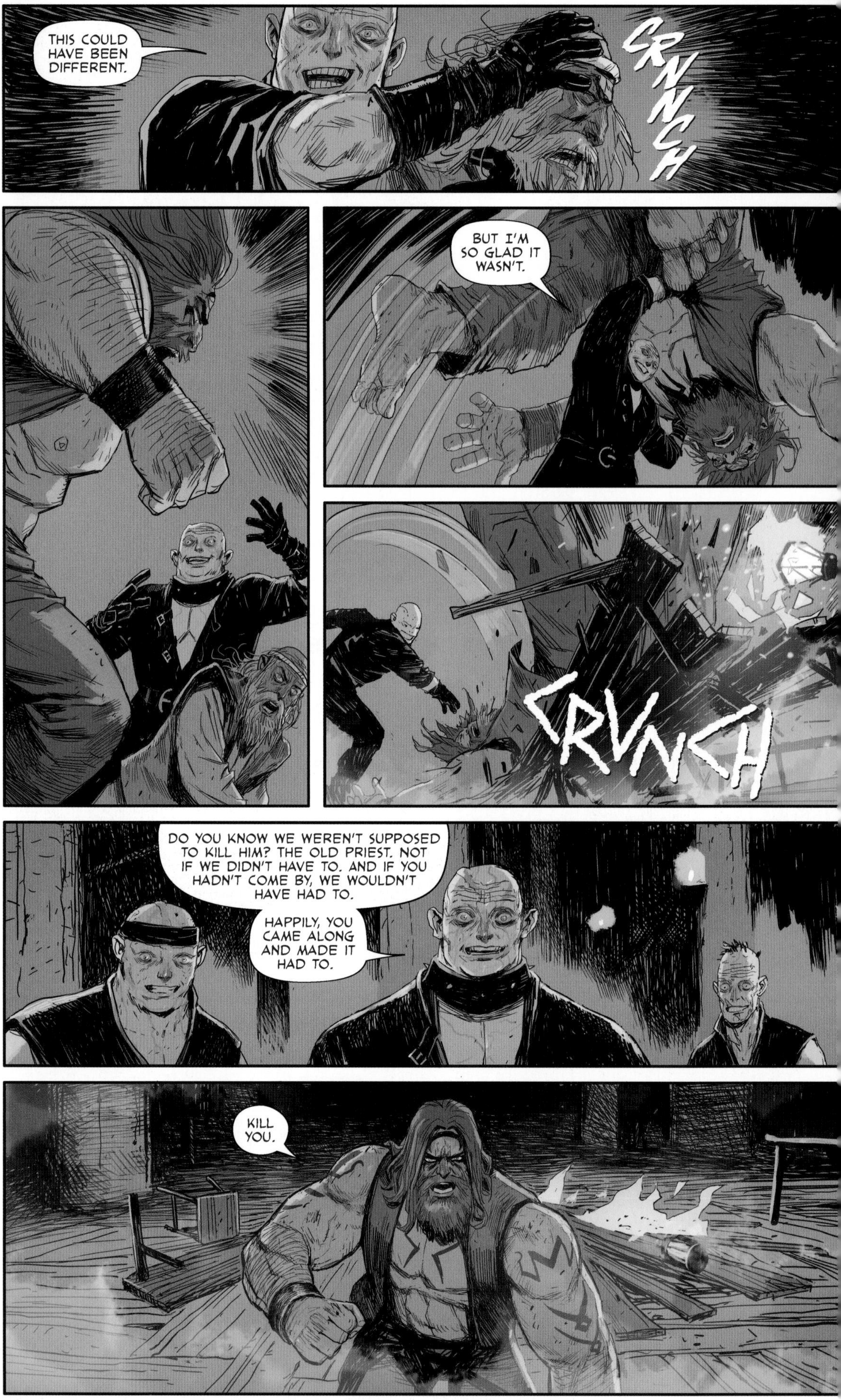
THIS COULD HAVE BEEN DIFFERENT.
CRNNCH
BUT I'M SO GLAD IT WASN'T.
CRUNCH
DO YOU KNOW WE WEREN'T SUPPOSED TO KILL HIM? THE OLD PRIEST. NOT IF WE DIDN'T HAVE TO. AND IF YOU HADN'T COME BY, WE WOULDN'T HAVE HAD TO.
HAPPILY, YOU CAME ALONG AND MADE IT HAD TO.
KILL YOU.

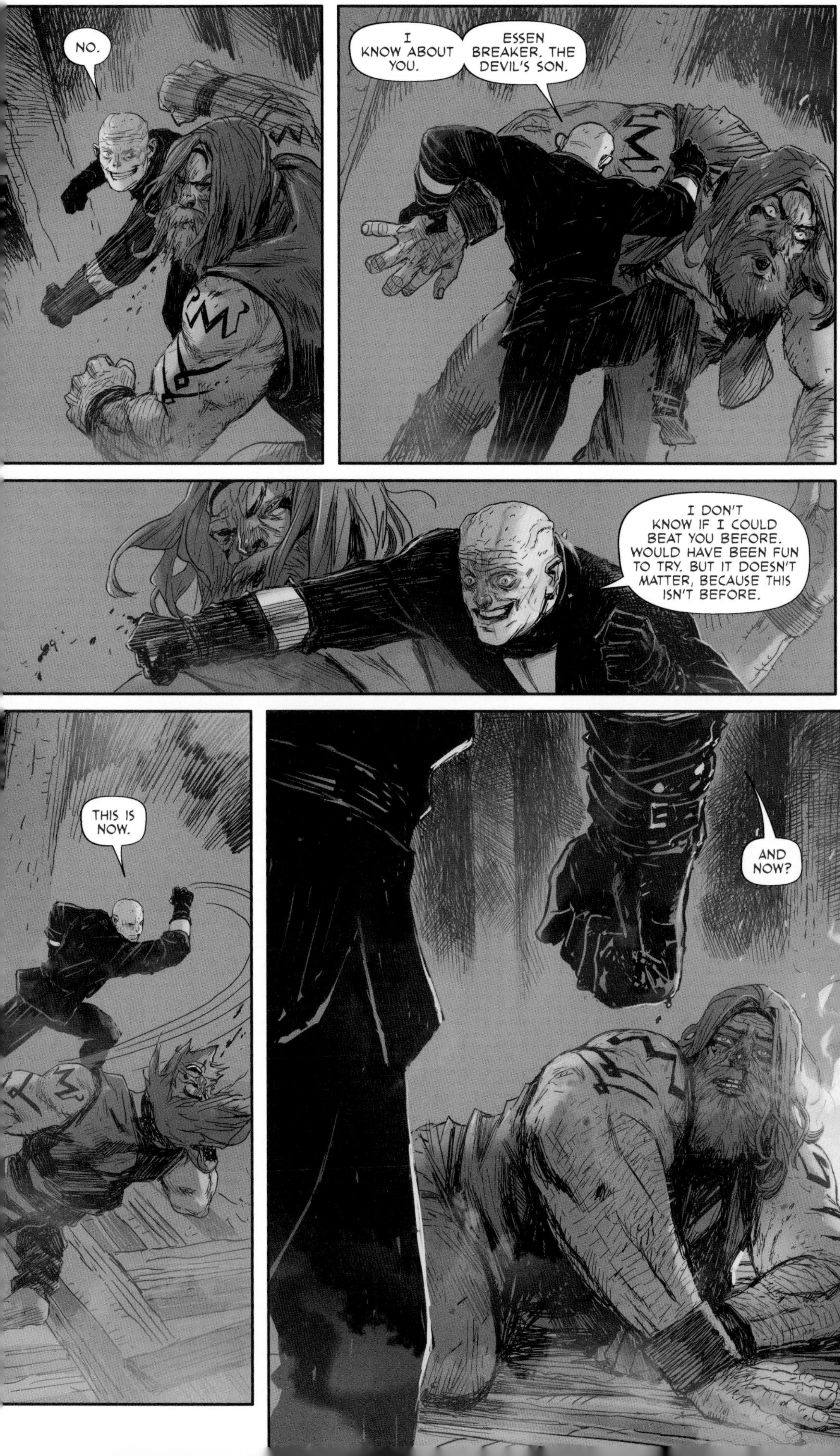
NO.
I KNOW ABOUT YOU.
ESSEN BREAKER. THE DEVIL'S SON.
I DON'T KNOW IF I COULD BEAT YOU BEFORE. WOULD HAVE BEEN FUN TO TRY. BUT IT DOESN'T MATTER, BECAUSE THIS ISN'T BEFORE.
THIS IS NOW.
AND NOW?

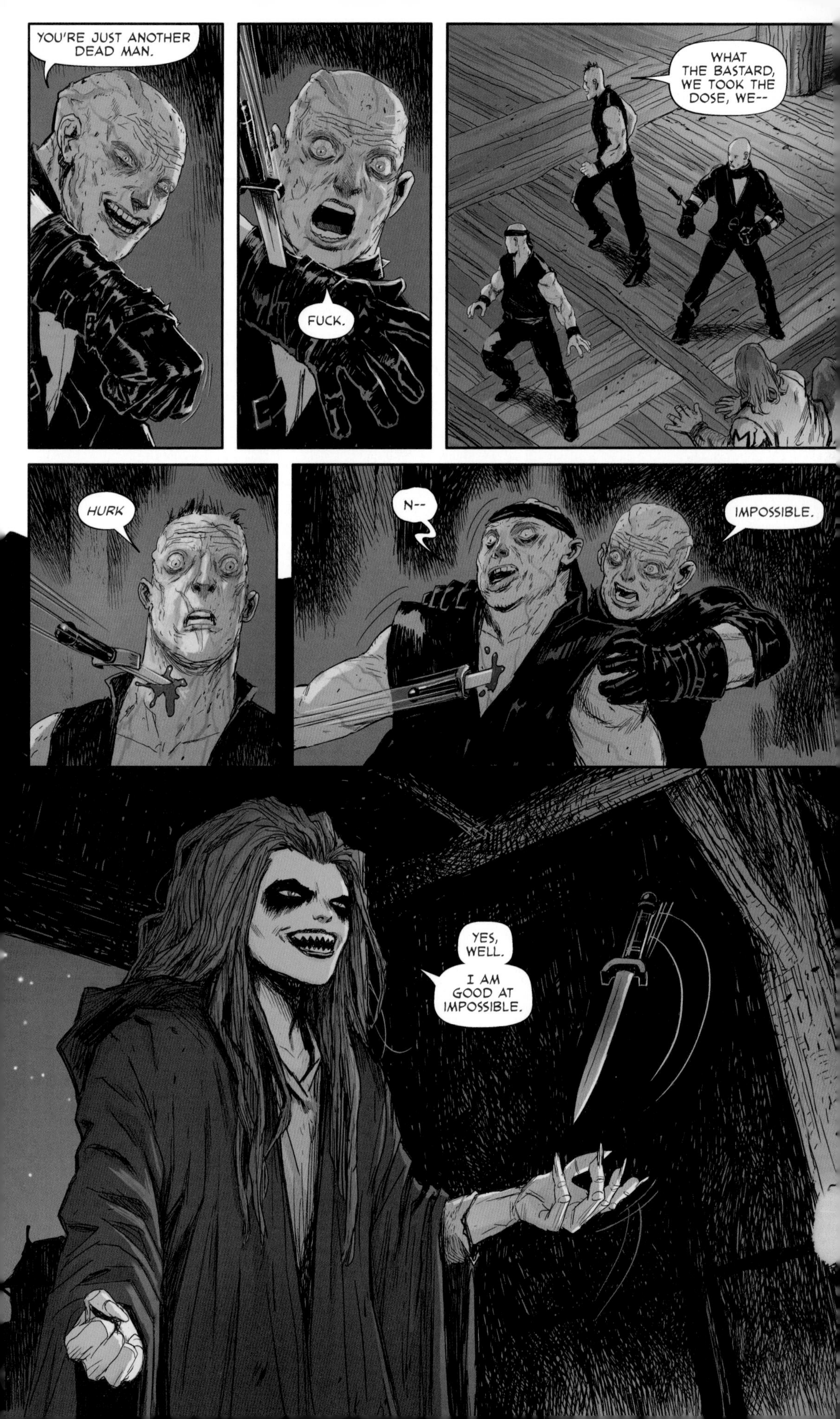
YOU'RE JUST ANOTHER DEAD MAN.
FUCK.
WHAT THE BASTARD, WE TOOK THE DOSE, WE--
HURK
N--
IMPOSSIBLE.
YES, WELL.
I AM GOOD AT IMPOSSIBLE.

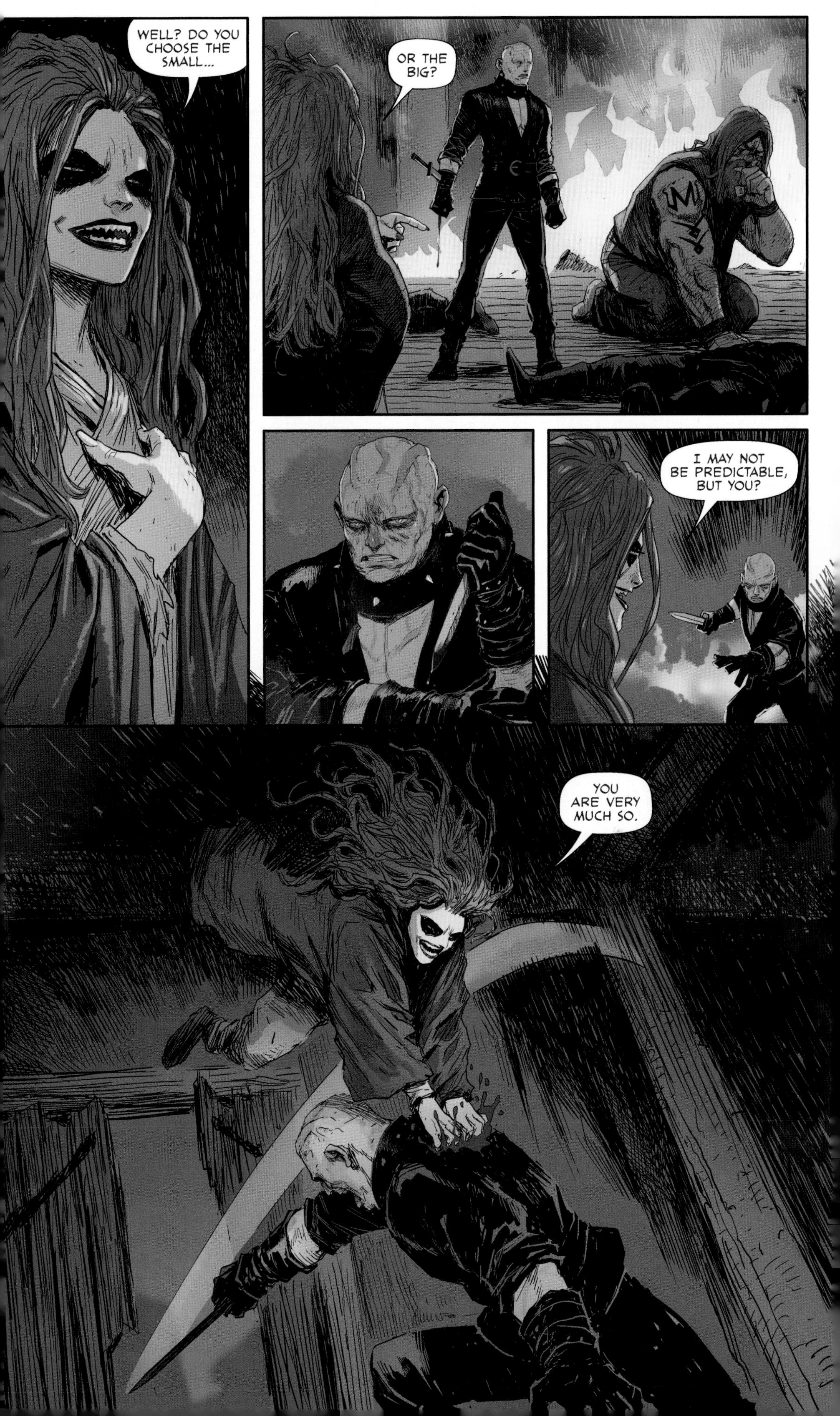
WELL? DO YOU CHOOSE THE SMALL...
OR THE BIG?
I MAY NOT BE PREDICTABLE, BUT YOU?
YOU ARE VERY MUCH SO.

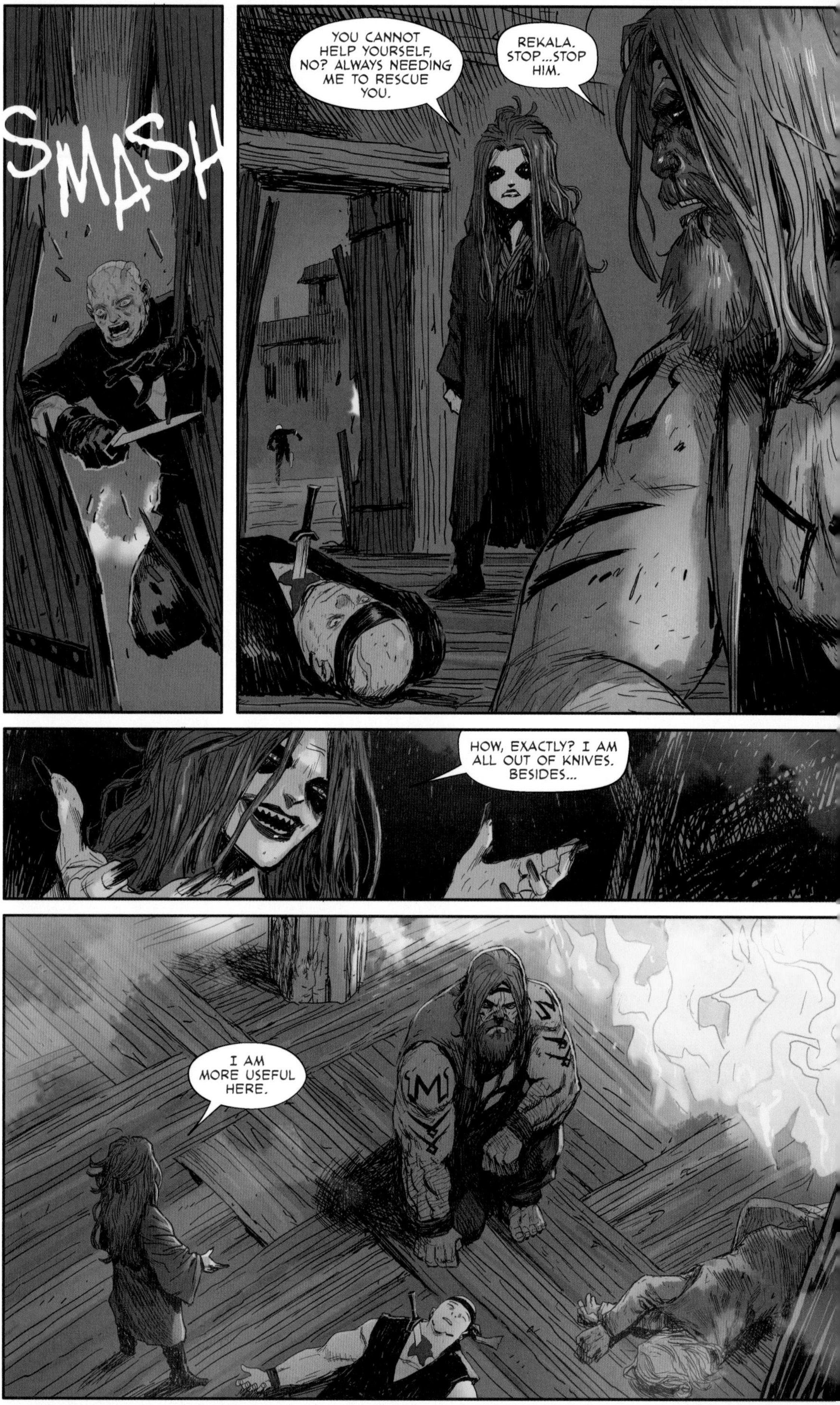
SMASH
YOU CANNOT HELP YOURSELF, NO? ALWAYS NEEDING ME TO RESCUE YOU.
REKALA. STOP...STOP HIM.
HOW, EXACTLY? I AM ALL OUT OF KNIVES. BESIDES...
I AM MORE USEFUL HERE.

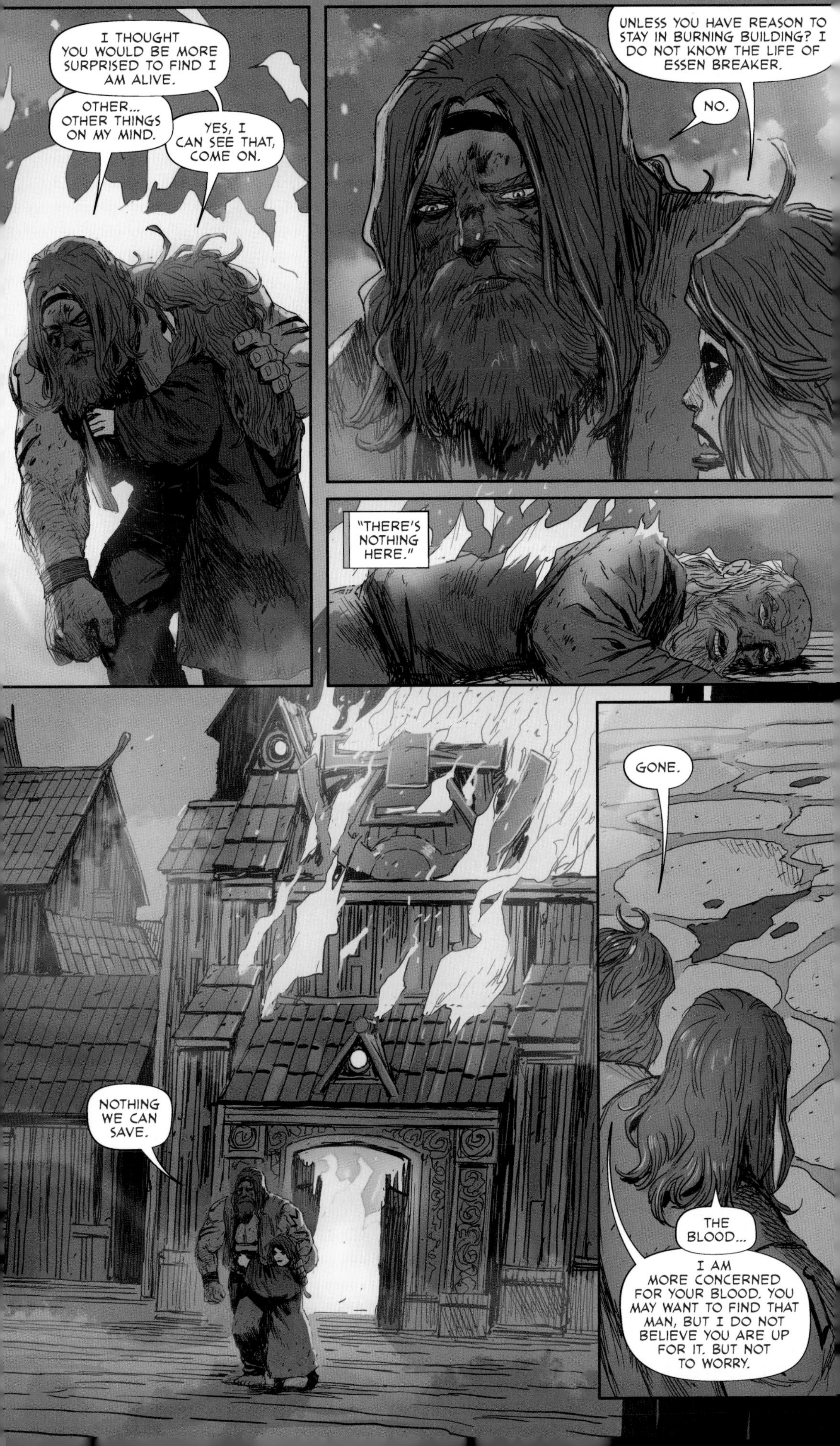
I THOUGHT YOU WOULD BE MORE SURPRISED TO FIND I AM ALIVE.
OTHER... OTHER THINGS ON MY MIND.
YES, I CAN SEE THAT, COME ON.
UNLESS YOU HAVE REASON TO STAY IN BURNING BUILDING? I DO NOT KNOW THE LIFE OF ESSEN BREAKER.
NO.
"THERE'S NOTHING HERE."
NOTHING WE CAN SAVE.
GONE.
THE BLOOD...
I AM MORE CONCERNED FOR YOUR BLOOD. YOU MAY WANT TO FIND THAT MAN, BUT I DO NOT BELIEVE YOU ARE UP FOR IT. BUT NOT TO WORRY.

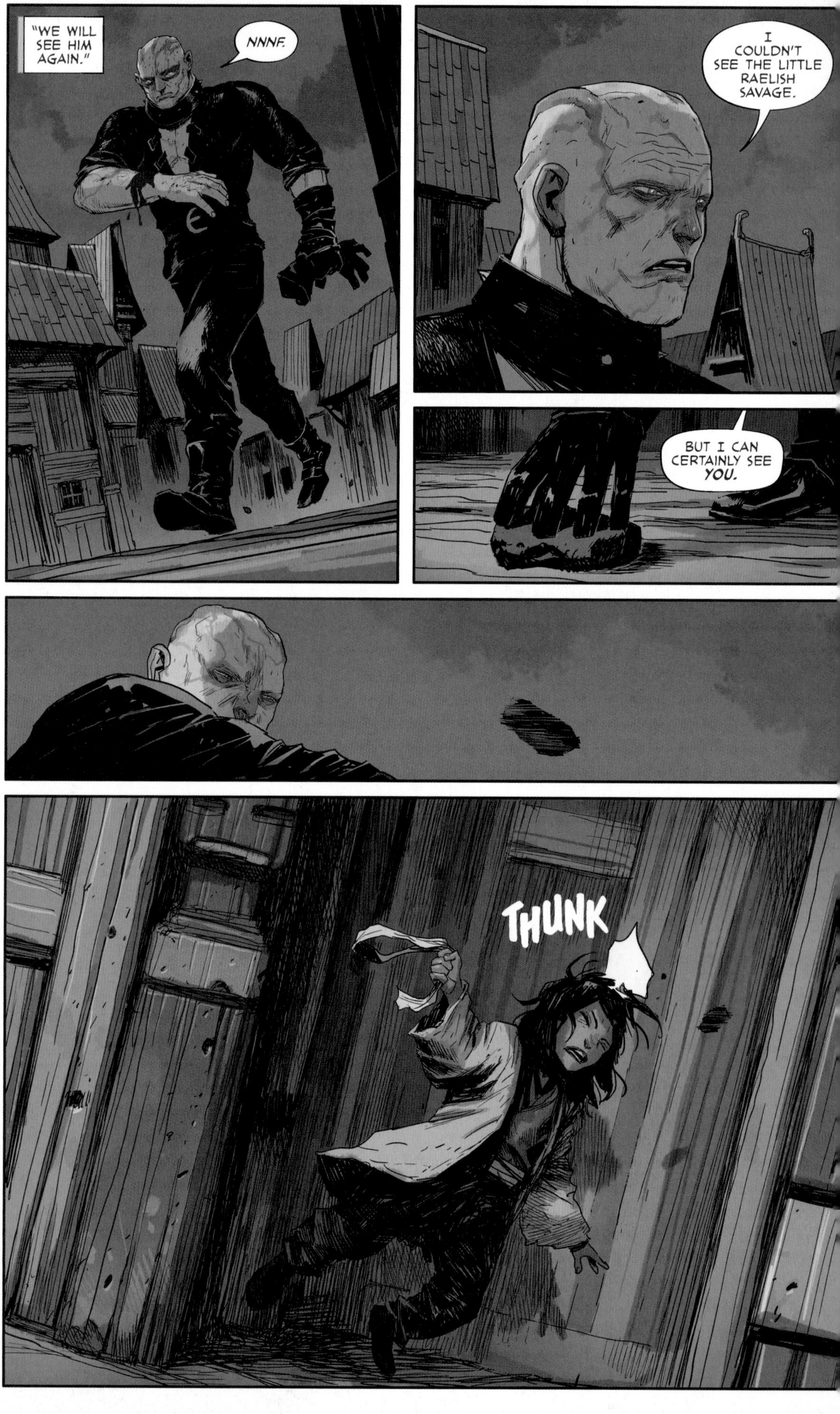
"WE WILL SEE HIM AGAIN."
NNNF.
I COULDN'T SEE THE LITTLE RAELISH SAVAGE.
BUT I CAN CERTAINLY SEE YOU.
THUNK

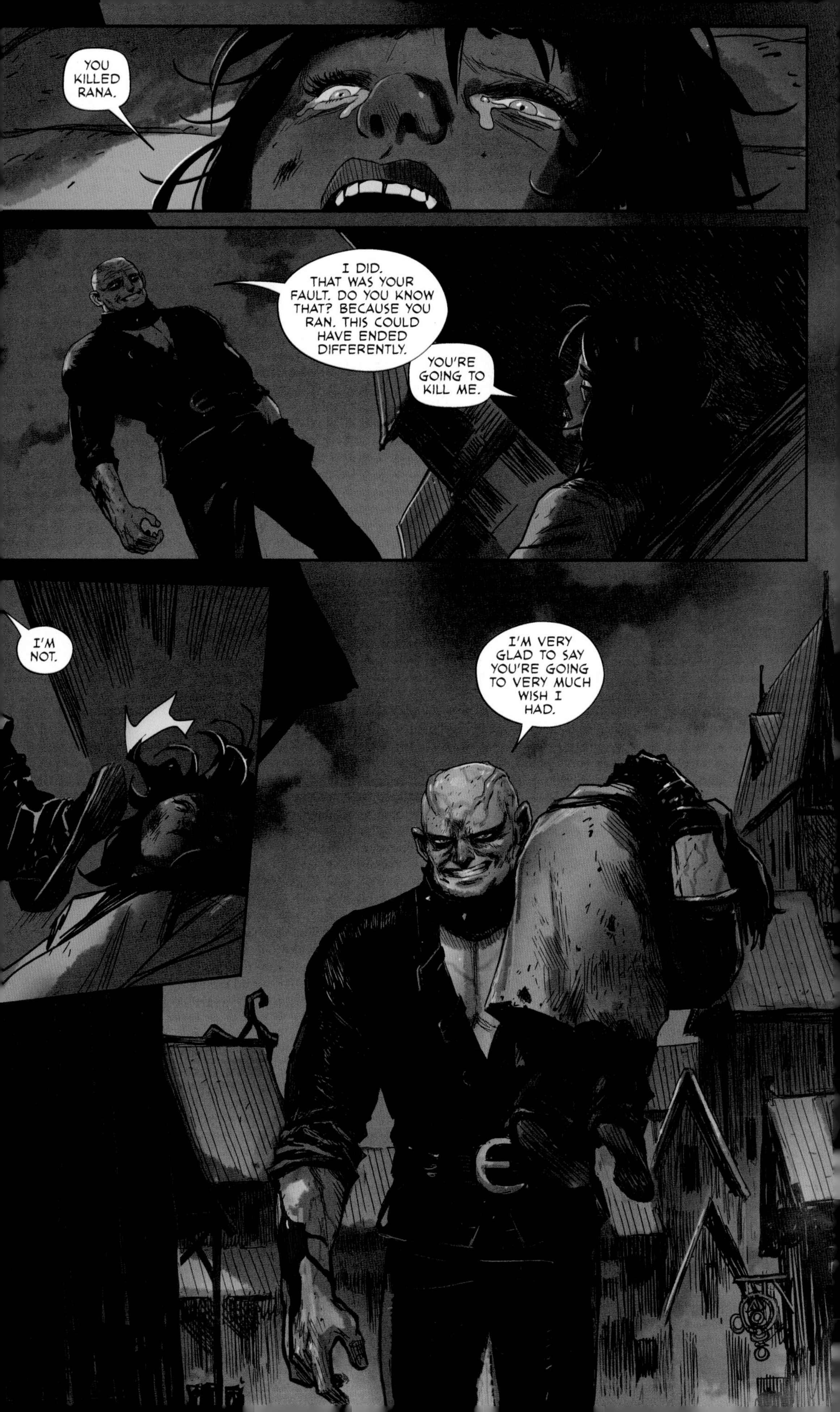
YOU KILLED RANA.
I DID. THAT WAS YOUR FAULT. DO YOU KNOW THAT? BECAUSE YOU RAN. THIS COULD HAVE ENDED DIFFERENTLY.
YOU'RE GOING TO KILL ME.
I'M NOT.
I'M VERY GLAD TO SAY YOU'RE GOING TO VERY MUCH WISH I HAD.

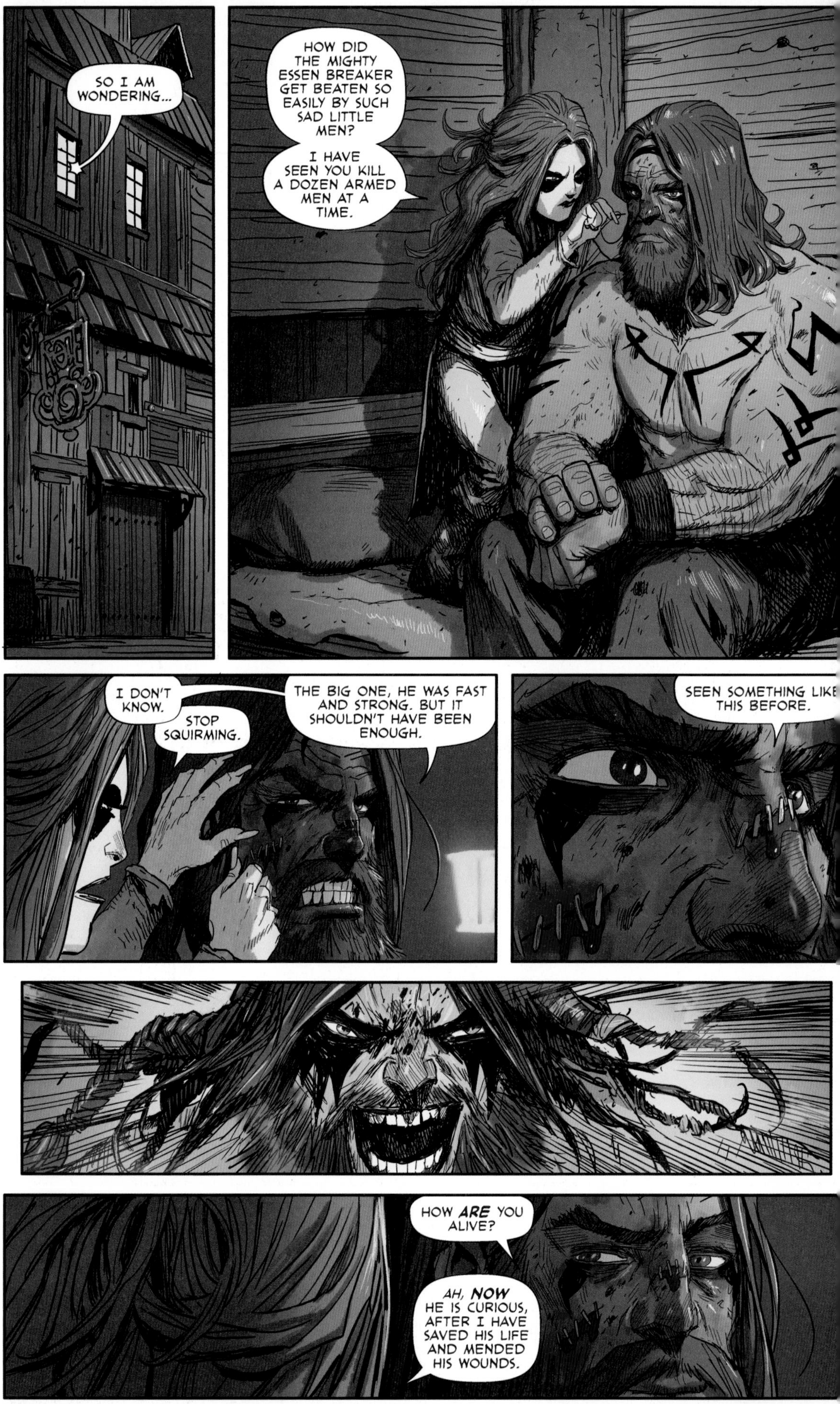
SO I AM WONDERING...
HOW DID THE MIGHTY ESSEN BREAKER GET BEATEN SO EASILY BY SUCH SAD LITTLE MEN?
I HAVE SEEN YOU KILL A DOZEN ARMED MEN AT A TIME.
I DON'T KNOW.
STOP SQUIRMING.
THE BIG ONE, HE WAS FAST AND STRONG. BUT IT SHOULDN'T HAVE BEEN ENOUGH.
SEEN SOMETHING LIKE THIS BEFORE.
HOW *ARE* YOU ALIVE?
*AH, **NOW*** HE IS CURIOUS, AFTER I HAVE SAVED HIS LIFE AND MENDED HIS WOUNDS.

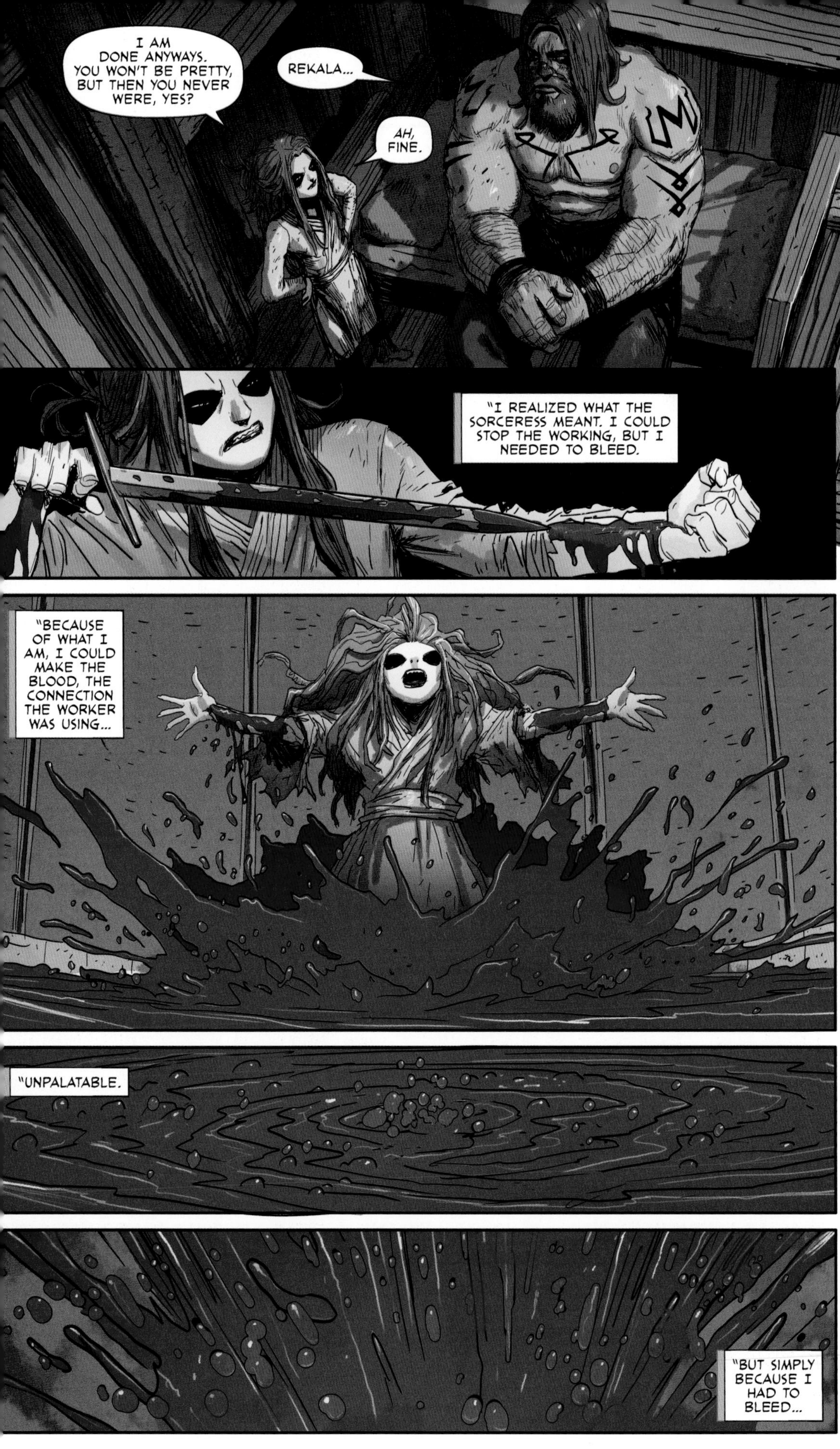
I AM DONE ANYWAYS. YOU WON'T BE PRETTY, BUT THEN YOU NEVER WERE, YES?
REKALA...
AH, FINE.
"I REALIZED WHAT THE SORCERESS MEANT. I COULD STOP THE WORKING, BUT I NEEDED TO BLEED.
"BECAUSE OF WHAT I AM, I COULD MAKE THE BLOOD, THE CONNECTION THE WORKER WAS USING...
"UNPALATABLE.
"BUT SIMPLY BECAUSE I HAD TO BLEED...

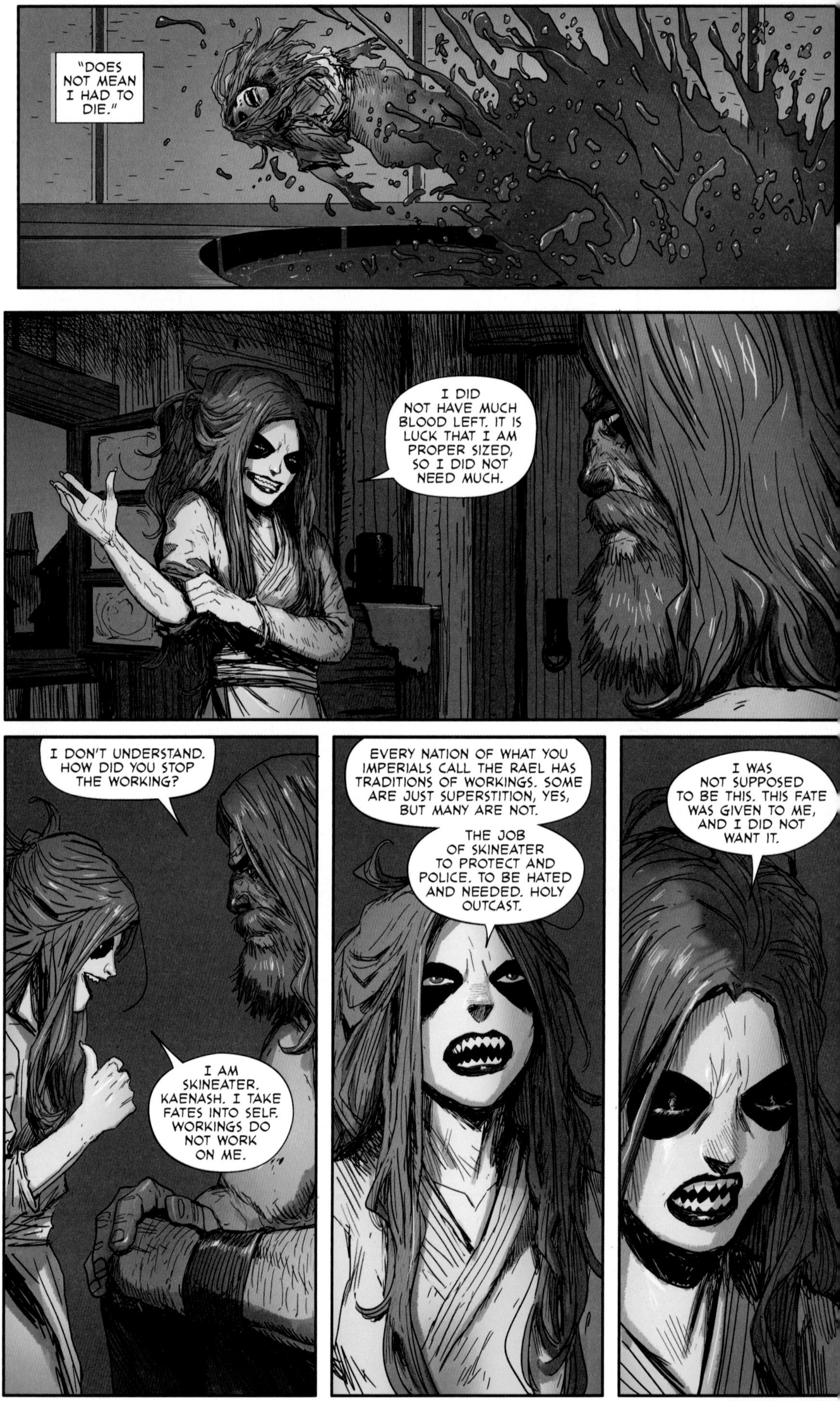
"DOES NOT MEAN I HAD TO DIE."
I DID NOT HAVE MUCH BLOOD LEFT. IT IS LUCK THAT I AM PROPER SIZED, SO I DID NOT NEED MUCH.
I DON'T UNDERSTAND. HOW DID YOU STOP THE WORKING?
I AM SKINEATER. KAENASH. I TAKE FATES INTO SELF. WORKINGS DO NOT WORK ON ME.
EVERY NATION OF WHAT YOU IMPERIALS CALL THE RAEL HAS TRADITIONS OF WORKINGS. SOME ARE JUST SUPERSTITION, YES, BUT MANY ARE NOT.
THE JOB OF SKINEATER TO PROTECT AND POLICE. TO BE HATED AND NEEDED. HOLY OUTCAST.
I WAS NOT SUPPOSED TO BE THIS. THIS FATE WAS GIVEN TO ME, AND I DID NOT WANT IT.

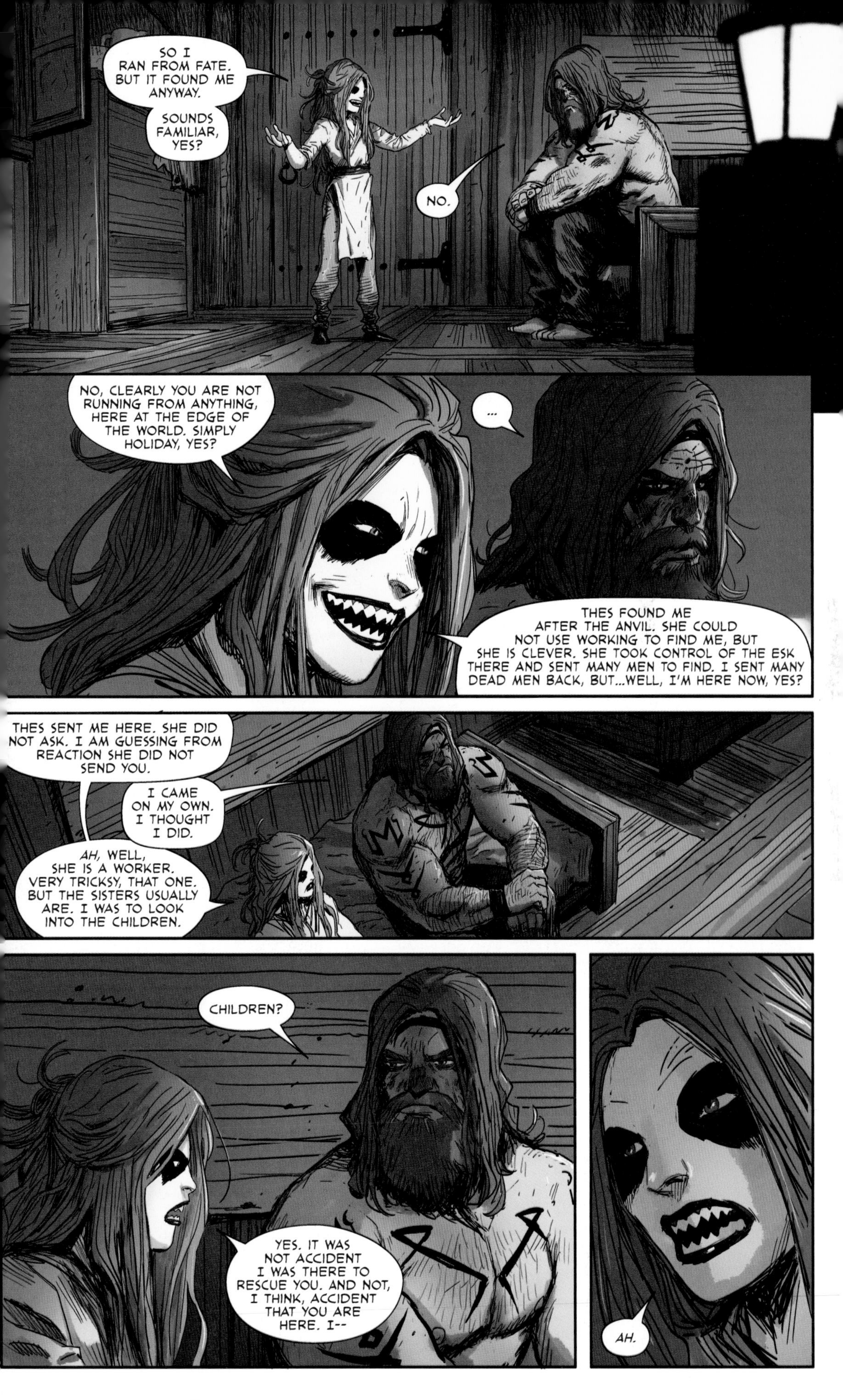
SO I RAN FROM FATE. BUT IT FOUND ME ANYWAY.
SOUNDS FAMILIAR, YES?
NO.
NO, CLEARLY YOU ARE NOT RUNNING FROM ANYTHING, HERE AT THE EDGE OF THE WORLD. SIMPLY HOLIDAY, YES?
...
THES FOUND ME AFTER THE ANVIL. SHE COULD NOT USE WORKING TO FIND ME, BUT SHE IS CLEVER. SHE TOOK CONTROL OF THE ESK THERE AND SENT MANY MEN TO FIND. I SENT MANY DEAD MEN BACK, BUT...WELL, I'M HERE NOW, YES?
THES SENT ME HERE. SHE DID NOT ASK. I AM GUESSING FROM REACTION SHE DID NOT SEND YOU.
I CAME ON MY OWN. I THOUGHT I DID.
AH, WELL, SHE IS A WORKER. VERY TRICKSY, THAT ONE. BUT THE SISTERS USUALLY ARE. I WAS TO LOOK INTO THE CHILDREN.
CHILDREN?
YES. IT WAS NOT ACCIDENT I WAS THERE TO RESCUE YOU. AND NOT, I THINK, ACCIDENT THAT YOU ARE HERE. I--
AH.

OH, WONDERFUL, YOU'RE HERE.

WHERE ELSE WOULD I BE?

ISN'T THAT THE QUESTION...

THERE'S A FIRE AT RANA'S. THE WHOLE STREET'S IN DANGER OF BURNING DOWN. BUT YOU KNOW THAT, DON'T YOU?

DON'T BOTHER. YOU NEVER COULD LIE PROPERLY, FOR ALL THAT I TRIED TO TEACH YOU.

LOOK AT YOU. BEAT TO FUCK AND A FIRE RAGING? YOU CAN'T EXPECT ME TO BELIEVE THOSE AREN'T CONNECTED.

FUCK, ESS. JUST...FUCK. HOW DID THEY FUCKING KICK YOUR GIANT ARSE?

I DON'T KNOW.

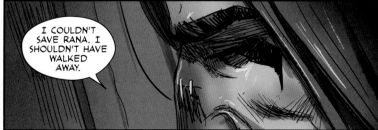

I COULDN'T SAVE RANA. I SHOULDN'T HAVE WALKED AWAY.

YOU DID THE RIGHT THING. I KNOW YOU THINK YOU NEED TO ATONE. I EVEN HEARD TELL WHY YOU THINK, WHAT YOU DID TO THE SOLDIERS AT THE REACH, BUT YOU DON'T. YOU DON'T OWE THE WORLD ANYTHING. NONE OF US DO. WE'VE ALREADY PAID.

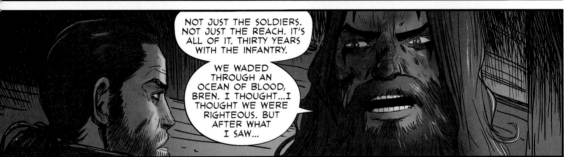

NOT JUST THE SOLDIERS. NOT JUST THE REACH. IT'S ALL OF IT. THIRTY YEARS WITH THE INFANTRY.

WE WADED THROUGH AN OCEAN OF BLOOD, BREN. I THOUGHT...I THOUGHT WE WERE RIGHTEOUS. BUT AFTER WHAT I SAW...

WHAT *WE* SAW. AFTER THE WAR, WHEN THEY SENT US TO *"MAKE PEACE"* WITH THE RAEL IN THE TERRITORIES.

THEY DIDN'T GO EASY. AND MAYBE THEY SHOULDN'T HAVE WENT AT ALL.

IT'S WHY YOU LEFT.

IT WASN'T JUST THAT. IT WAS ALL OF IT. IT WAS THE SHIT AND THE MUD AND THE BLOOD AND...IT WAS EVERYTHING. I SAW THE WAR, JUST NEVER THE SPOILS.

WE SHOULD HAVE DONE BETTER. EVERYONE SHOULD DO BETTER. I WANT TO DO BETTER. I JUST DON'T KNOW HOW.

WHO THE FUCK DOES? YOU DO THE BEST YOU CAN FOR YOU AND YOURS, AND FUCK EVERYONE ELSE.

IT'S JUST THE WAY OF THE WORLD.

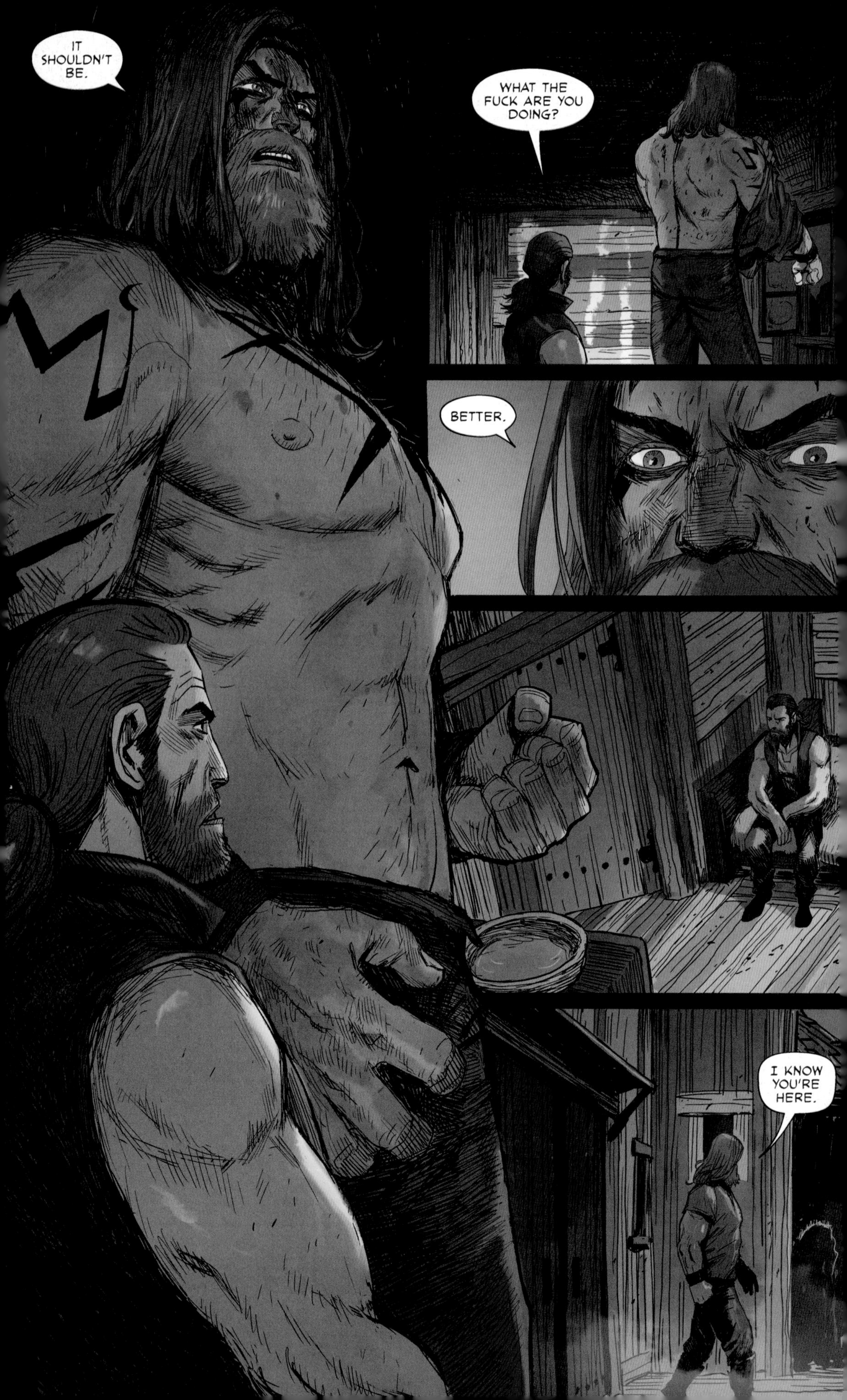
IT SHOULDN'T BE.
WHAT THE FUCK ARE YOU DOING?
BETTER.
I KNOW YOU'RE HERE.

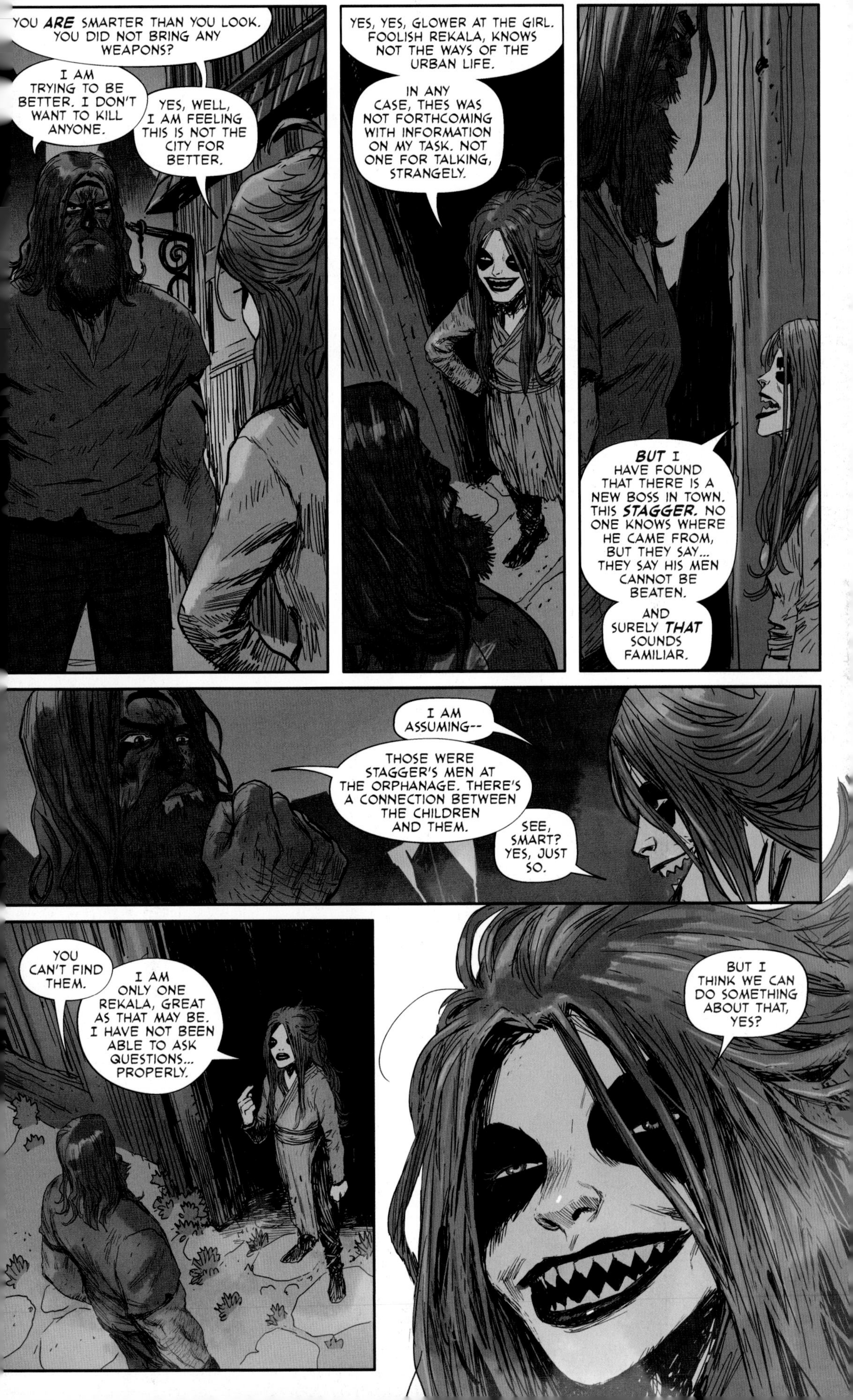
YOU *ARE* SMARTER THAN YOU LOOK. YOU DID NOT BRING ANY WEAPONS?
I AM TRYING TO BE BETTER. I DON'T WANT TO KILL ANYONE.
YES, WELL, I AM FEELING THIS IS NOT THE CITY FOR BETTER.
YES, YES, GLOWER AT THE GIRL. FOOLISH REKALA, KNOWS NOT THE WAYS OF THE URBAN LIFE.
IN ANY CASE, THES WAS NOT FORTHCOMING WITH INFORMATION ON MY TASK. NOT ONE FOR TALKING, STRANGELY.
BUT I HAVE FOUND THAT THERE IS A NEW BOSS IN TOWN. THIS *STAGGER.* NO ONE KNOWS WHERE HE CAME FROM, BUT THEY SAY... THEY SAY HIS MEN CANNOT BE BEATEN.
AND SURELY *THAT* SOUNDS FAMILIAR.
I AM ASSUMING--
THOSE WERE STAGGER'S MEN AT THE ORPHANAGE. THERE'S A CONNECTION BETWEEN THE CHILDREN AND THEM.
SEE, SMART? YES, JUST SO.
YOU CAN'T FIND THEM.
I AM ONLY ONE REKALA, GREAT AS THAT MAY BE. I HAVE NOT BEEN ABLE TO ASK QUESTIONS... PROPERLY.
BUT I THINK WE CAN DO SOMETHING ABOUT THAT, YES?

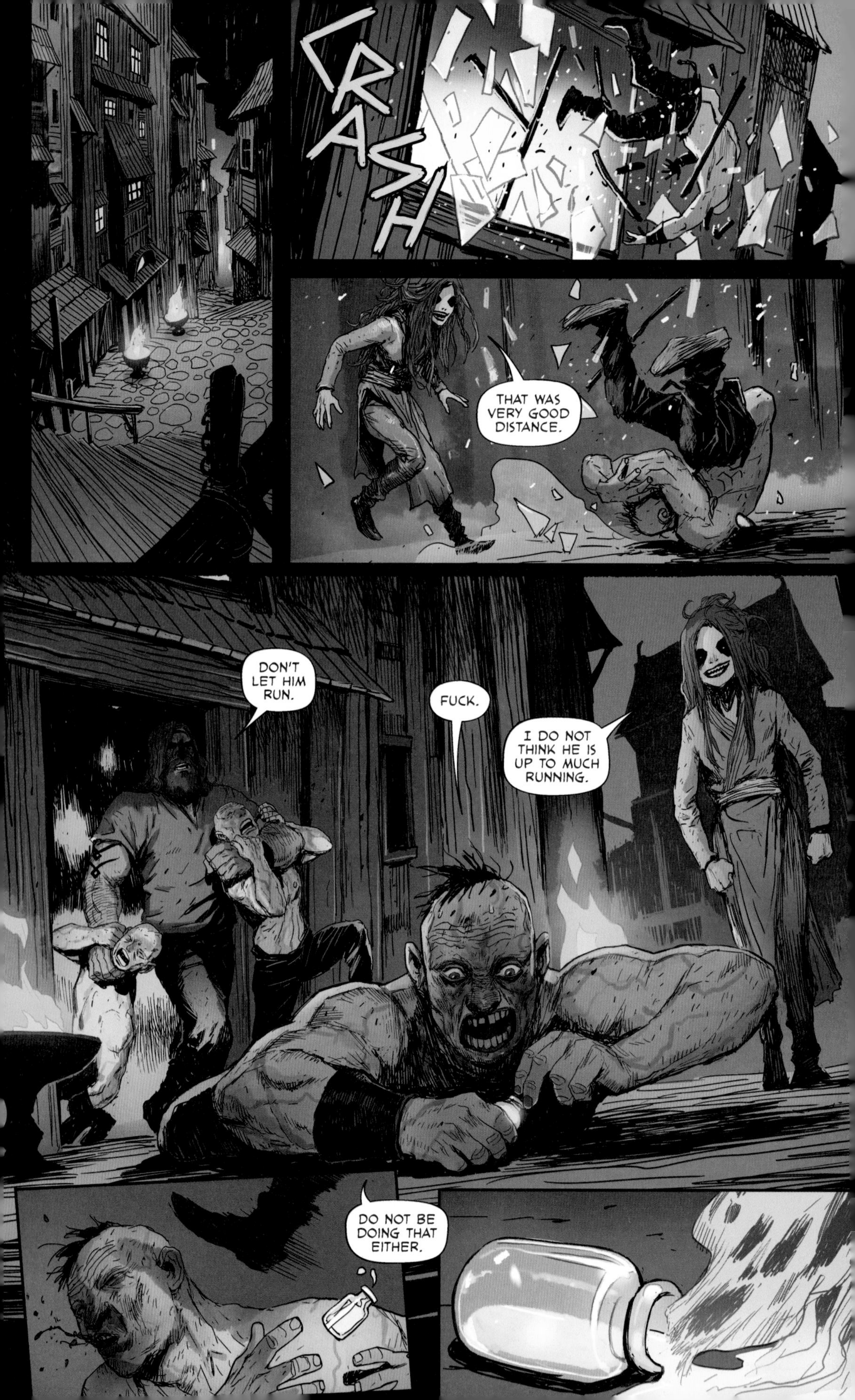
CRASH
THAT WAS VERY GOOD DISTANCE.
DON'T LET HIM RUN.
FUCK.
I DO NOT THINK HE IS UP TO MUCH RUNNING.
DO NOT BE DOING THAT EITHER.

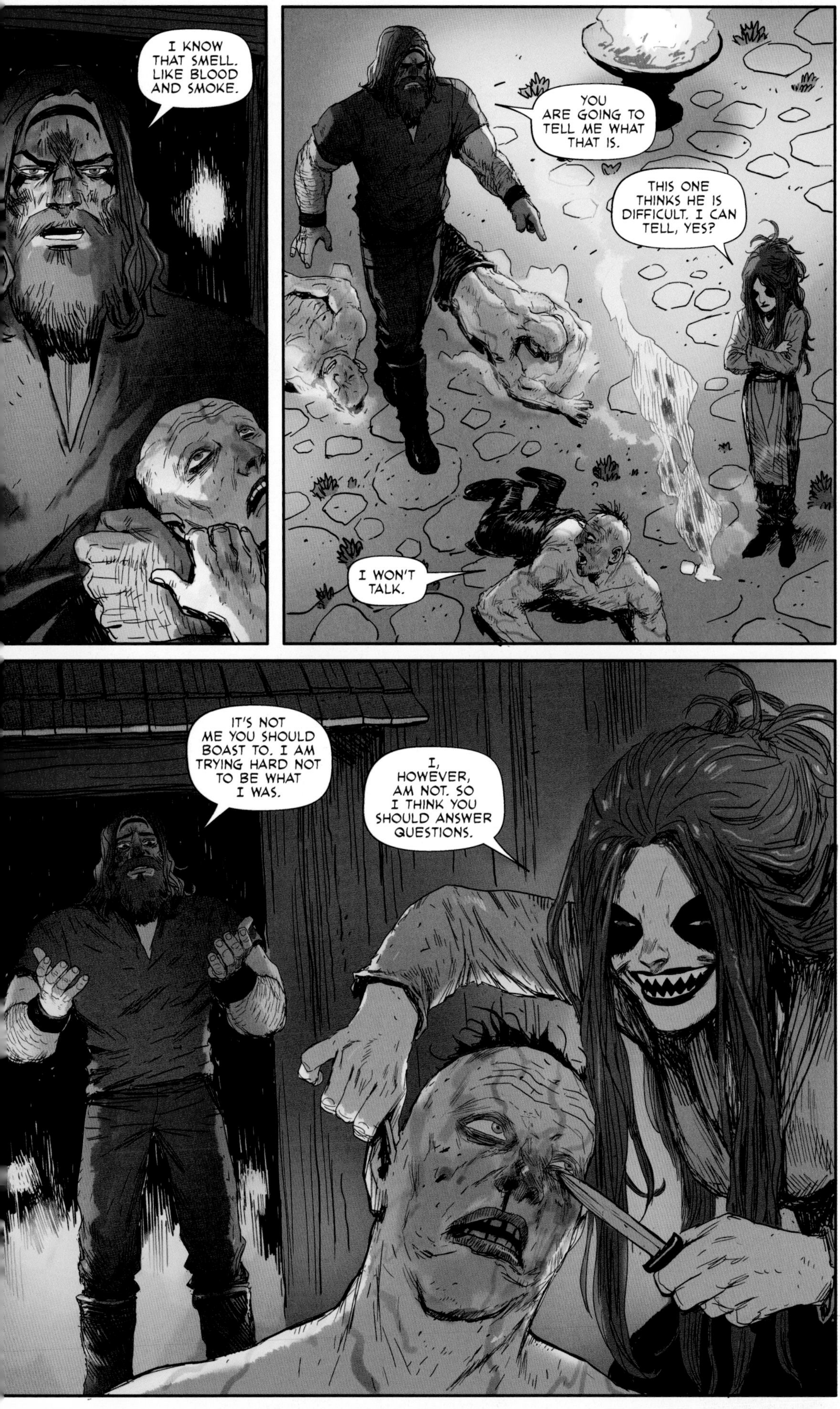

I KNOW THAT SMELL. LIKE BLOOD AND SMOKE.
YOU ARE GOING TO TELL ME WHAT THAT IS.
THIS ONE THINKS HE IS DIFFICULT. I CAN TELL, YES?
I WON'T TALK.
IT'S NOT ME YOU SHOULD BOAST TO. I AM TRYING HARD NOT TO BE WHAT I WAS.
I, HOWEVER, AM NOT. SO I THINK YOU SHOULD ANSWER QUESTIONS.

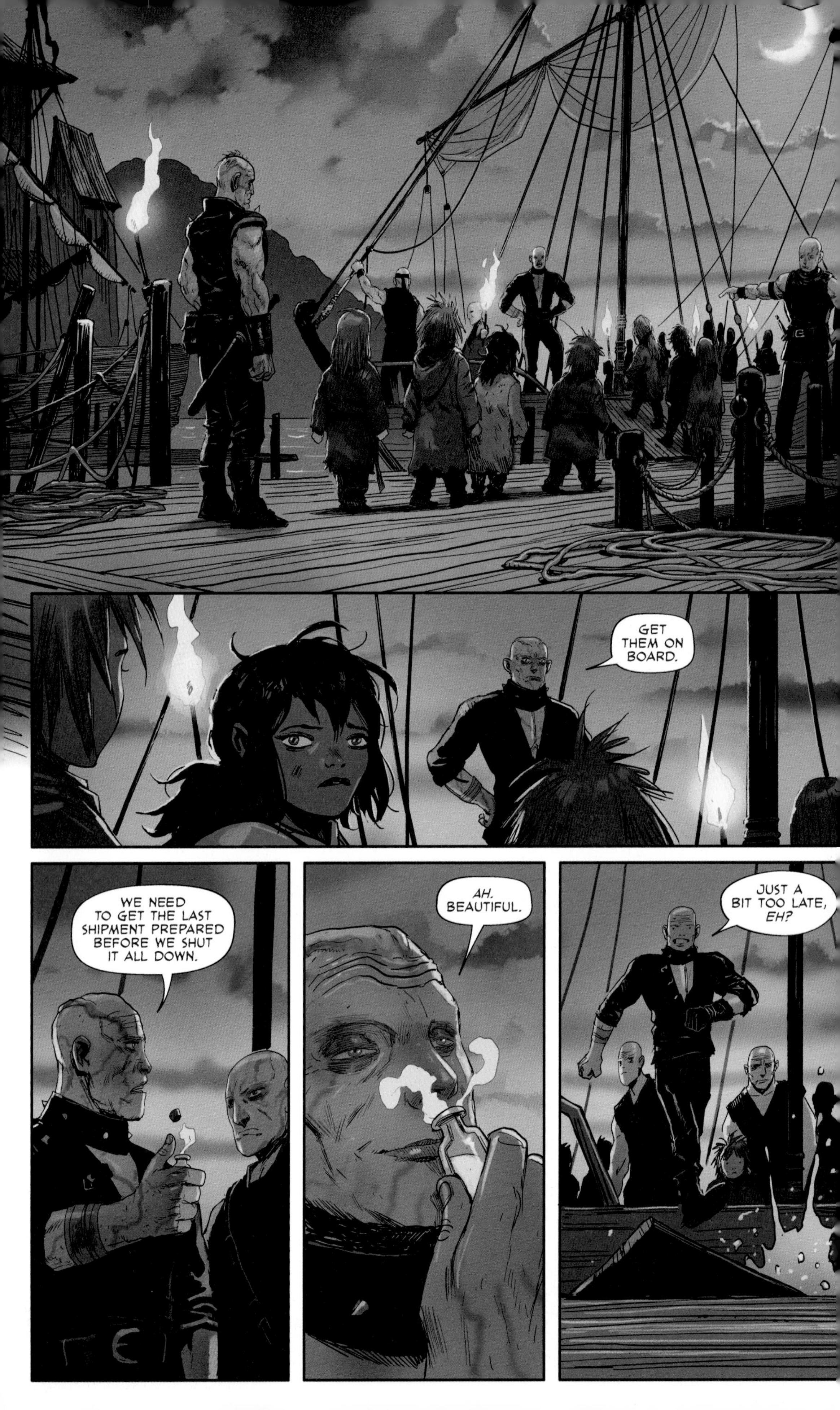
GET THEM ON BOARD.
WE NEED TO GET THE LAST SHIPMENT PREPARED BEFORE WE SHUT IT ALL DOWN.
AH. BEAUTIFUL.
JUST A BIT TOO LATE, EH?

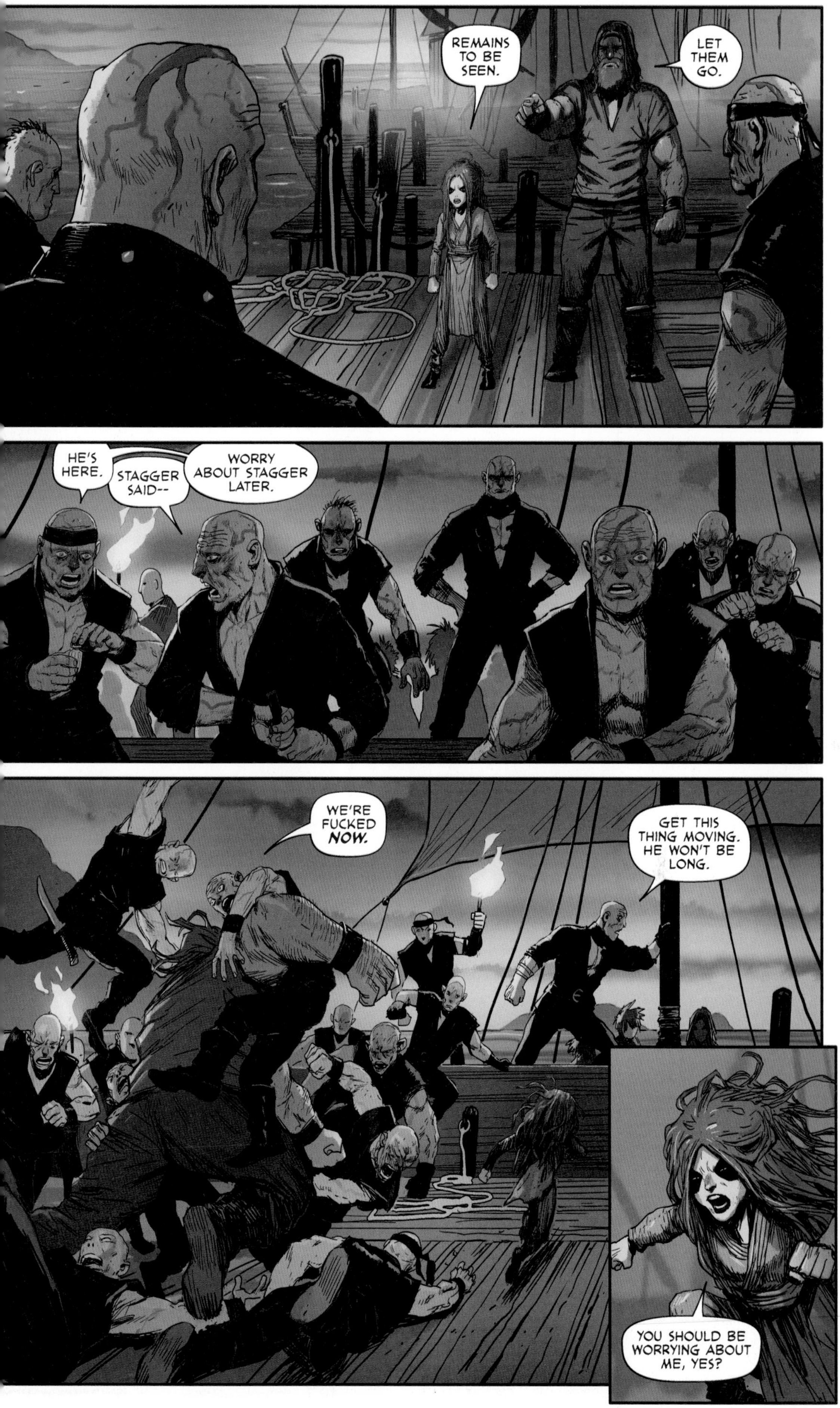
REMAINS TO BE SEEN.
LET THEM GO.
HE'S HERE.
STAGGER SAID--
WORRY ABOUT STAGGER LATER.
WE'RE FUCKED *NOW.*
GET THIS THING MOVING. HE WON'T BE LONG.
YOU SHOULD BE WORRYING ABOUT ME, YES?

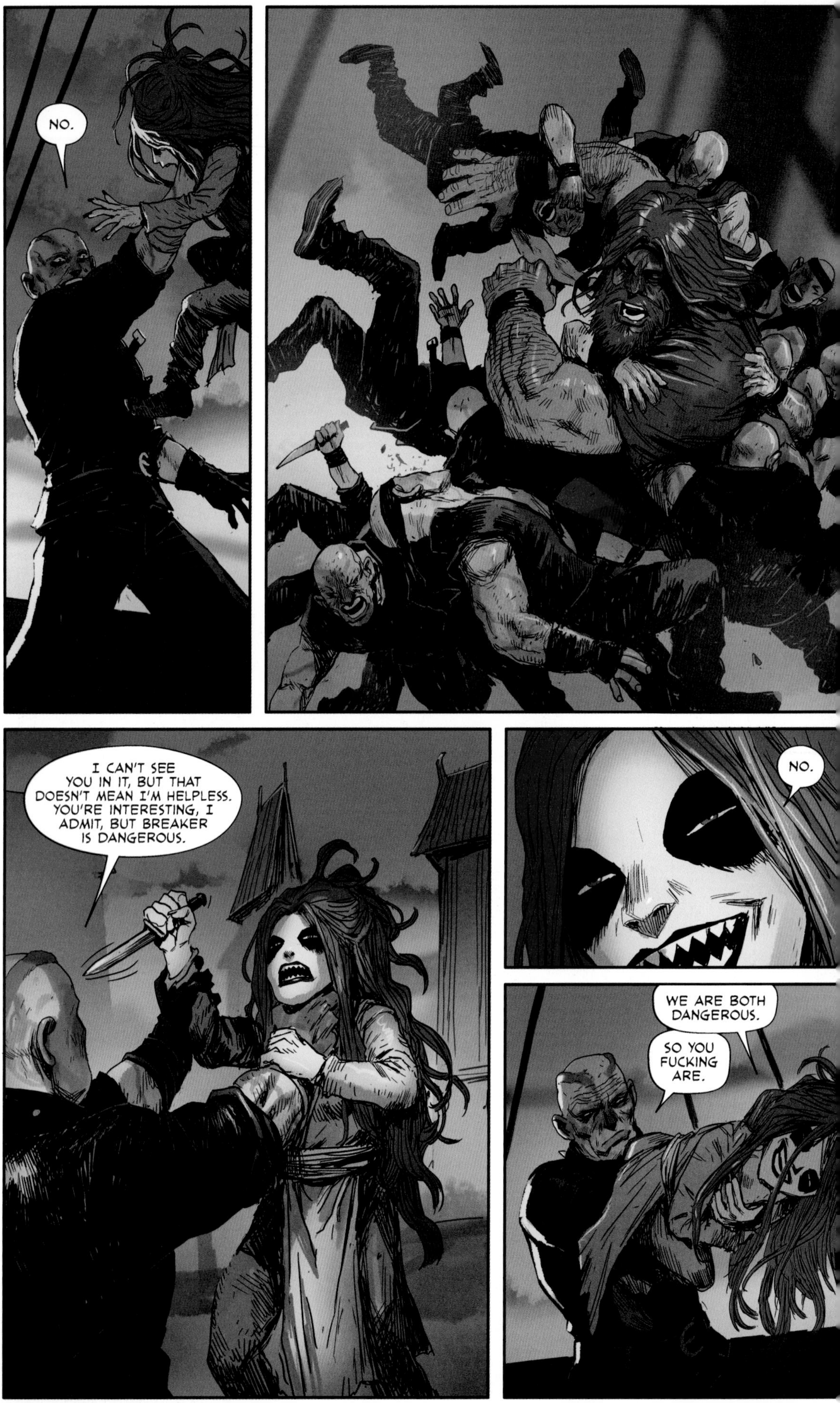
NO.
I CAN'T SEE YOU IN IT, BUT THAT DOESN'T MEAN I'M HELPLESS. YOU'RE INTERESTING, I ADMIT, BUT BREAKER IS DANGEROUS.
NO.
WE ARE BOTH DANGEROUS.
SO YOU FUCKING ARE.

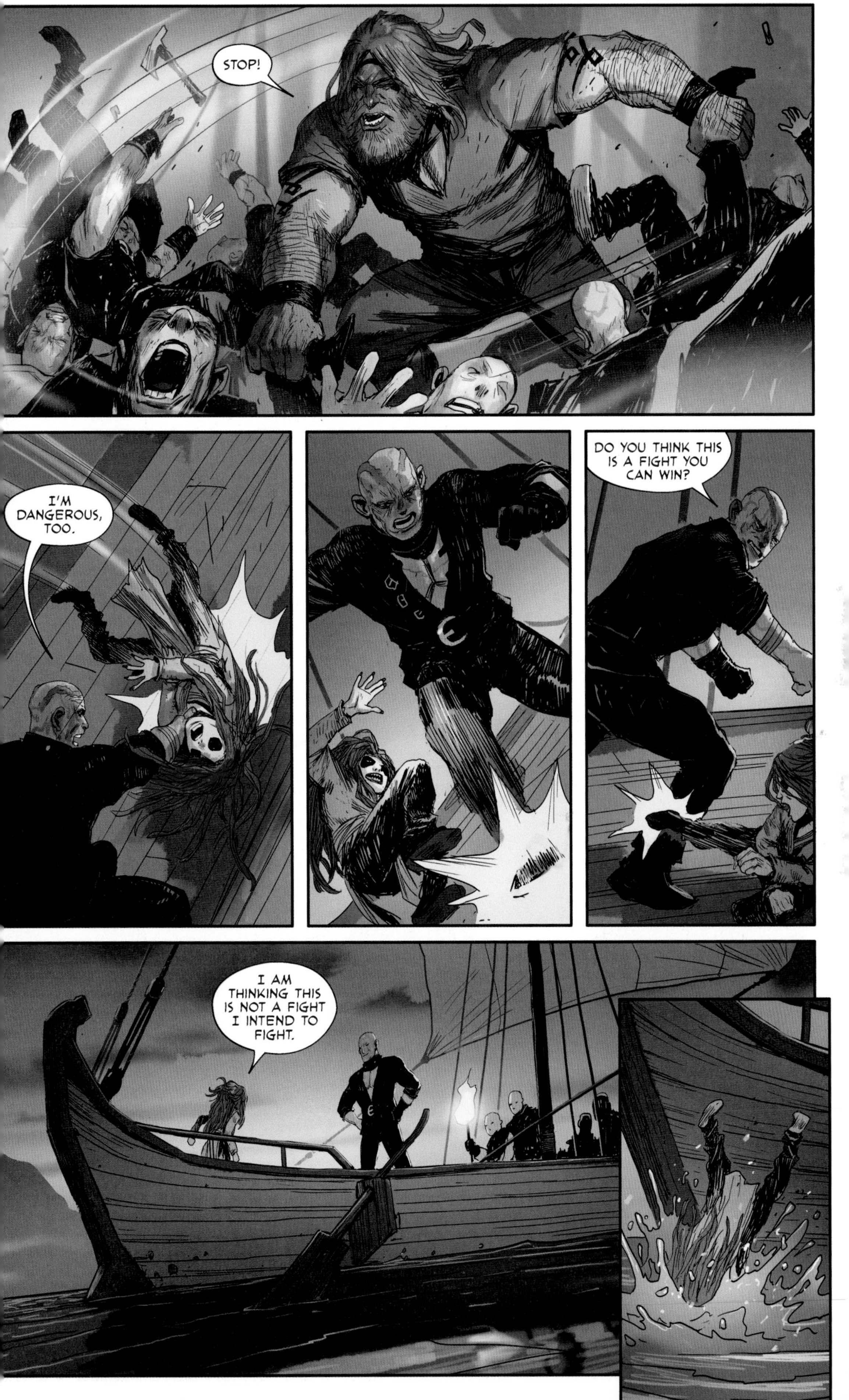
STOP!
I'M DANGEROUS, TOO.
DO YOU THINK THIS IS A FIGHT YOU CAN WIN?
I AM THINKING THIS IS NOT A FIGHT I INTEND TO FIGHT.

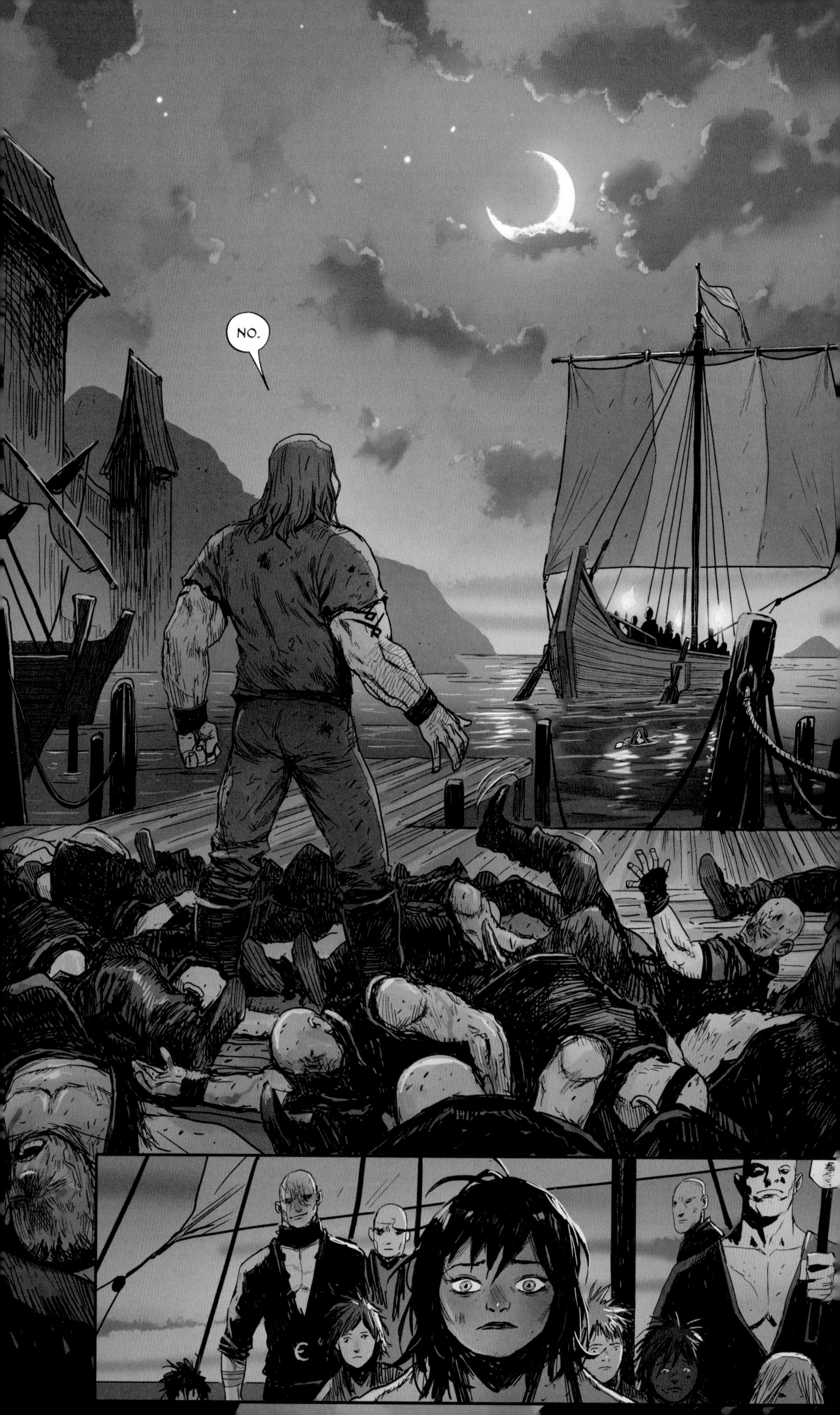
NO.

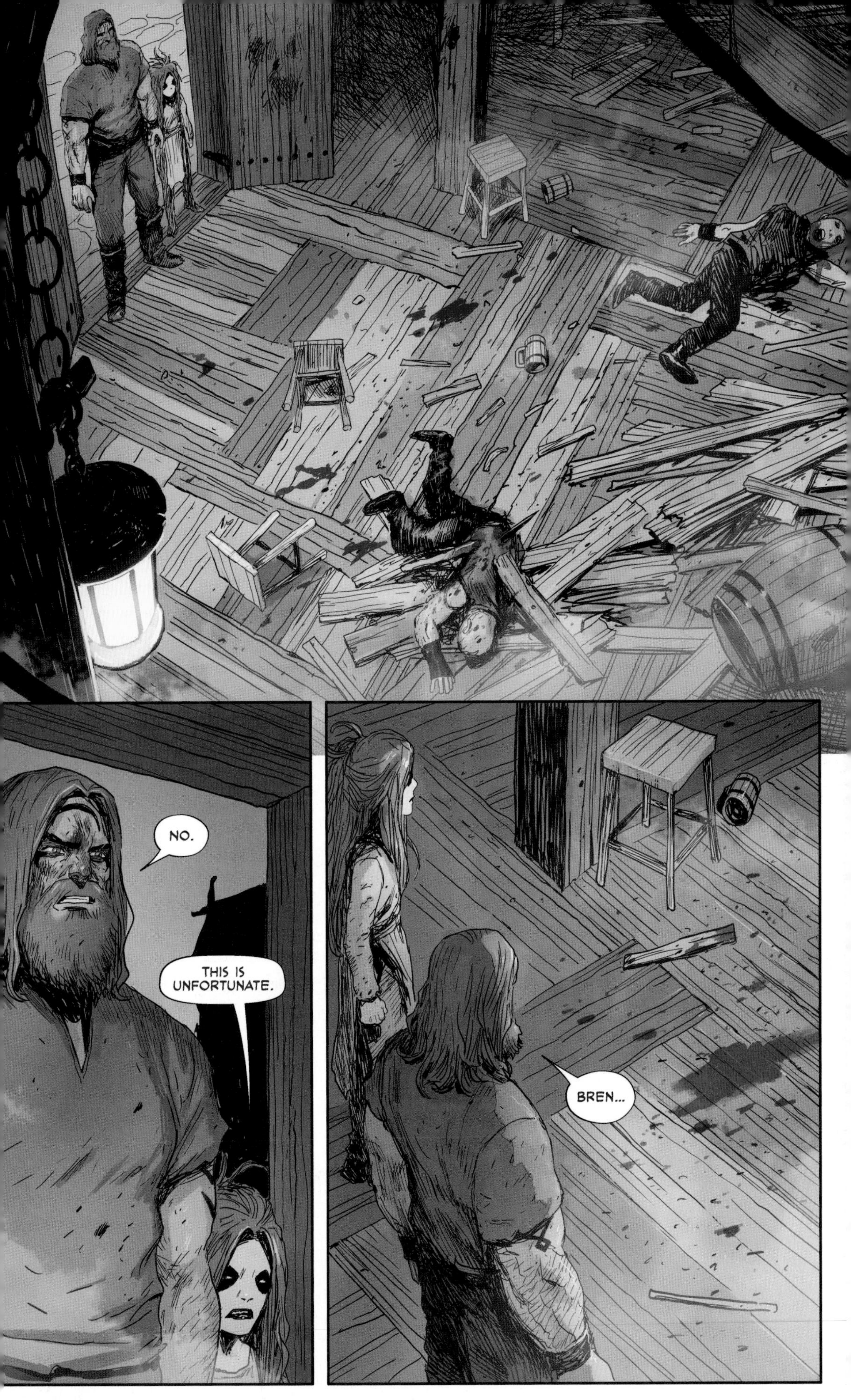
NO.
THIS IS UNFORTUNATE.
BREN...

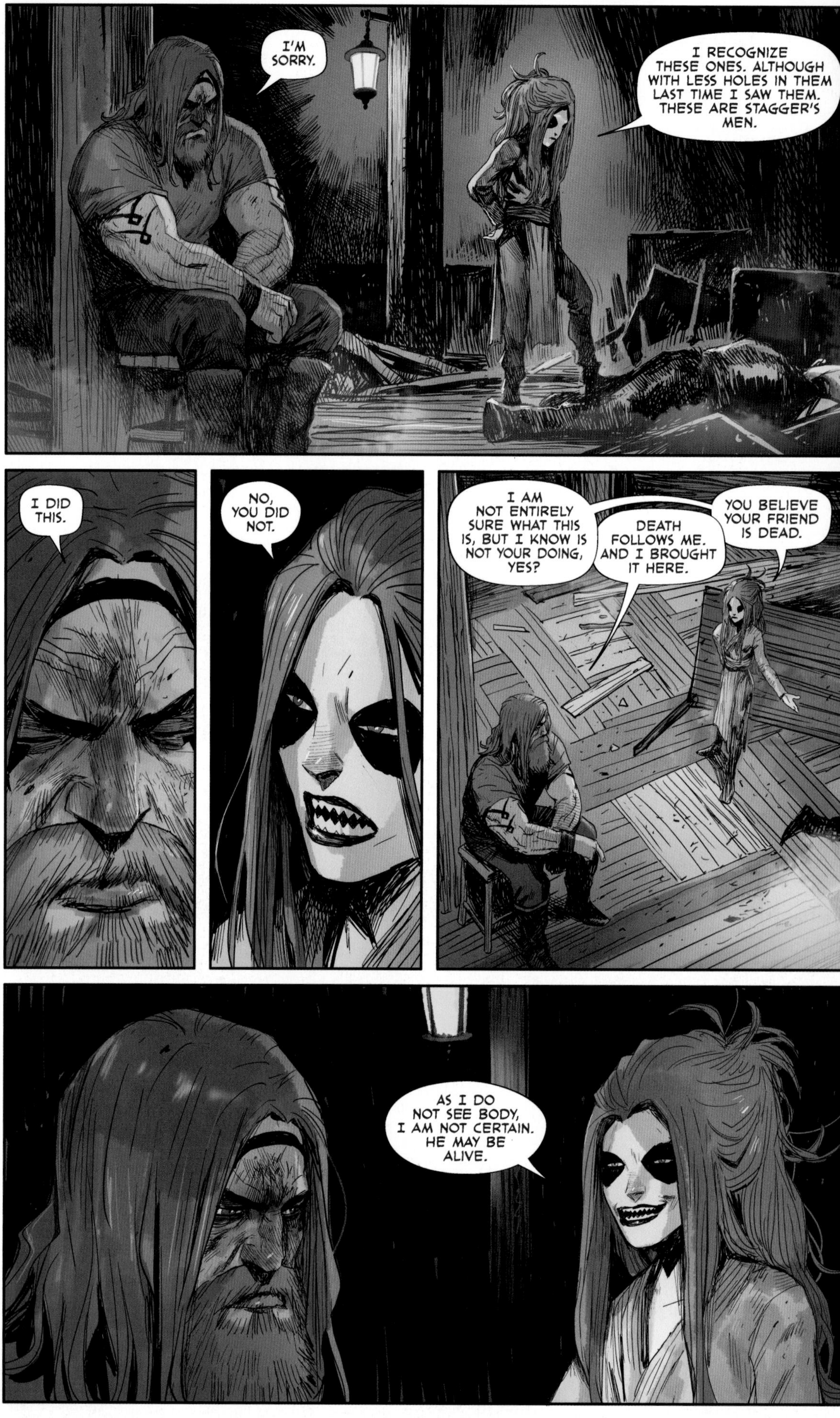
I'M SORRY.
I RECOGNIZE THESE ONES. ALTHOUGH WITH LESS HOLES IN THEM LAST TIME I SAW THEM. THESE ARE STAGGER'S MEN.
I DID THIS.
NO, YOU DID NOT.
I AM NOT ENTIRELY SURE WHAT THIS IS, BUT I KNOW IS NOT YOUR DOING, YES?
DEATH FOLLOWS ME. AND I BROUGHT IT HERE.
YOU BELIEVE YOUR FRIEND IS DEAD.
AS I DO NOT SEE BODY, I AM NOT CERTAIN. HE MAY BE ALIVE.

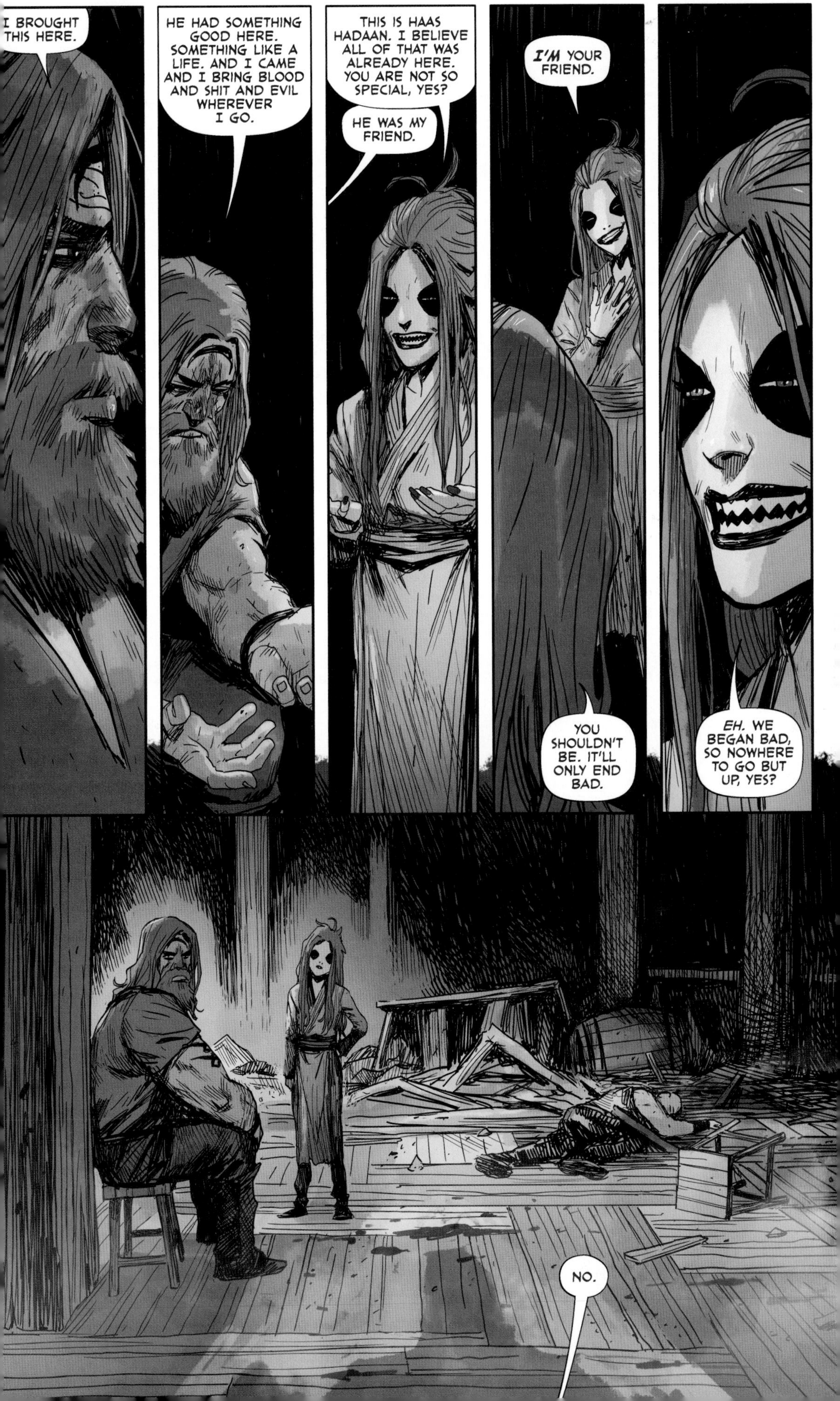
I BROUGHT THIS HERE.
HE HAD SOMETHING GOOD HERE. SOMETHING LIKE A LIFE. AND I CAME AND I BRING BLOOD AND SHIT AND EVIL WHEREVER I GO.
THIS IS HAAS HADAAN. I BELIEVE ALL OF THAT WAS ALREADY HERE. YOU ARE NOT SO SPECIAL, YES?
HE WAS MY FRIEND.
I'M YOUR FRIEND.
YOU SHOULDN'T BE. IT'LL ONLY END BAD.
EH. WE BEGAN BAD, SO NOWHERE TO GO BUT UP, YES?
NO.

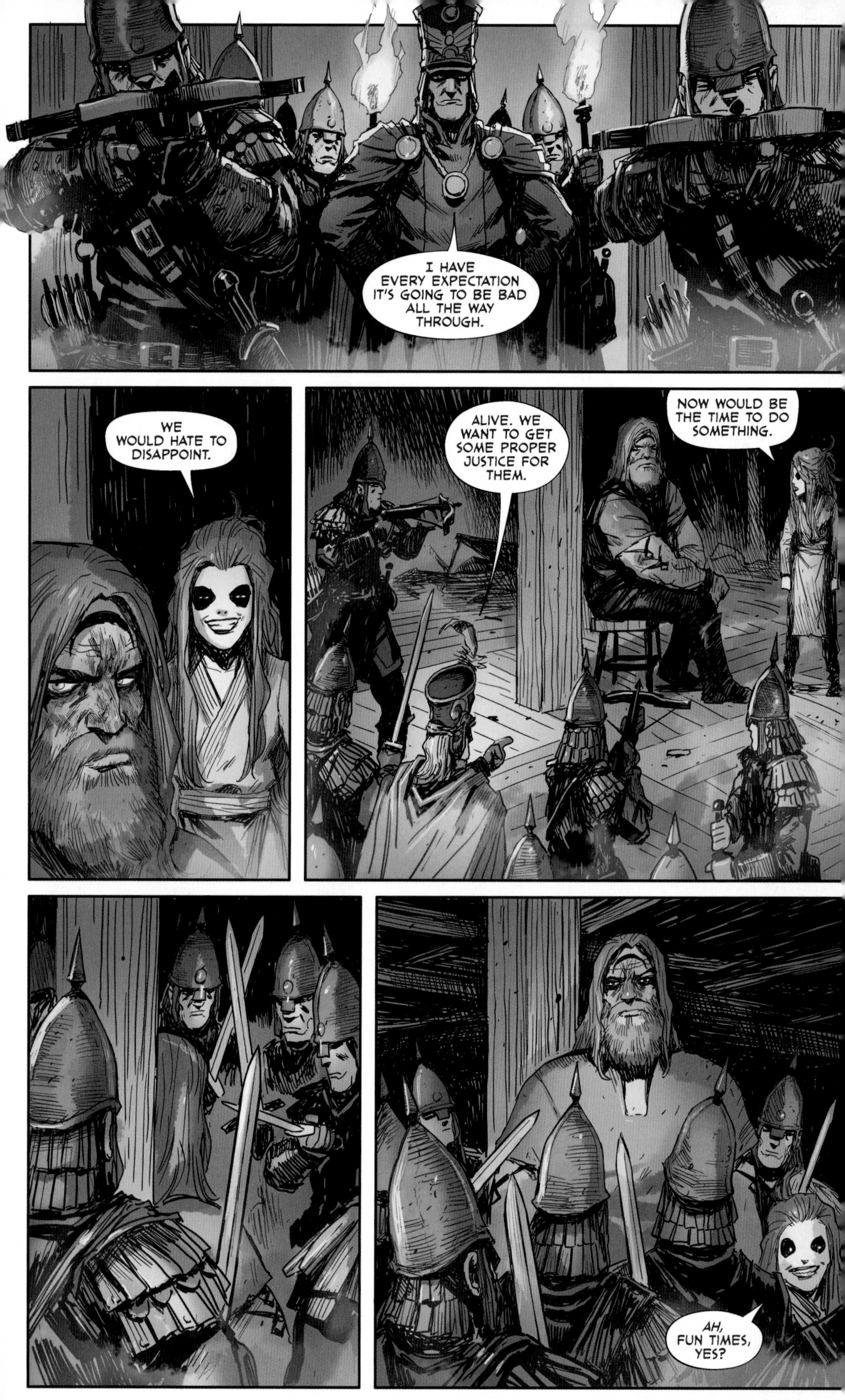
I HAVE EVERY EXPECTATION IT'S GOING TO BE BAD ALL THE WAY THROUGH.
WE WOULD HATE TO DISAPPOINT.
ALIVE. WE WANT TO GET SOME PROPER JUSTICE FOR THEM.
NOW WOULD BE THE TIME TO DO SOMETHING.
AH, FUN TIMES, YES?

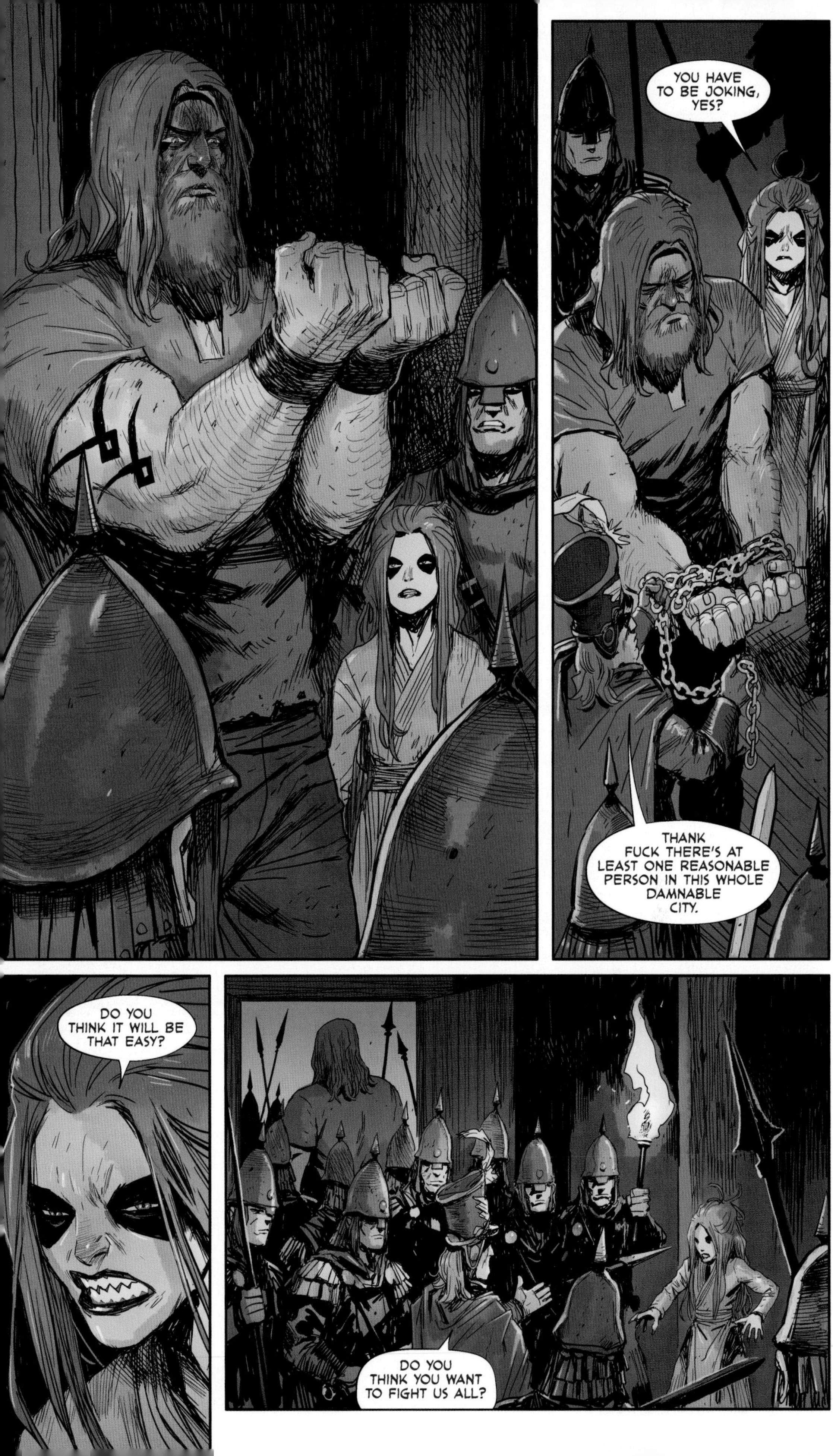
YOU HAVE TO BE JOKING, YES?
THANK FUCK THERE'S AT LEAST ONE REASONABLE PERSON IN THIS WHOLE DAMNABLE CITY.
DO YOU THINK IT WILL BE THAT EASY?
DO YOU THINK YOU WANT TO FIGHT US ALL?

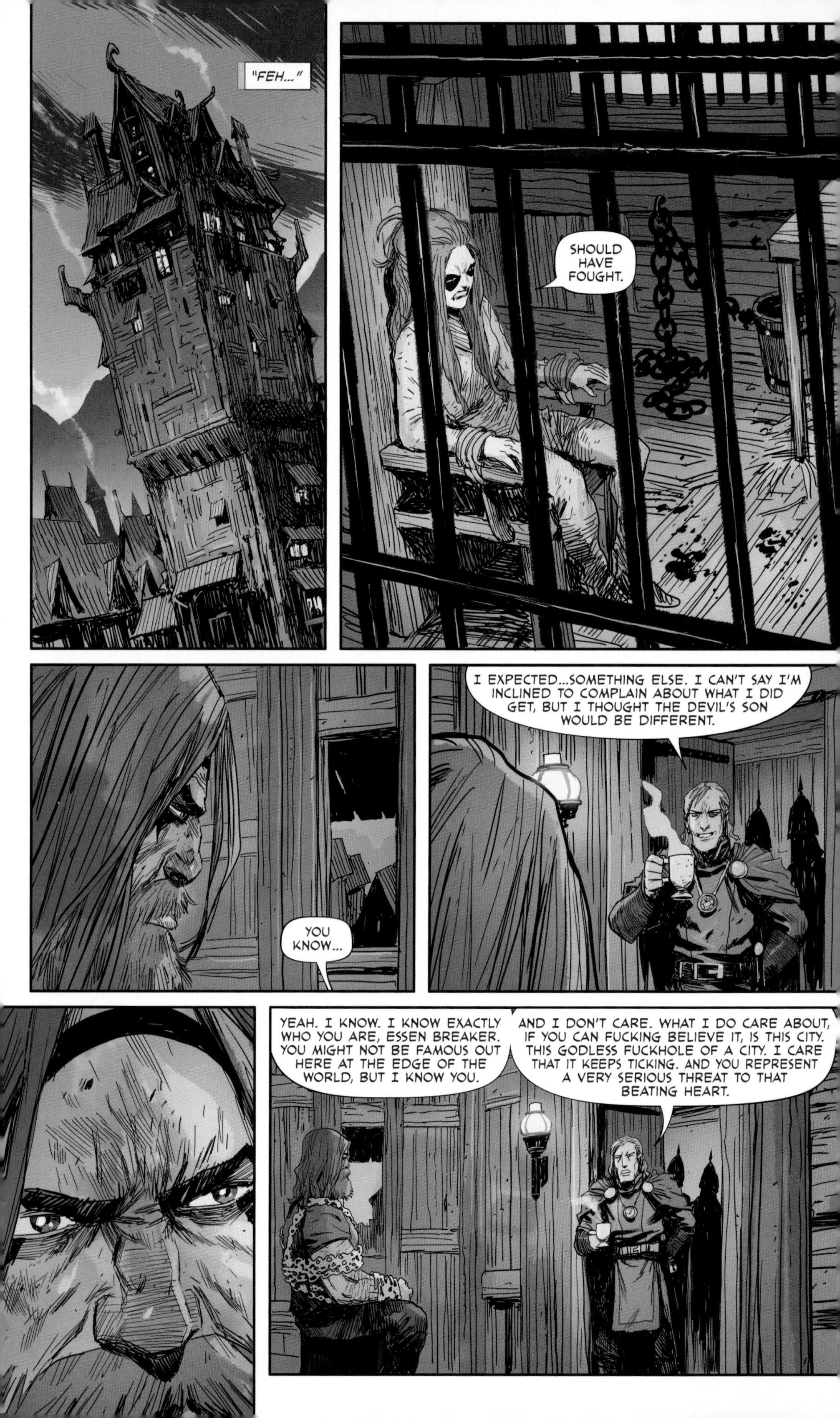
"FEH..."
SHOULD HAVE FOUGHT.
YOU KNOW...
I EXPECTED...SOMETHING ELSE. I CAN'T SAY I'M INCLINED TO COMPLAIN ABOUT WHAT I DID GET, BUT I THOUGHT THE DEVIL'S SON WOULD BE DIFFERENT.
YEAH. I KNOW. I KNOW EXACTLY WHO YOU ARE, ESSEN BREAKER. YOU MIGHT NOT BE FAMOUS OUT HERE AT THE EDGE OF THE WORLD, BUT I KNOW YOU.
AND I DON'T CARE. WHAT I DO CARE ABOUT, IF YOU CAN FUCKING BELIEVE IT, IS THIS CITY. THIS GODLESS FUCKHOLE OF A CITY. I CARE THAT IT KEEPS TICKING. AND YOU REPRESENT A VERY SERIOUS THREAT TO THAT BEATING HEART.

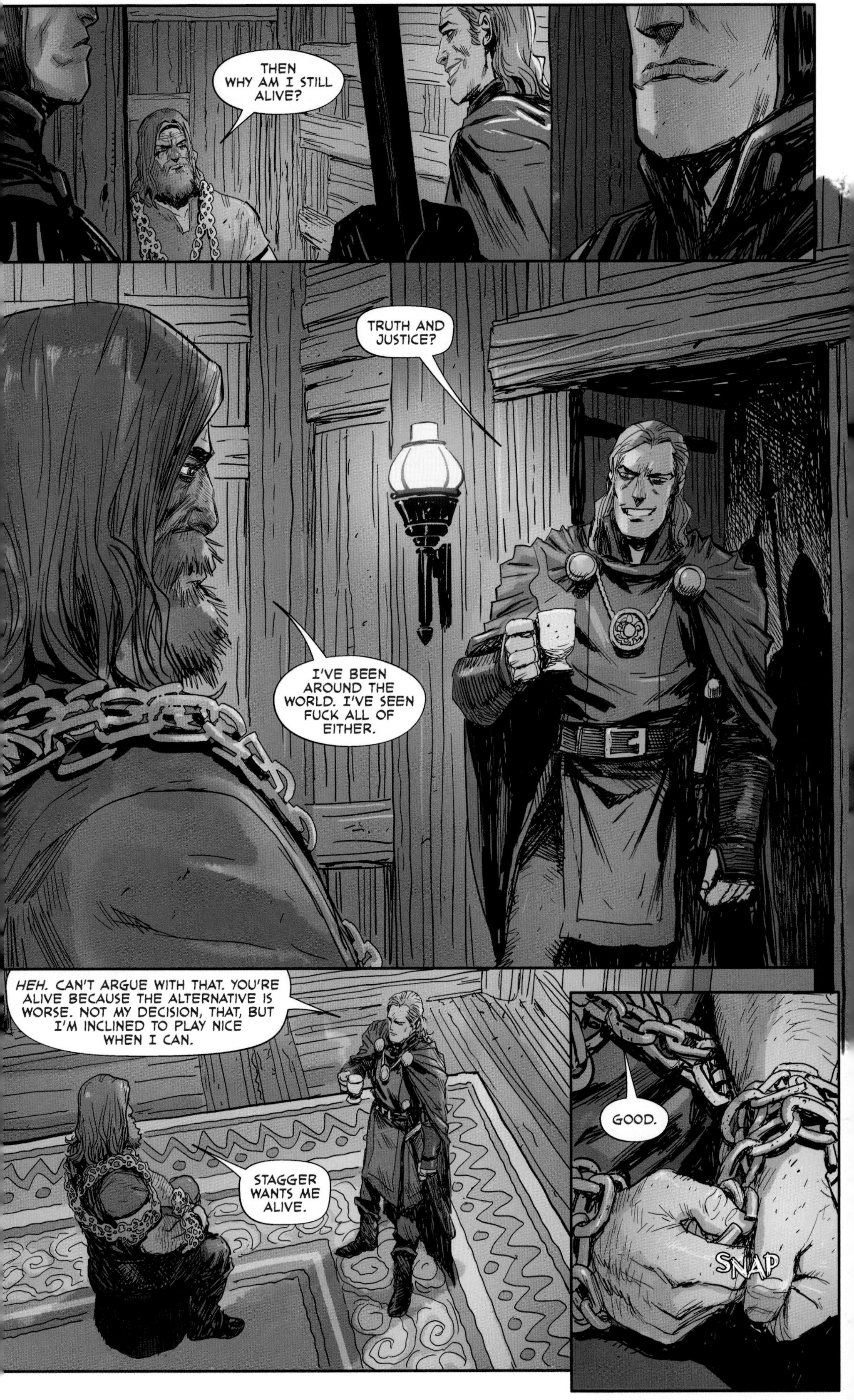
THEN WHY AM I STILL ALIVE?
TRUTH AND JUSTICE?
I'VE BEEN AROUND THE WORLD. I'VE SEEN FUCK ALL OF EITHER.
HEH. CAN'T ARGUE WITH THAT. YOU'RE ALIVE BECAUSE THE ALTERNATIVE IS WORSE. NOT MY DECISION, THAT, BUT I'M INCLINED TO PLAY NICE WHEN I CAN.
STAGGER WANTS ME ALIVE.
GOOD.
SNAP

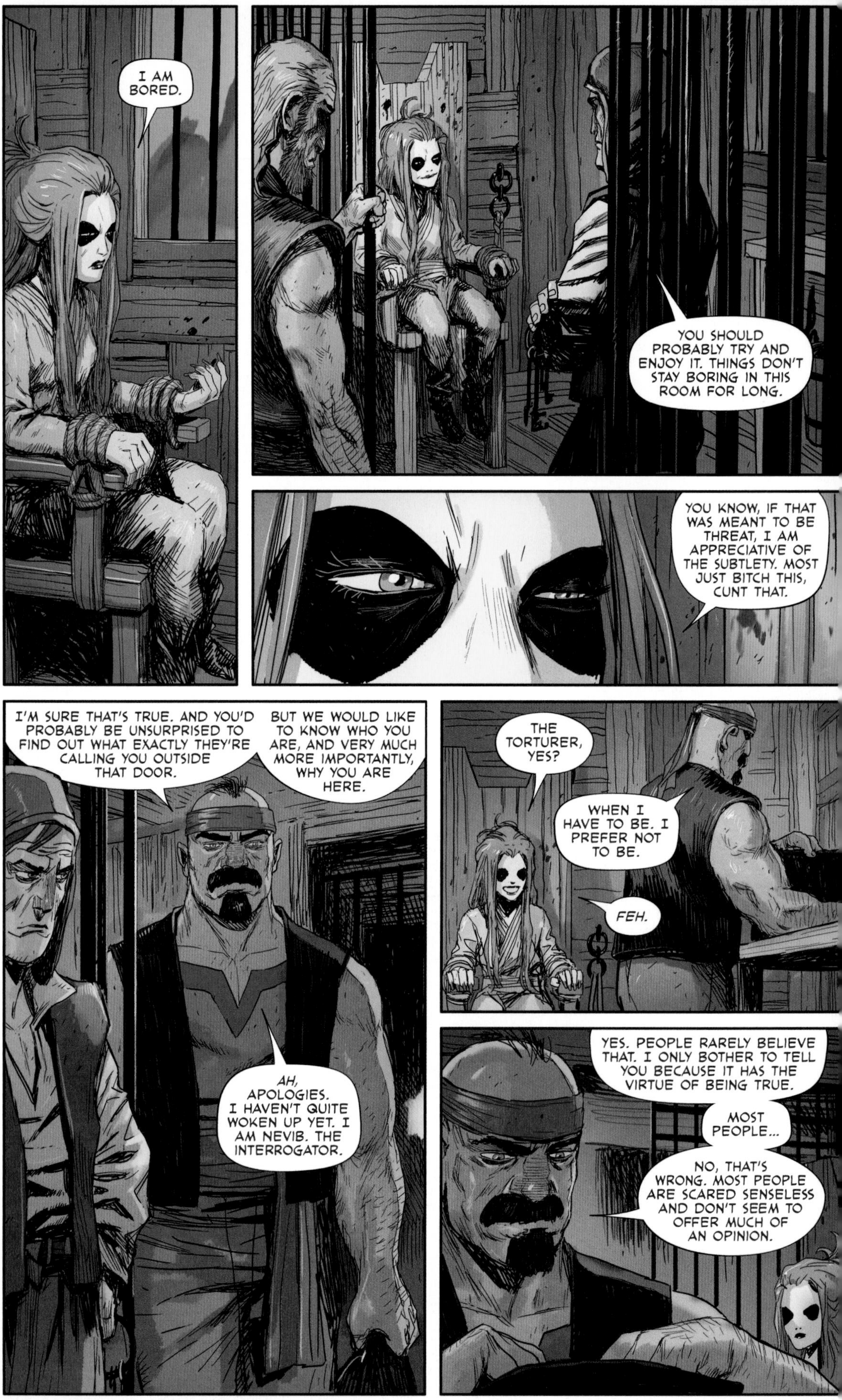
I AM BORED.
YOU SHOULD PROBABLY TRY AND ENJOY IT. THINGS DON'T STAY BORING IN THIS ROOM FOR LONG.
YOU KNOW, IF THAT WAS MEANT TO BE THREAT, I AM APPRECIATIVE OF THE SUBTLETY. MOST JUST BITCH THIS, CUNT THAT.
I'M SURE THAT'S TRUE. AND YOU'D PROBABLY BE UNSURPRISED TO FIND OUT WHAT EXACTLY THEY'RE CALLING YOU OUTSIDE THAT DOOR.
BUT WE WOULD LIKE TO KNOW WHO YOU ARE, AND VERY MUCH MORE IMPORTANTLY, WHY YOU ARE HERE.
AH, APOLOGIES. I HAVEN'T QUITE WOKEN UP YET. I AM NEVIB. THE INTERROGATOR.
THE TORTURER, YES?
WHEN I HAVE TO BE. I PREFER NOT TO BE.
FEH.
YES. PEOPLE RARELY BELIEVE THAT. I ONLY BOTHER TO TELL YOU BECAUSE IT HAS THE VIRTUE OF BEING TRUE.
MOST PEOPLE...
NO, THAT'S WRONG. MOST PEOPLE ARE SCARED SENSELESS AND DON'T SEEM TO OFFER MUCH OF AN OPINION.

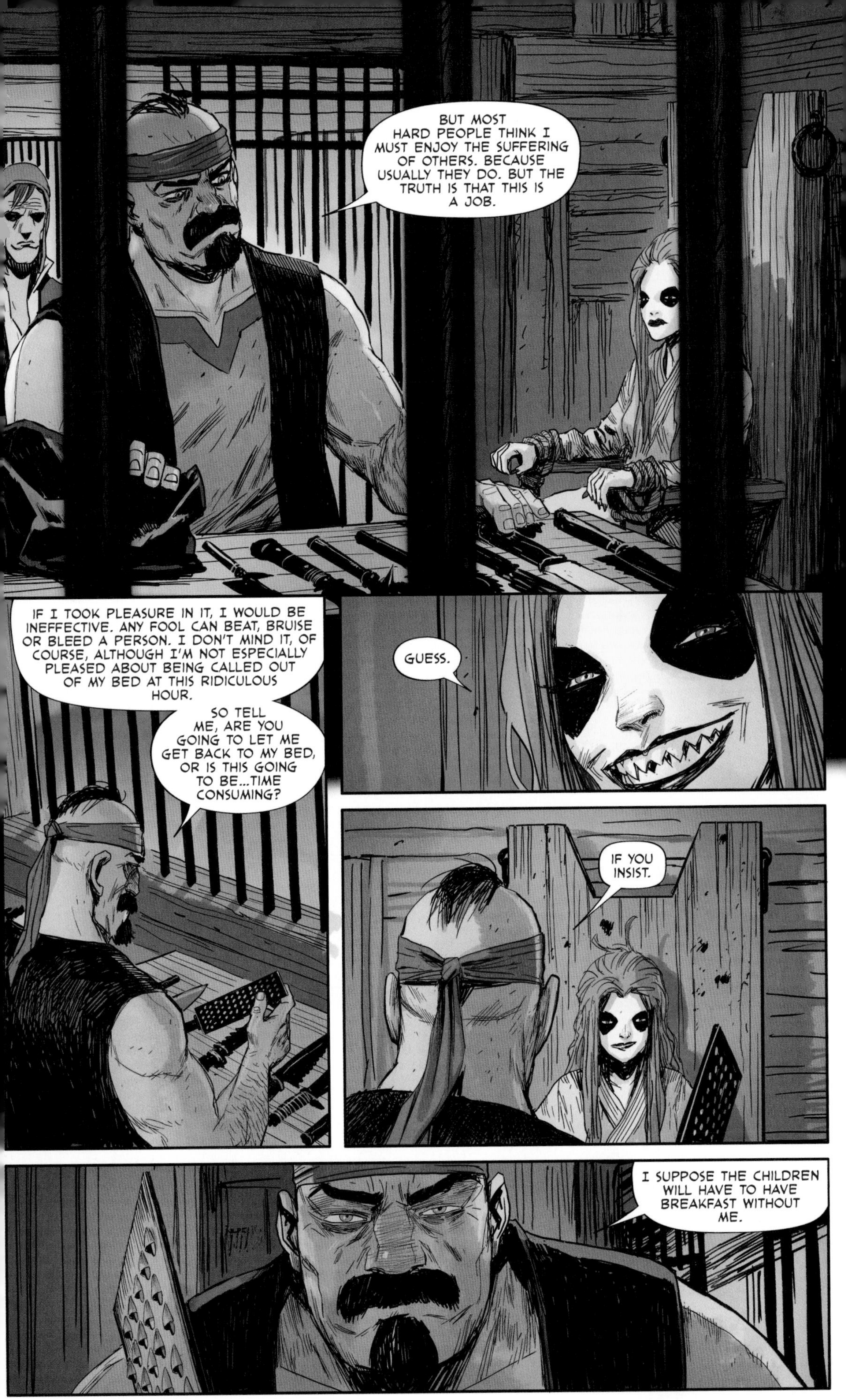
BUT MOST HARD PEOPLE THINK I MUST ENJOY THE SUFFERING OF OTHERS. BECAUSE USUALLY THEY DO. BUT THE TRUTH IS THAT THIS IS A JOB.
IF I TOOK PLEASURE IN IT, I WOULD BE INEFFECTIVE. ANY FOOL CAN BEAT, BRUISE OR BLEED A PERSON. I DON'T MIND IT, OF COURSE, ALTHOUGH I'M NOT ESPECIALLY PLEASED ABOUT BEING CALLED OUT OF MY BED AT THIS RIDICULOUS HOUR.
SO TELL ME, ARE YOU GOING TO LET ME GET BACK TO MY BED, OR IS THIS GOING TO BE...TIME CONSUMING?
GUESS.
IF YOU INSIST.
I SUPPOSE THE CHILDREN WILL HAVE TO HAVE BREAKFAST WITHOUT ME.

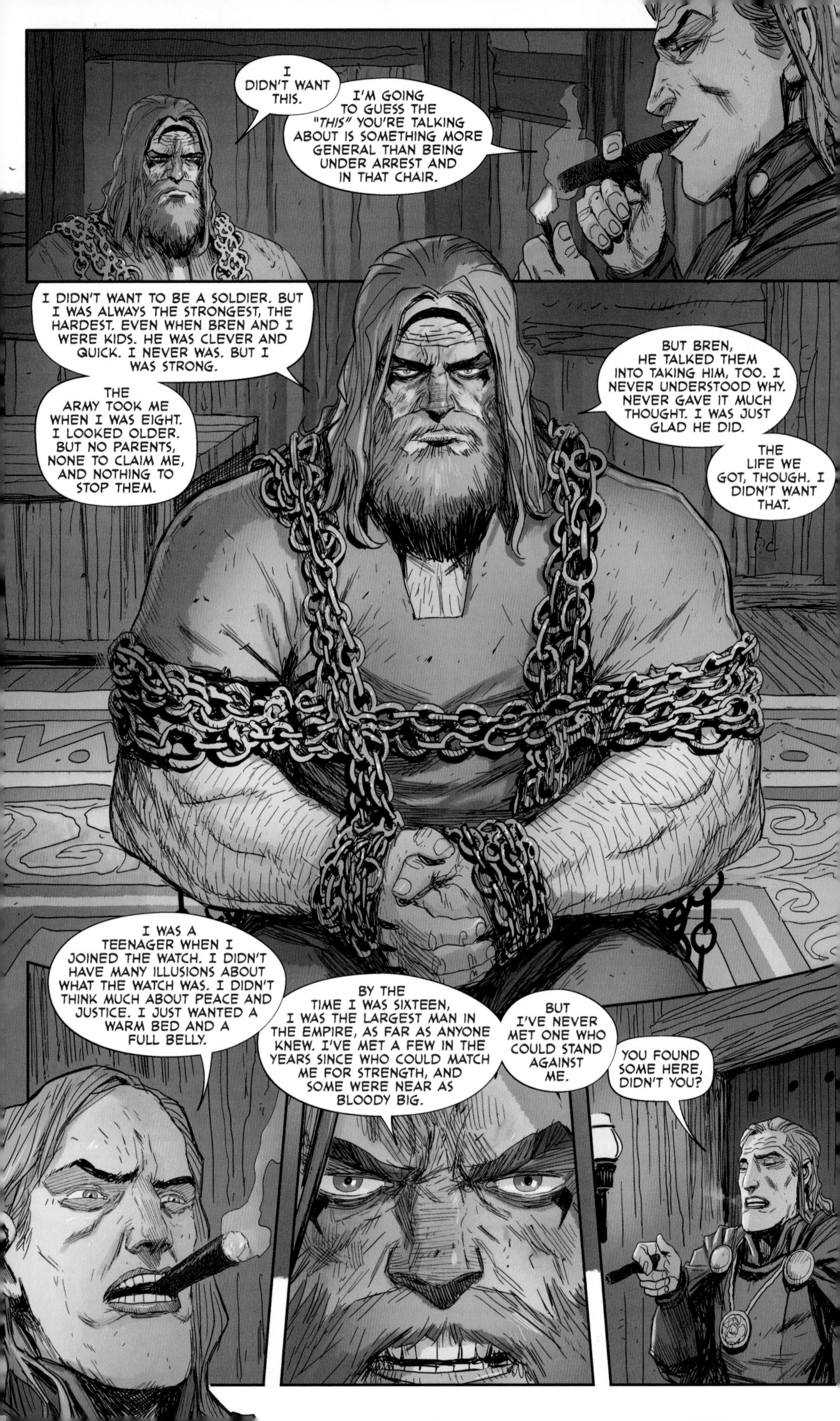
I DIDN'T WANT THIS.
I'M GOING TO GUESS THE "THIS" YOU'RE TALKING ABOUT IS SOMETHING MORE GENERAL THAN BEING UNDER ARREST AND IN THAT CHAIR.
I DIDN'T WANT TO BE A SOLDIER. BUT I WAS ALWAYS THE STRONGEST, THE HARDEST. EVEN WHEN BREN AND I WERE KIDS. HE WAS CLEVER AND QUICK. I NEVER WAS. BUT I WAS STRONG.
THE ARMY TOOK ME WHEN I WAS EIGHT. I LOOKED OLDER. BUT NO PARENTS, NONE TO CLAIM ME, AND NOTHING TO STOP THEM.
BUT BREN, HE TALKED THEM INTO TAKING HIM, TOO. I NEVER UNDERSTOOD WHY. NEVER GAVE IT MUCH THOUGHT. I WAS JUST GLAD HE DID.
THE LIFE WE GOT, THOUGH. I DIDN'T WANT THAT.
I WAS A TEENAGER WHEN I JOINED THE WATCH. I DIDN'T HAVE MANY ILLUSIONS ABOUT WHAT THE WATCH WAS. I DIDN'T THINK MUCH ABOUT PEACE AND JUSTICE. I JUST WANTED A WARM BED AND A FULL BELLY.
BY THE TIME I WAS SIXTEEN, I WAS THE LARGEST MAN IN THE EMPIRE, AS FAR AS ANYONE KNEW. I'VE MET A FEW IN THE YEARS SINCE WHO COULD MATCH ME FOR STRENGTH, AND SOME WERE NEAR AS BLOODY BIG.
BUT I'VE NEVER MET ONE WHO COULD STAND AGAINST ME.
YOU FOUND SOME HERE, DIDN'T YOU?

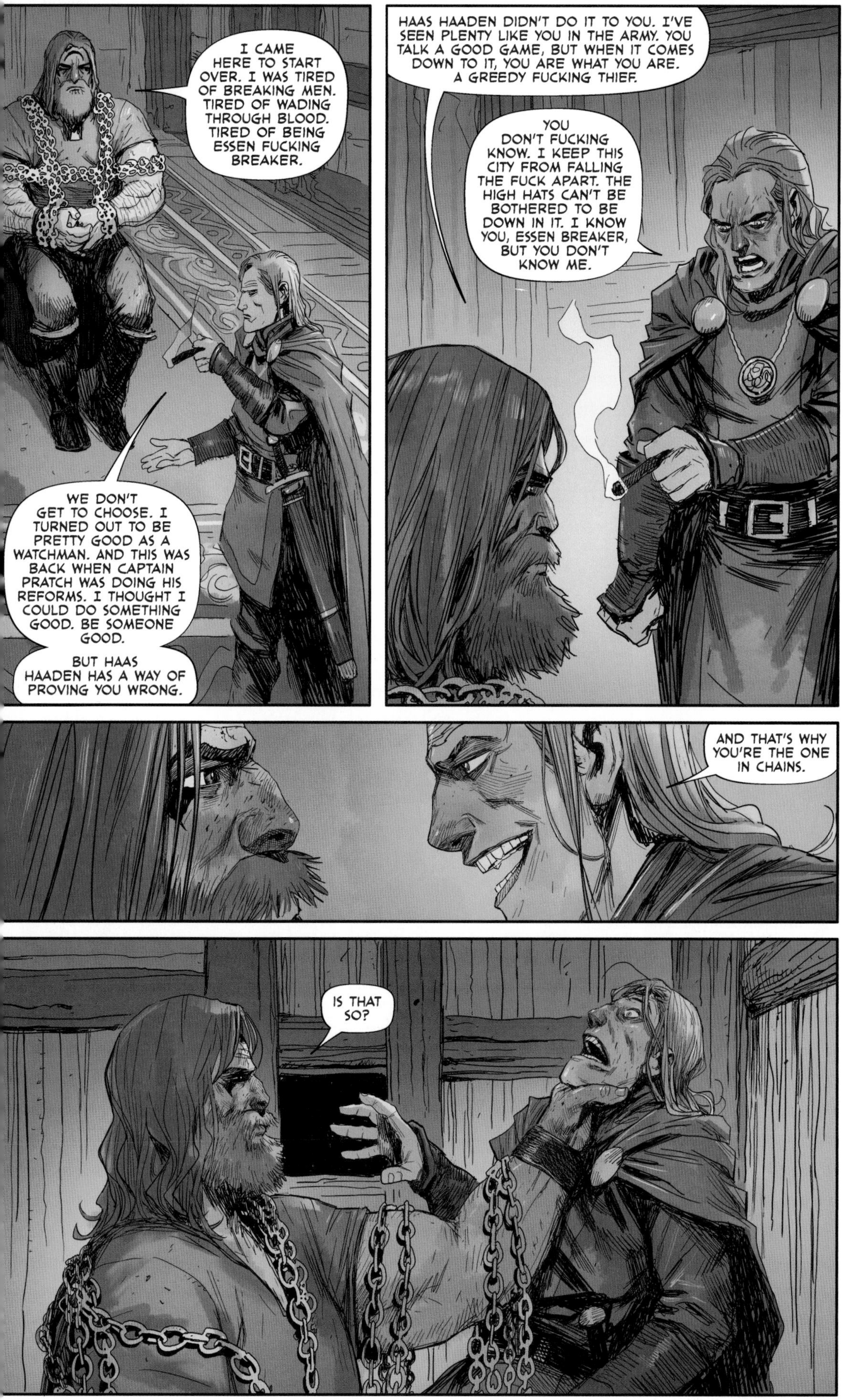
I CAME HERE TO START OVER. I WAS TIRED OF BREAKING MEN. TIRED OF WADING THROUGH BLOOD. TIRED OF BEING ESSEN FUCKING BREAKER.
WE DON'T GET TO CHOOSE. I TURNED OUT TO BE PRETTY GOOD AS A WATCHMAN. AND THIS WAS BACK WHEN CAPTAIN PRATCH WAS DOING HIS REFORMS. I THOUGHT I COULD DO SOMETHING GOOD. BE SOMEONE GOOD.
BUT HAAS HAADEN HAS A WAY OF PROVING YOU WRONG.
HAAS HAADEN DIDN'T DO IT TO YOU. I'VE SEEN PLENTY LIKE YOU IN THE ARMY. YOU TALK A GOOD GAME, BUT WHEN IT COMES DOWN TO IT, YOU ARE WHAT YOU ARE. A GREEDY FUCKING THIEF.
YOU DON'T FUCKING KNOW. I KEEP THIS CITY FROM FALLING THE FUCK APART. THE HIGH HATS CAN'T BE BOTHERED TO BE DOWN IN IT. I KNOW YOU, ESSEN BREAKER, BUT YOU DON'T KNOW ME.
AND THAT'S WHY YOU'RE THE ONE IN CHAINS.
IS THAT SO?

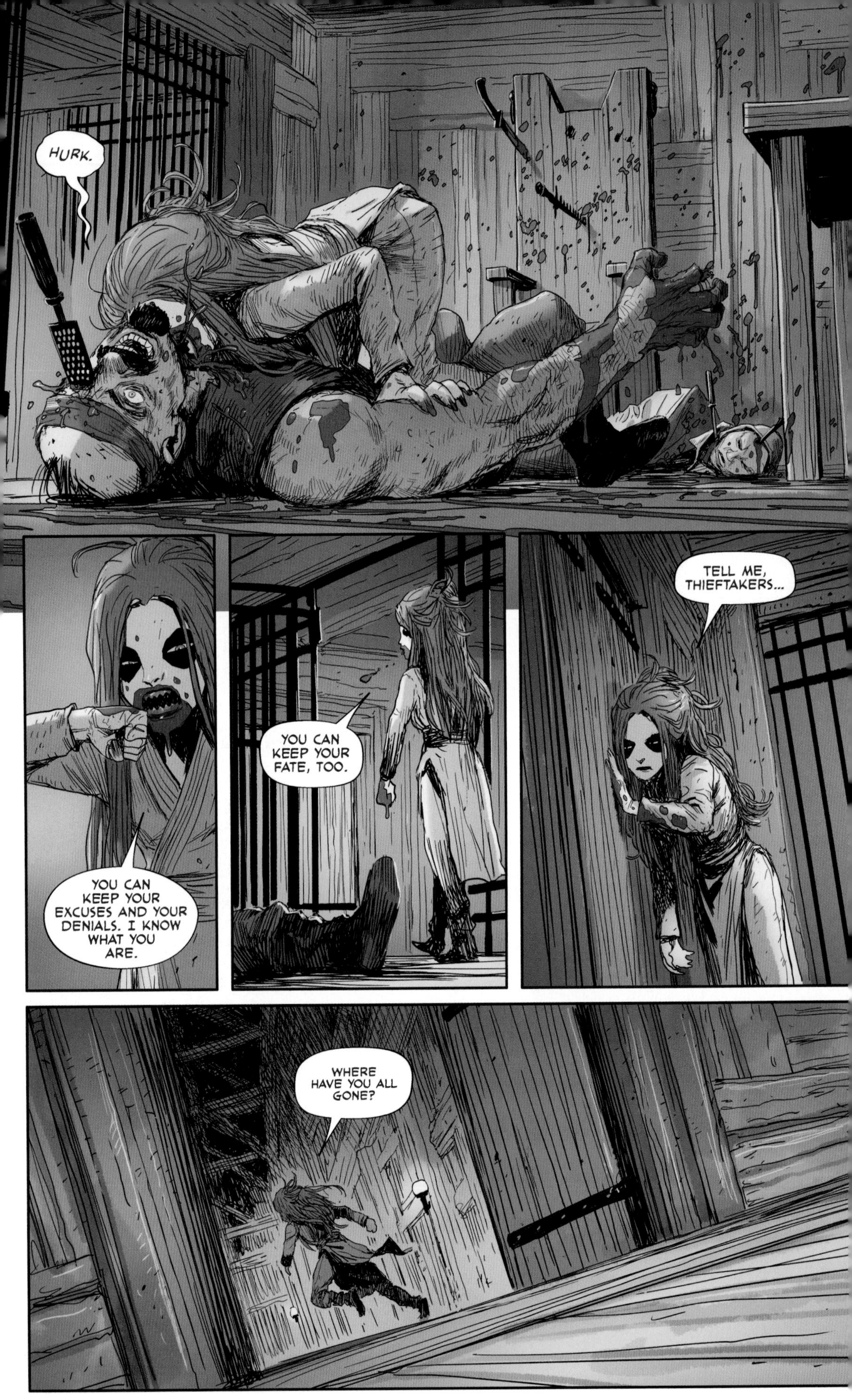
HURK.
YOU CAN KEEP YOUR EXCUSES AND YOUR DENIALS. I KNOW WHAT YOU ARE.
YOU CAN KEEP YOUR FATE, TOO.
TELL ME, THIEFTAKERS...
WHERE HAVE YOU ALL GONE?

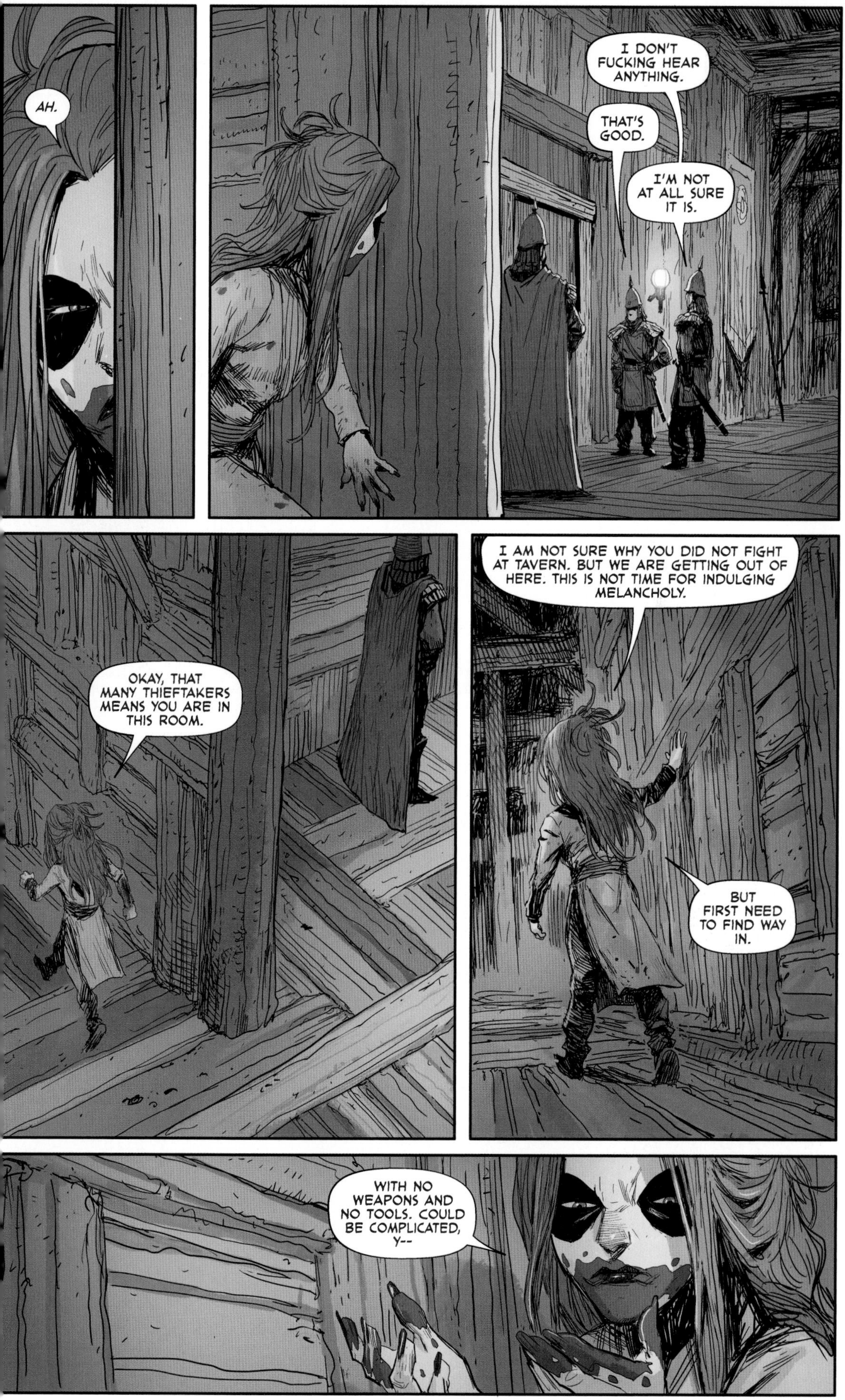
AH.
I DON'T FUCKING HEAR ANYTHING.
THAT'S GOOD.
I'M NOT AT ALL SURE IT IS.
OKAY, THAT MANY THIEFTAKERS MEANS YOU ARE IN THIS ROOM.
I AM NOT SURE WHY YOU DID NOT FIGHT AT TAVERN. BUT WE ARE GETTING OUT OF HERE. THIS IS NOT TIME FOR INDULGING MELANCHOLY.
BUT FIRST NEED TO FIND WAY IN.
WITH NO WEAPONS AND NO TOOLS. COULD BE COMPLICATED, Y--

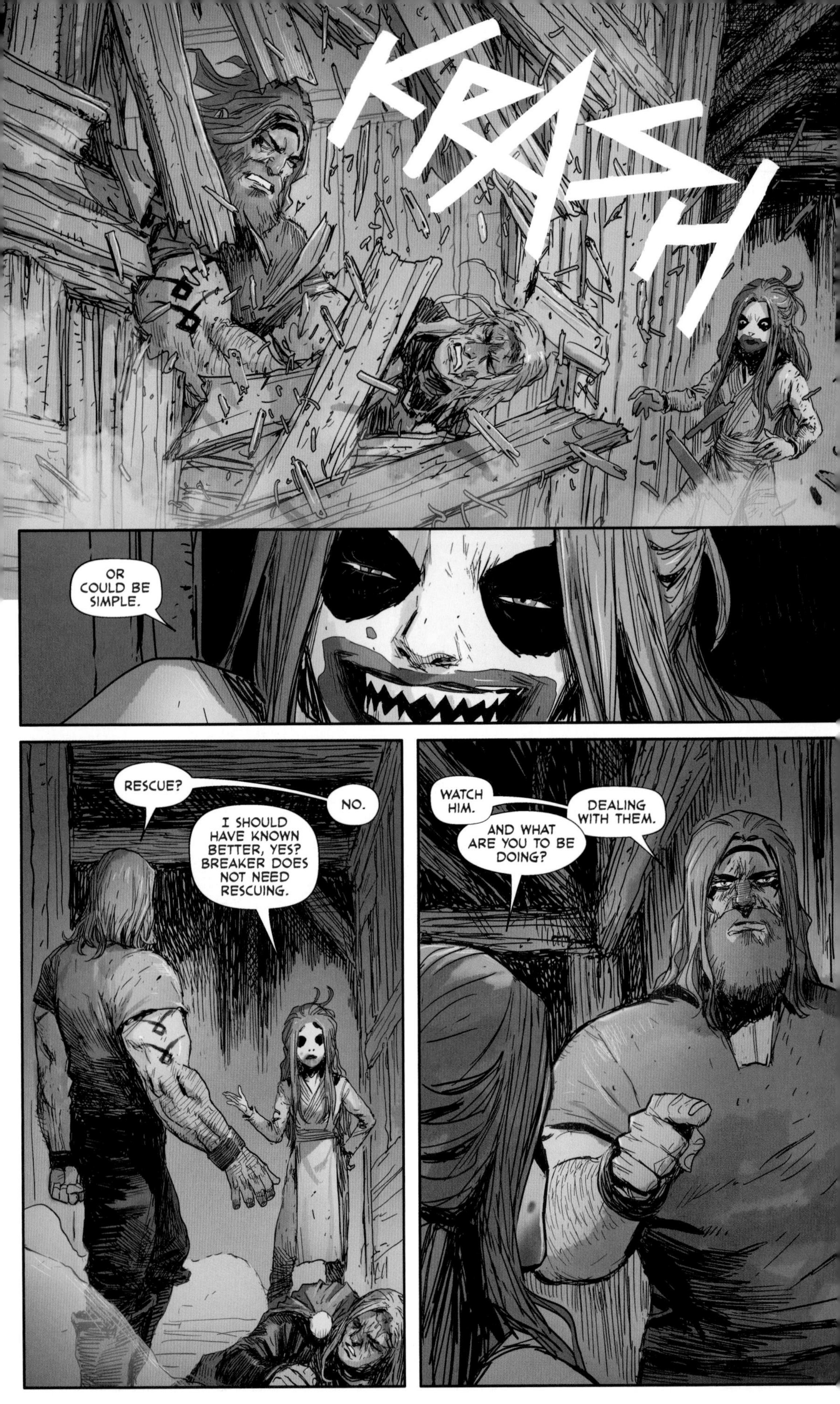
KRASH
OR COULD BE SIMPLE.
RESCUE?
NO.
I SHOULD HAVE KNOWN BETTER, YES? BREAKER DOES NOT NEED RESCUING.
WATCH HIM.
DEALING WITH THEM.
AND WHAT ARE YOU TO BE DOING?

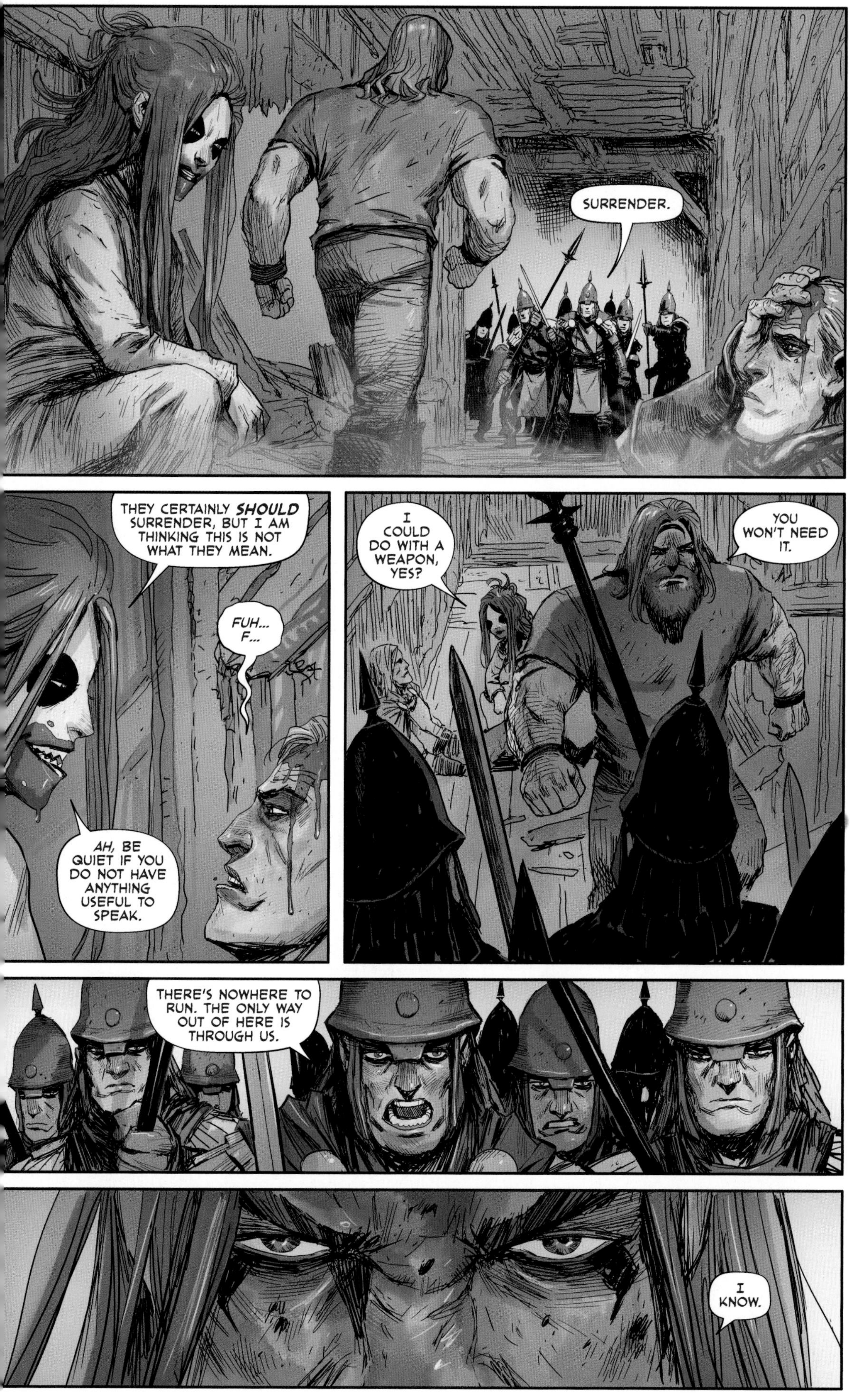
SURRENDER.
THEY CERTAINLY **SHOULD** SURRENDER, BUT I AM THINKING THIS IS NOT WHAT THEY MEAN.
FUH... F...
AH, BE QUIET IF YOU DO NOT HAVE ANYTHING USEFUL TO SPEAK.
I COULD DO WITH A WEAPON, YES?
YOU WON'T NEED IT.
THERE'S NOWHERE TO RUN. THE ONLY WAY OUT OF HERE IS THROUGH US.
I KNOW.

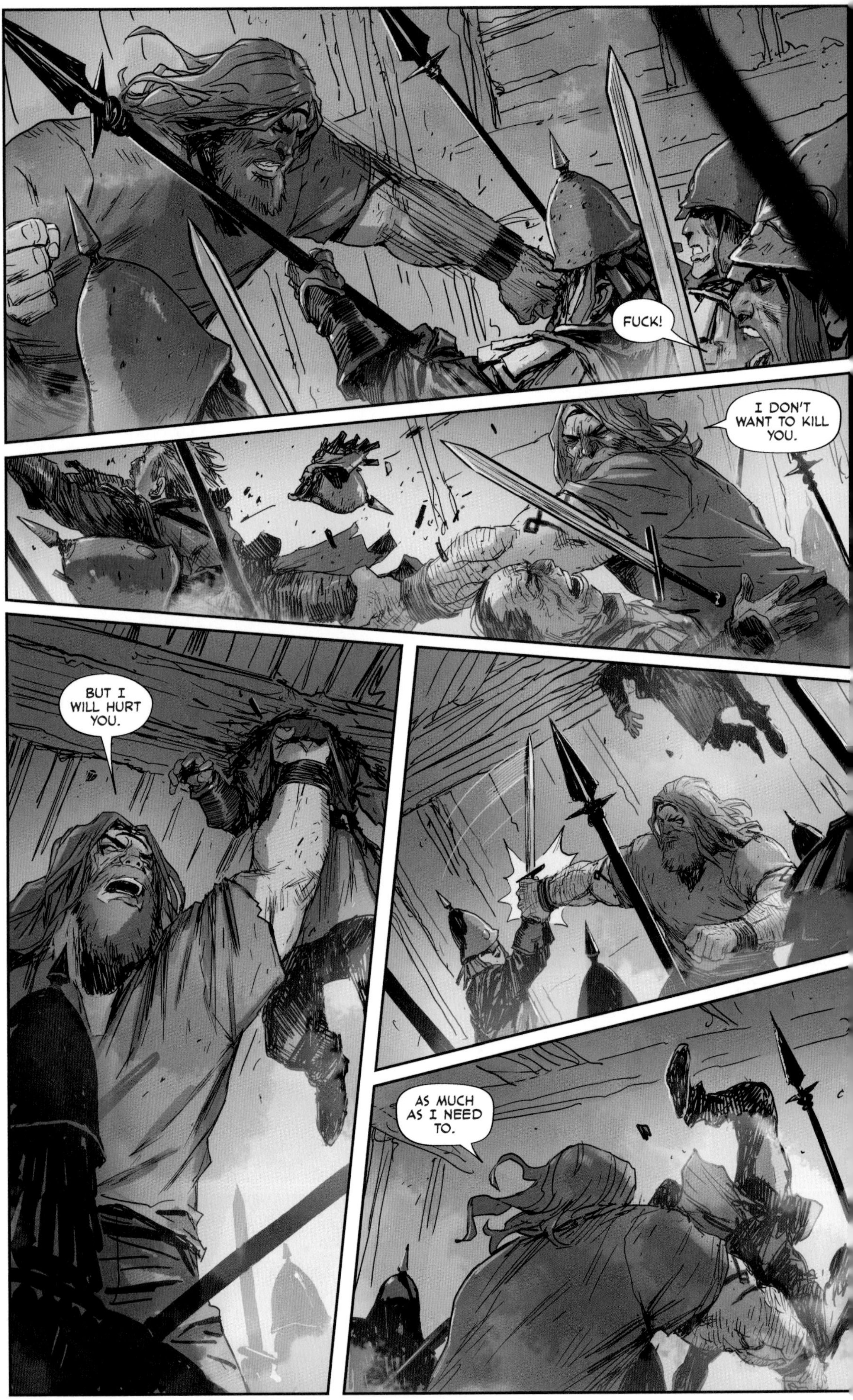
FUCK!
I DON'T WANT TO KILL YOU.
BUT I WILL HURT YOU.
AS MUCH AS I NEED TO.

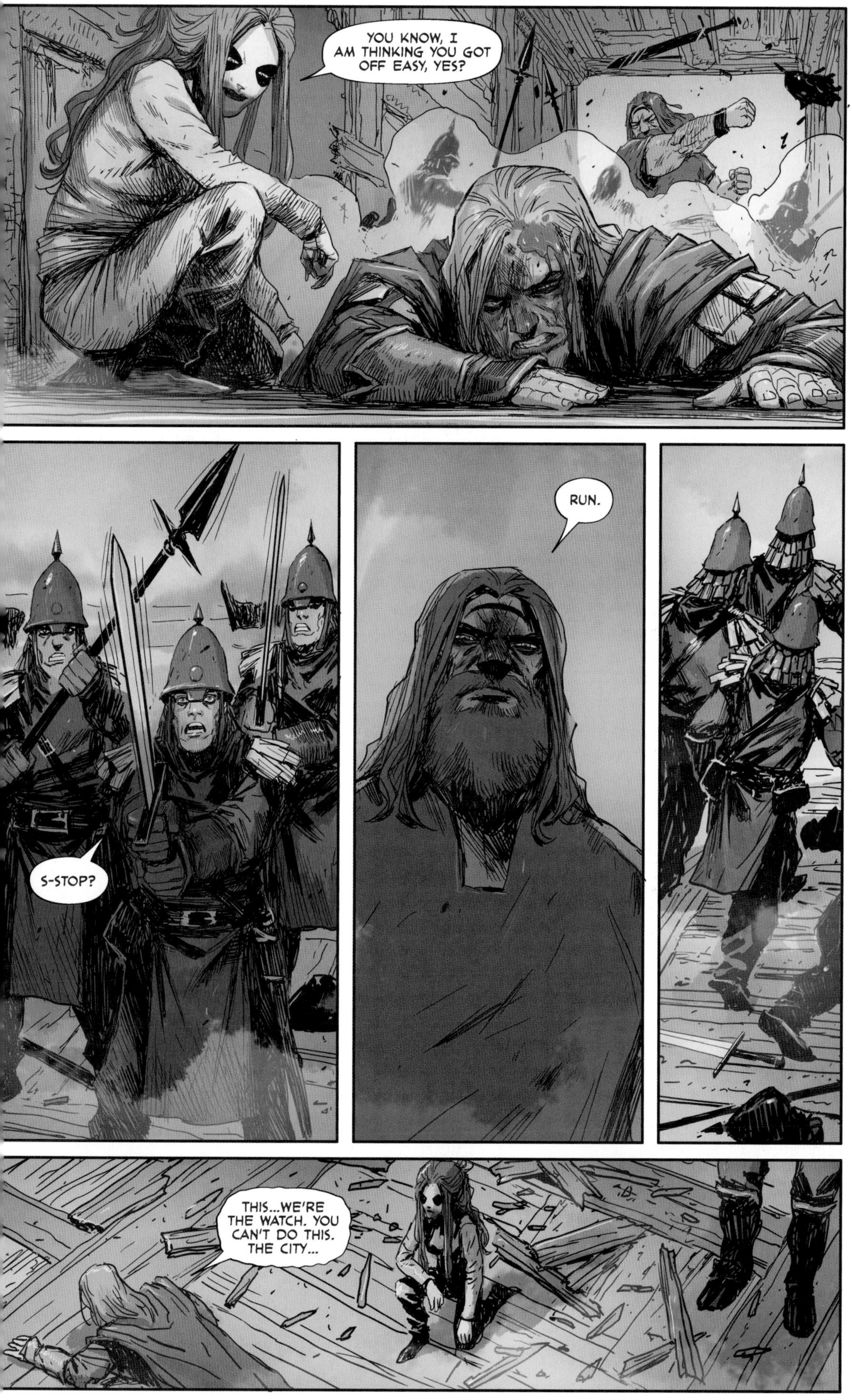
YOU KNOW, I AM THINKING YOU GOT OFF EASY, YES?
S-STOP?
RUN.
THIS...WE'RE THE WATCH. YOU CAN'T DO THIS. THE CITY...

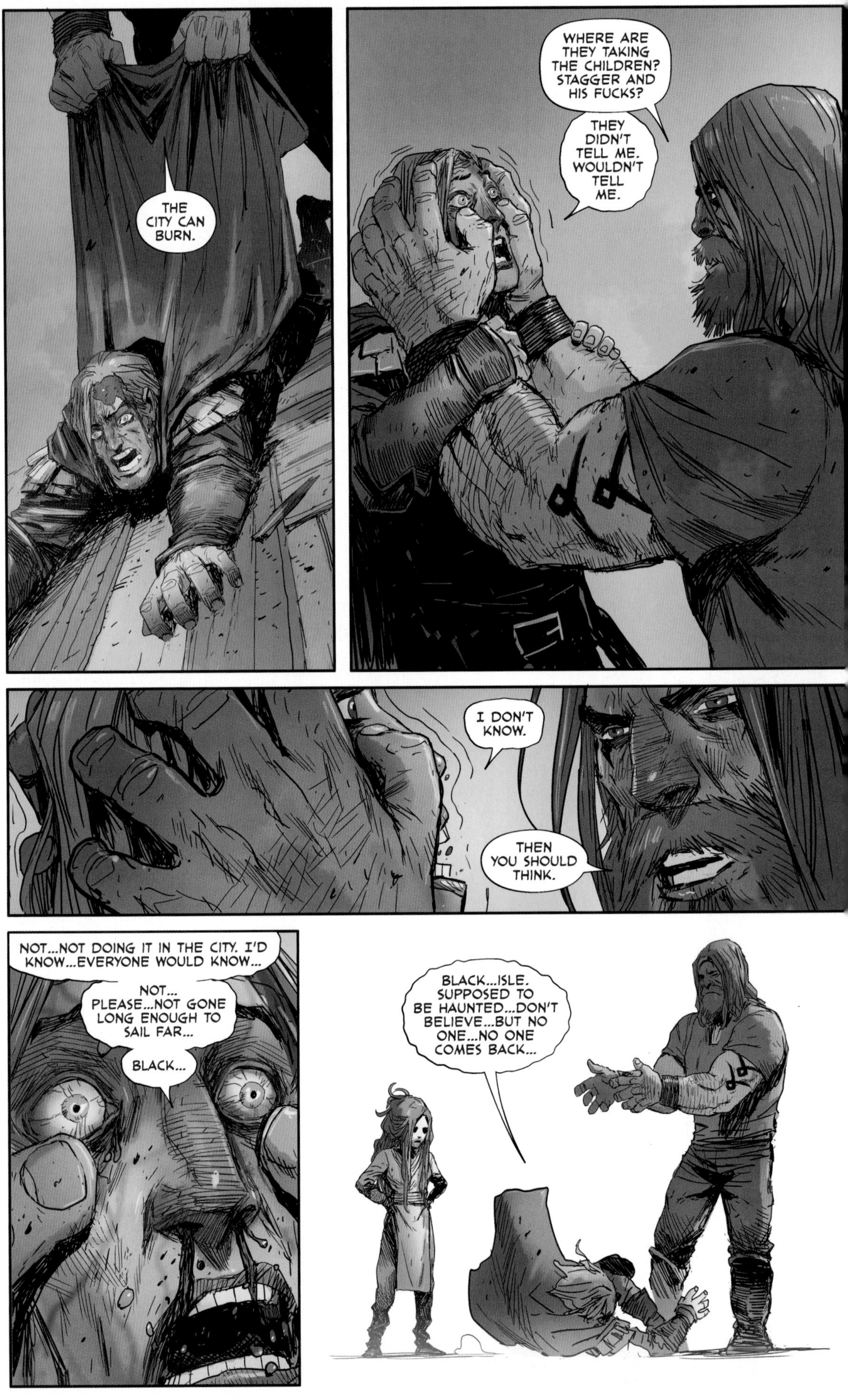
THE CITY CAN BURN.
WHERE ARE THEY TAKING THE CHILDREN? STAGGER AND HIS FUCKS?
THEY DIDN'T TELL ME. WOULDN'T TELL ME.
I DON'T KNOW.
THEN YOU SHOULD THINK.
NOT...NOT DOING IT IN THE CITY. I'D KNOW...EVERYONE WOULD KNOW...
NOT... PLEASE...NOT GONE LONG ENOUGH TO SAIL FAR...
BLACK...
BLACK...ISLE. SUPPOSED TO BE HAUNTED...DON'T BELIEVE...BUT NO ONE...NO ONE COMES BACK...

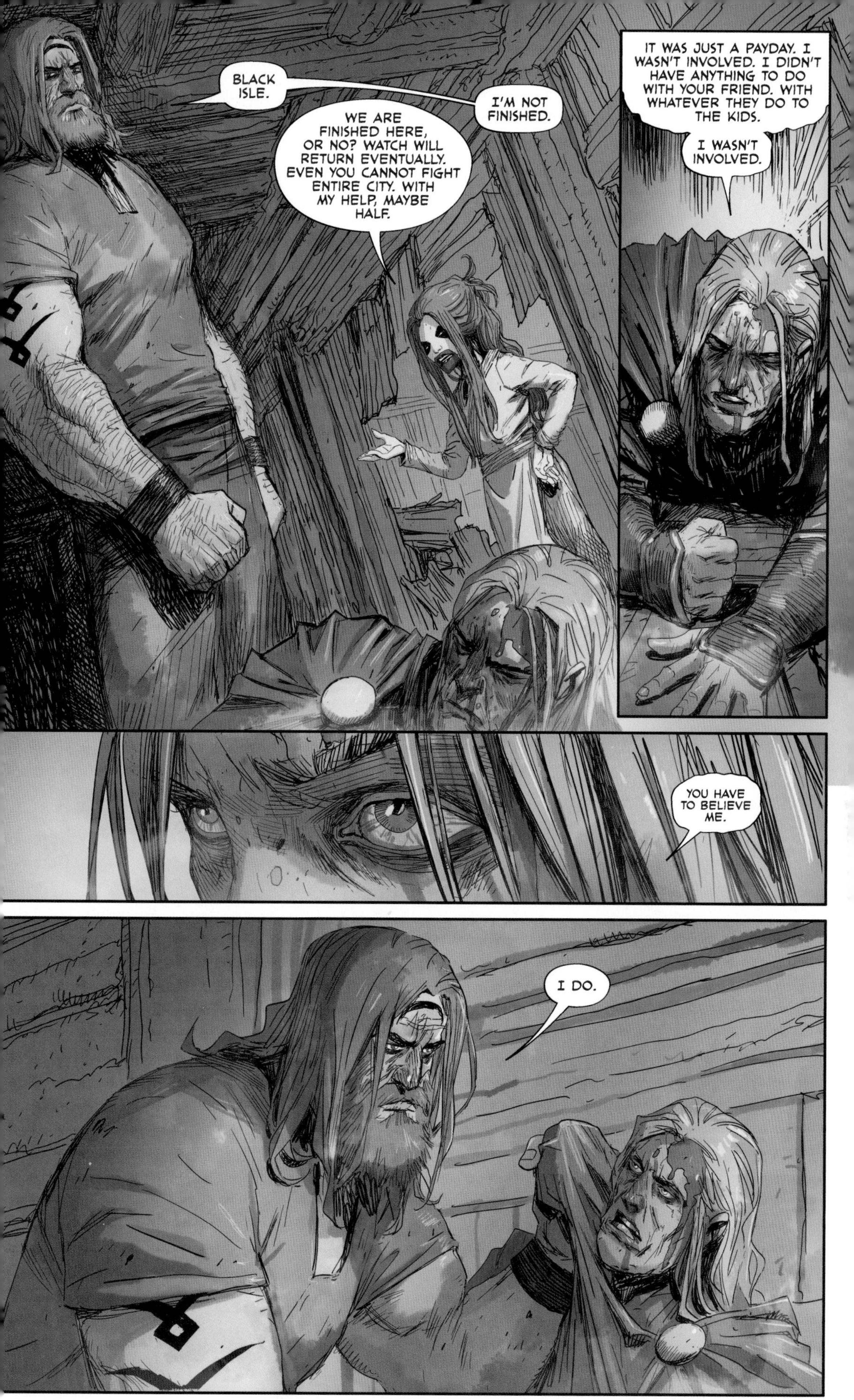
BLACK ISLE.
I'M NOT FINISHED.
WE ARE FINISHED HERE, OR NO? WATCH WILL RETURN EVENTUALLY. EVEN YOU CANNOT FIGHT ENTIRE CITY. WITH MY HELP, MAYBE HALF.
IT WAS JUST A PAYDAY. I WASN'T INVOLVED. I DIDN'T HAVE ANYTHING TO DO WITH YOUR FRIEND. WITH WHATEVER THEY DO TO THE KIDS.
I WASN'T INVOLVED.
YOU HAVE TO BELIEVE ME.
I DO.

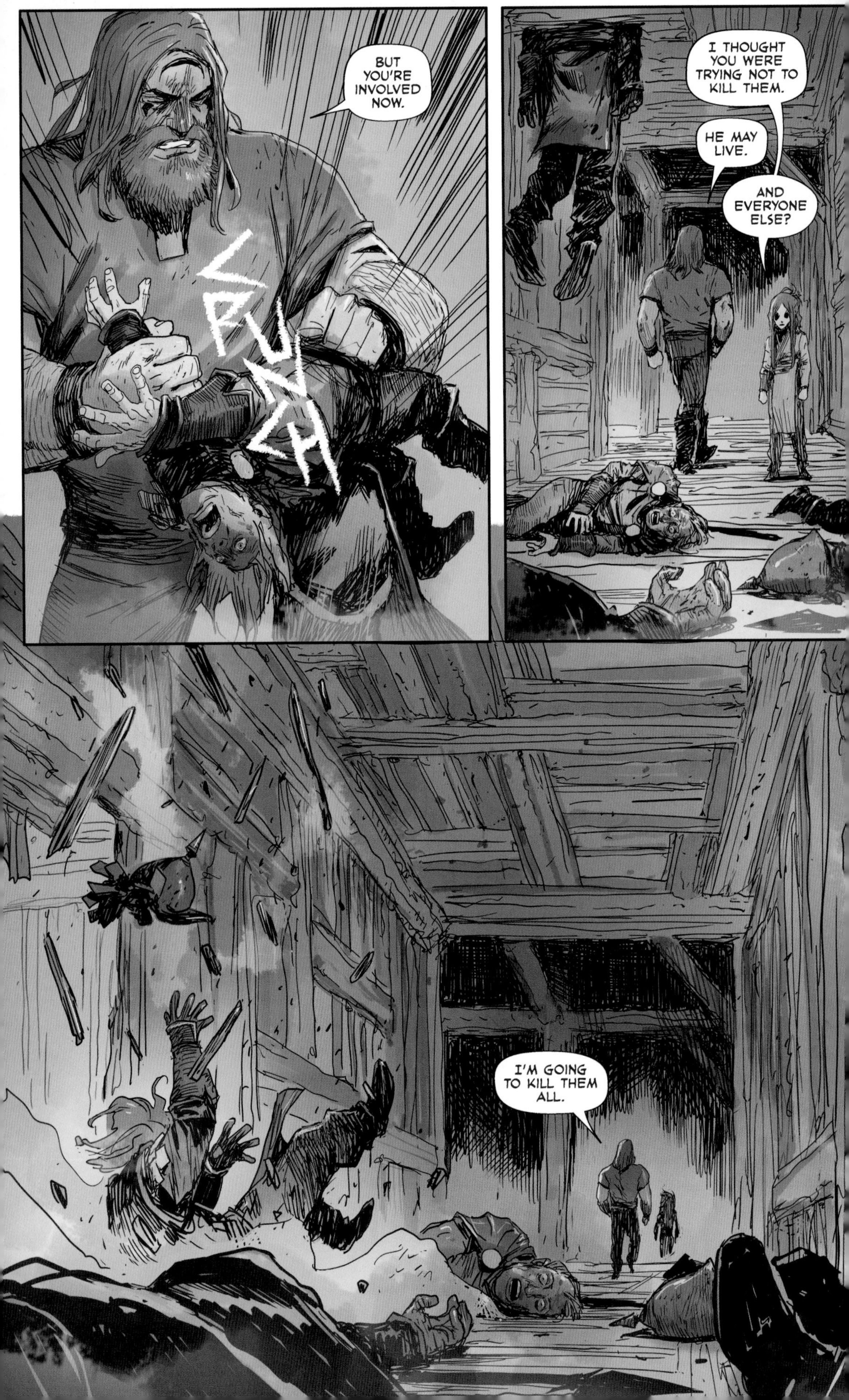
BUT YOU'RE INVOLVED NOW.
CRUNCH
I THOUGHT YOU WERE TRYING NOT TO KILL THEM.
HE MAY LIVE.
AND EVERYONE ELSE?
I'M GOING TO KILL THEM ALL.

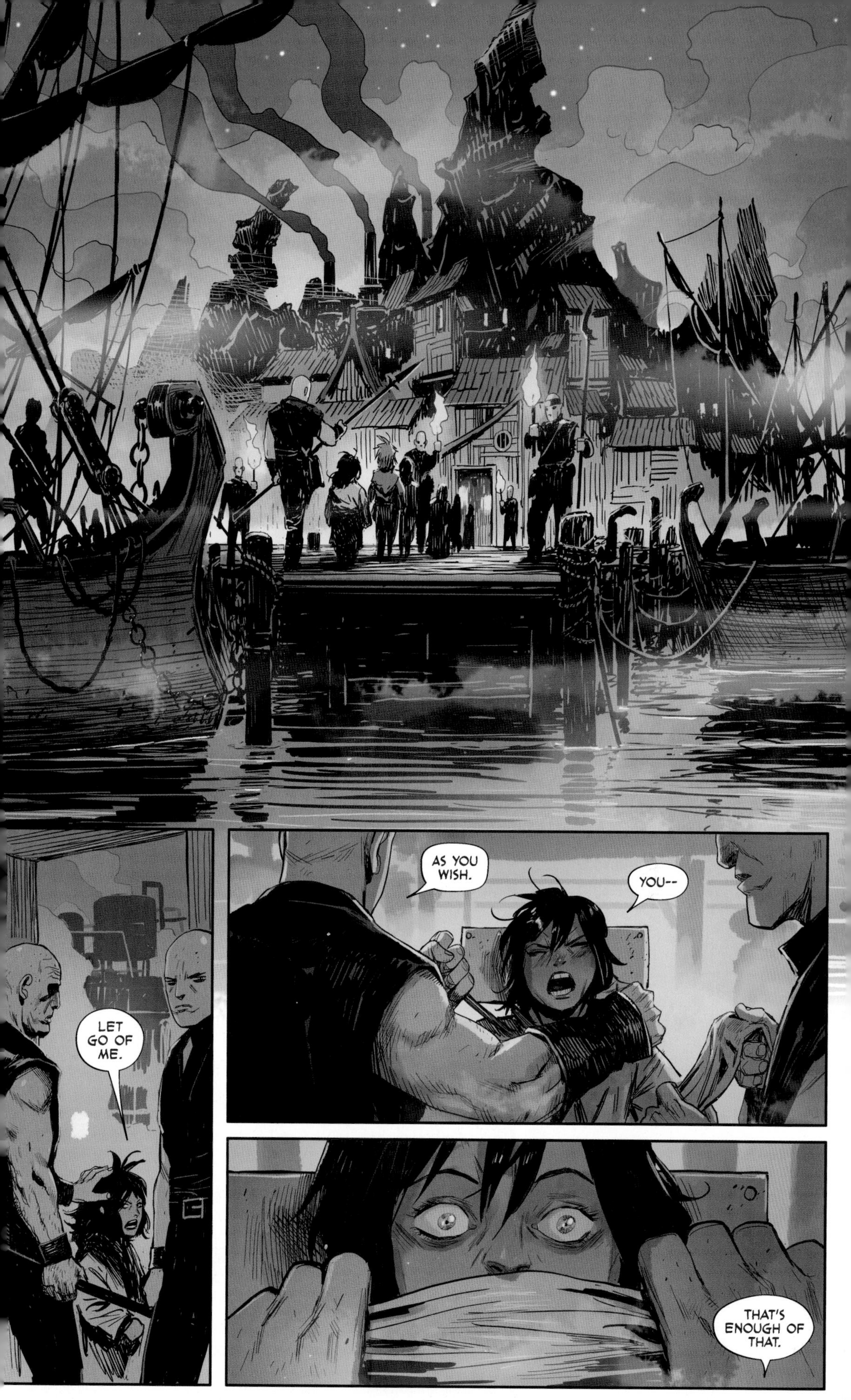
LET GO OF ME.
AS YOU WISH.
YOU--
THAT'S ENOUGH OF THAT.

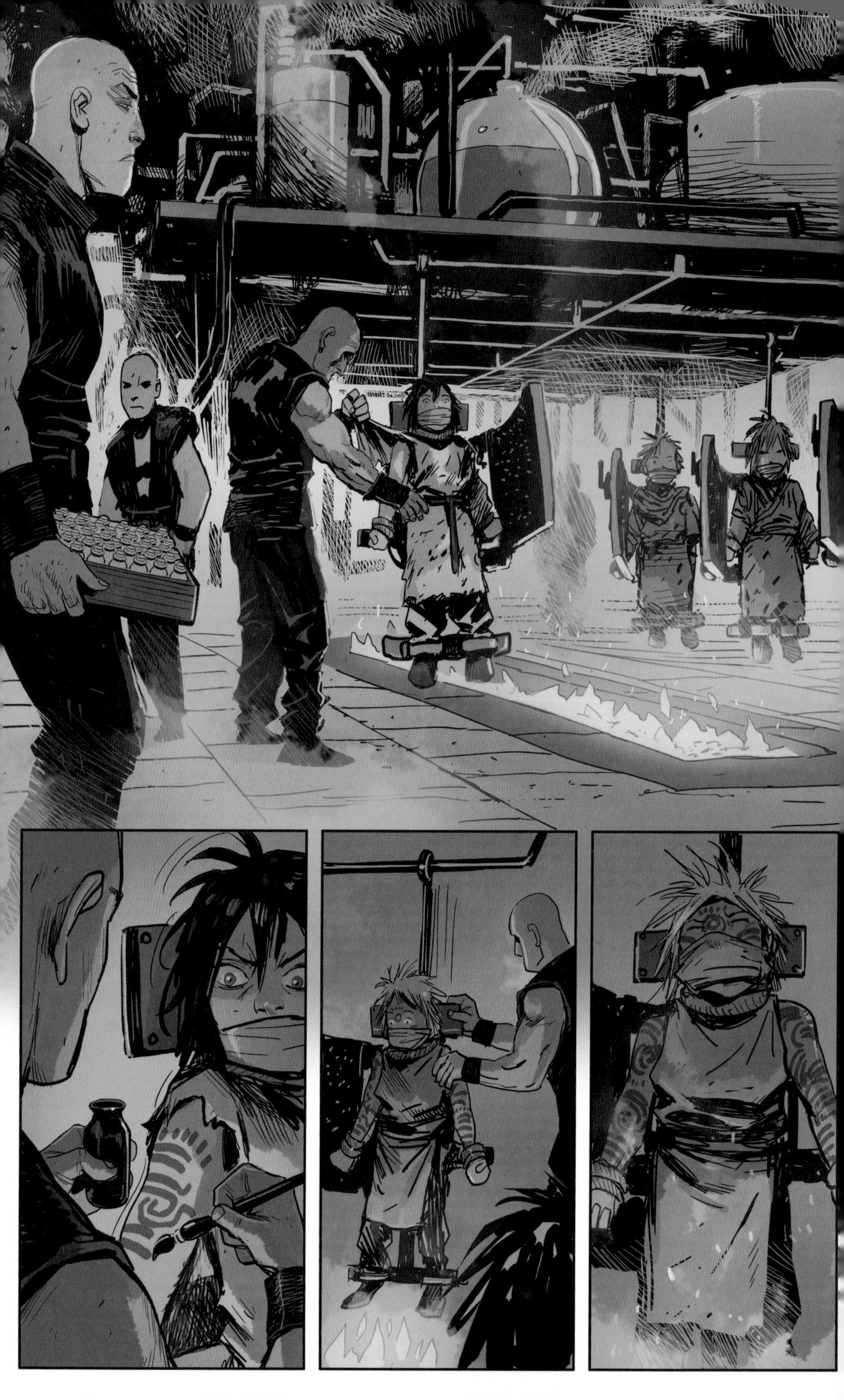

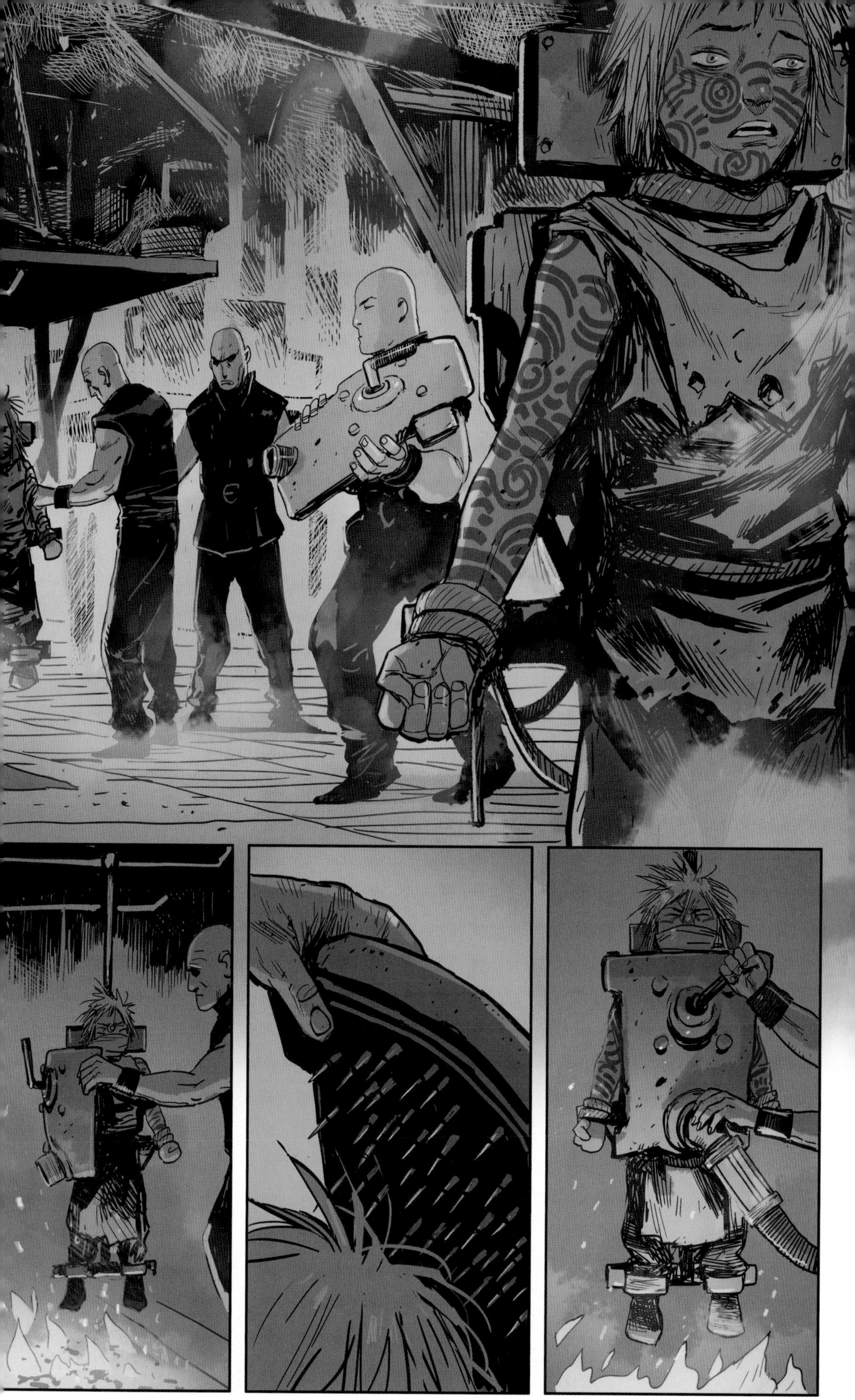

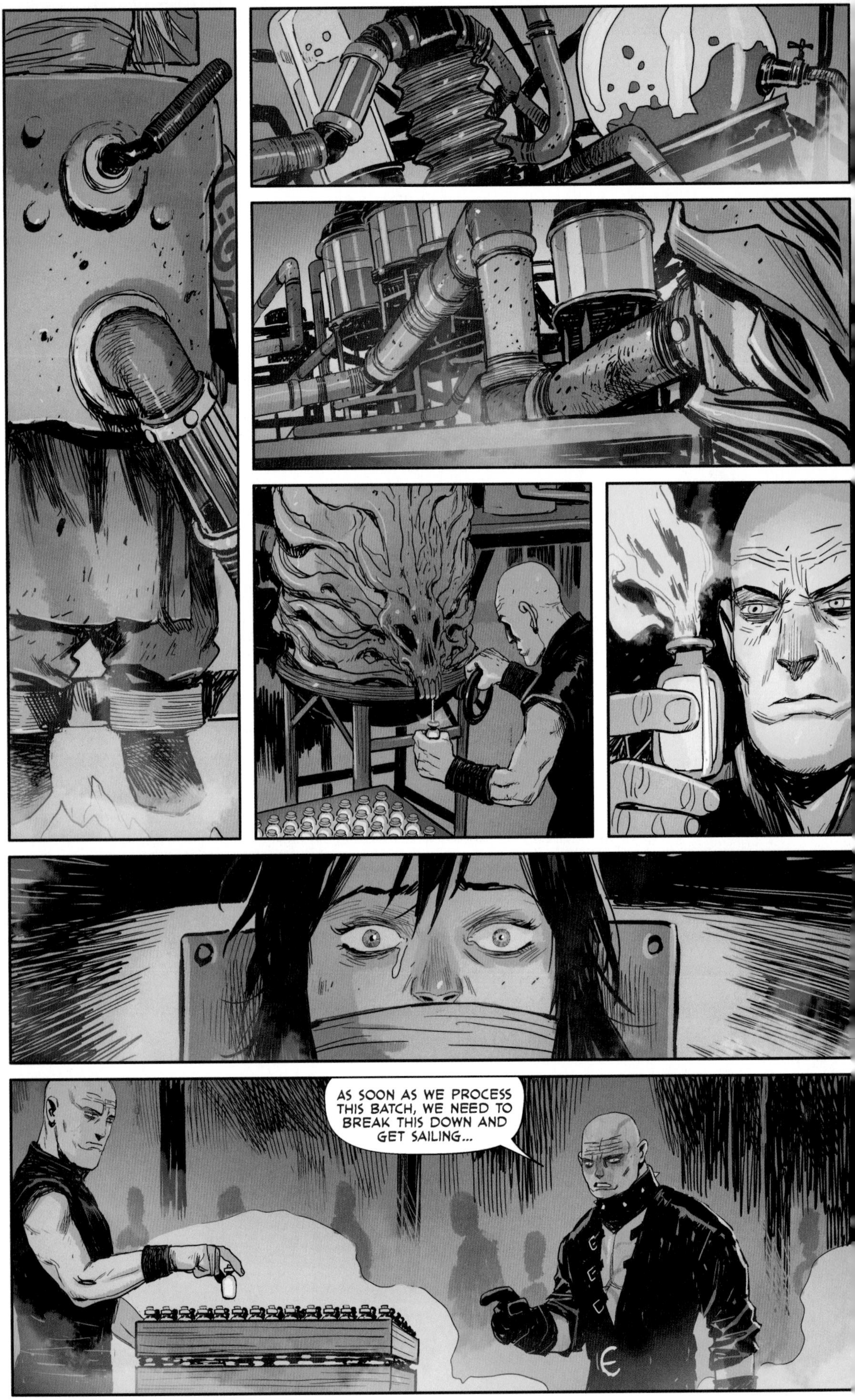
AS SOON AS WE PROCESS THIS BATCH, WE NEED TO BREAK THIS DOWN AND GET SAILING...

"BECAUSE SOMEONE WE CAN'T AFFORD TO FUCK WITH IS COMING."

THEY'RE HERE.

LIGHT IT UP.

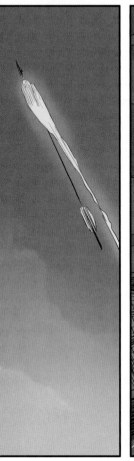

THEN I RECKON WE SHOULD GET READY TO RECEIVE OUR VISITORS.

NOT YET. THAT DOSE ONLY LASTS A COUPLE MINUTES. IT'LL TAKE THAT LONG BEFORE THE BOAT EVEN GETS...

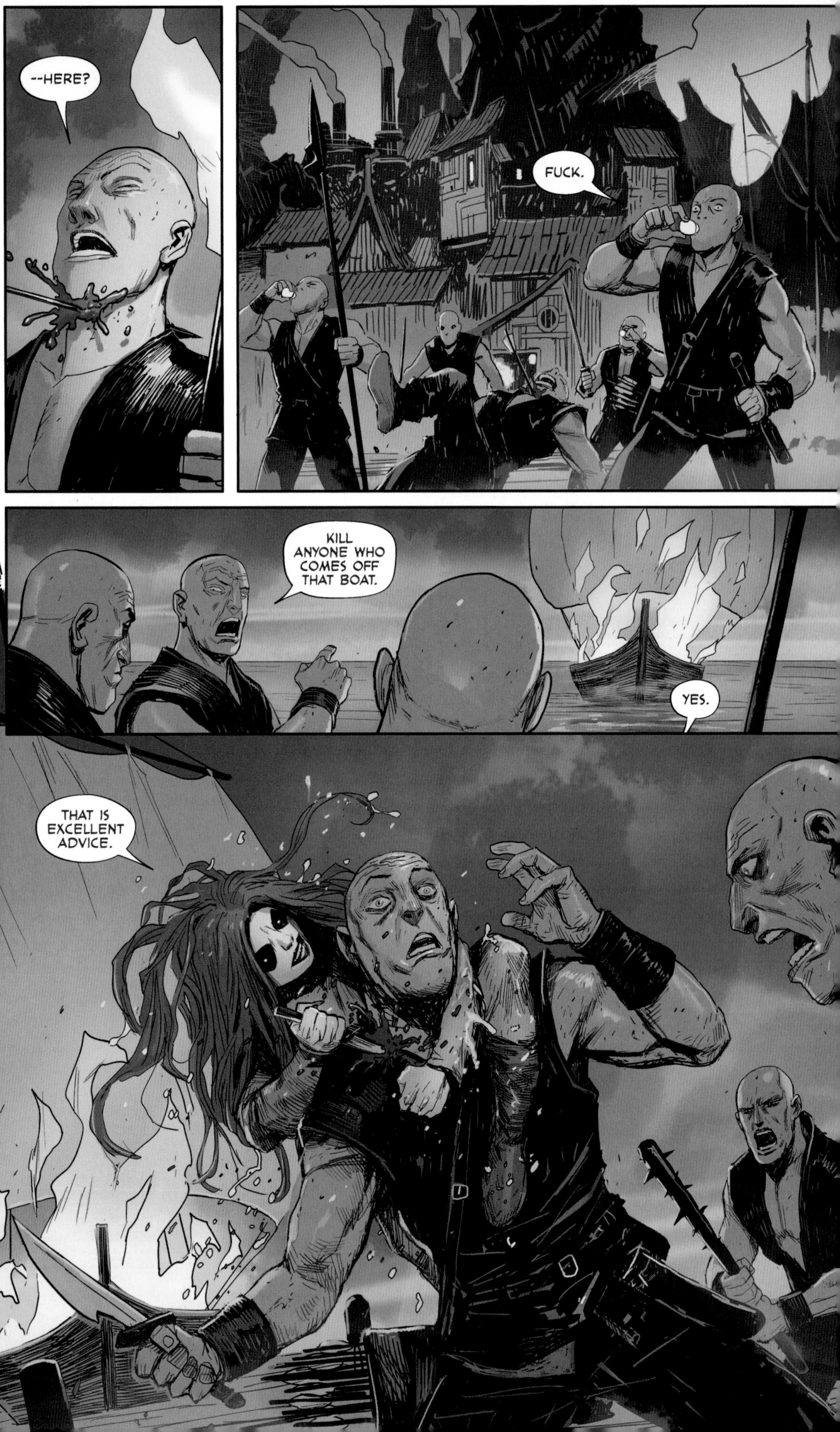
--HERE?
FUCK.
KILL ANYONE WHO COMES OFF THAT BOAT.
YES.
THAT IS EXCELLENT ADVICE.

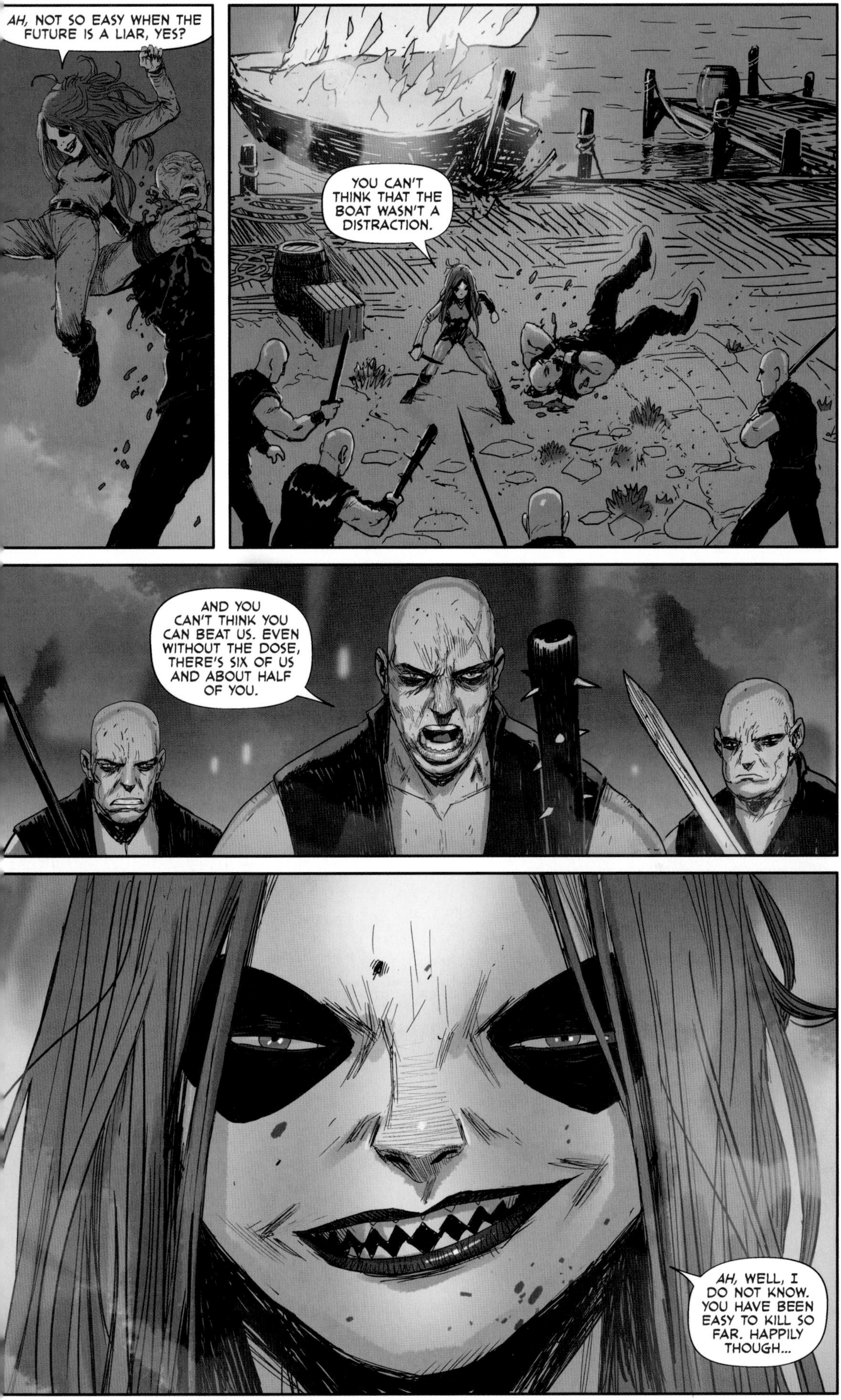
AH, NOT SO EASY WHEN THE FUTURE IS A LIAR, YES?
YOU CAN'T THINK THAT THE BOAT WASN'T A DISTRACTION.
AND YOU CAN'T THINK YOU CAN BEAT US. EVEN WITHOUT THE DOSE, THERE'S SIX OF US AND ABOUT HALF OF YOU.
AH, WELL, I DO NOT KNOW. YOU HAVE BEEN EASY TO KILL SO FAR. HAPPILY THOUGH...

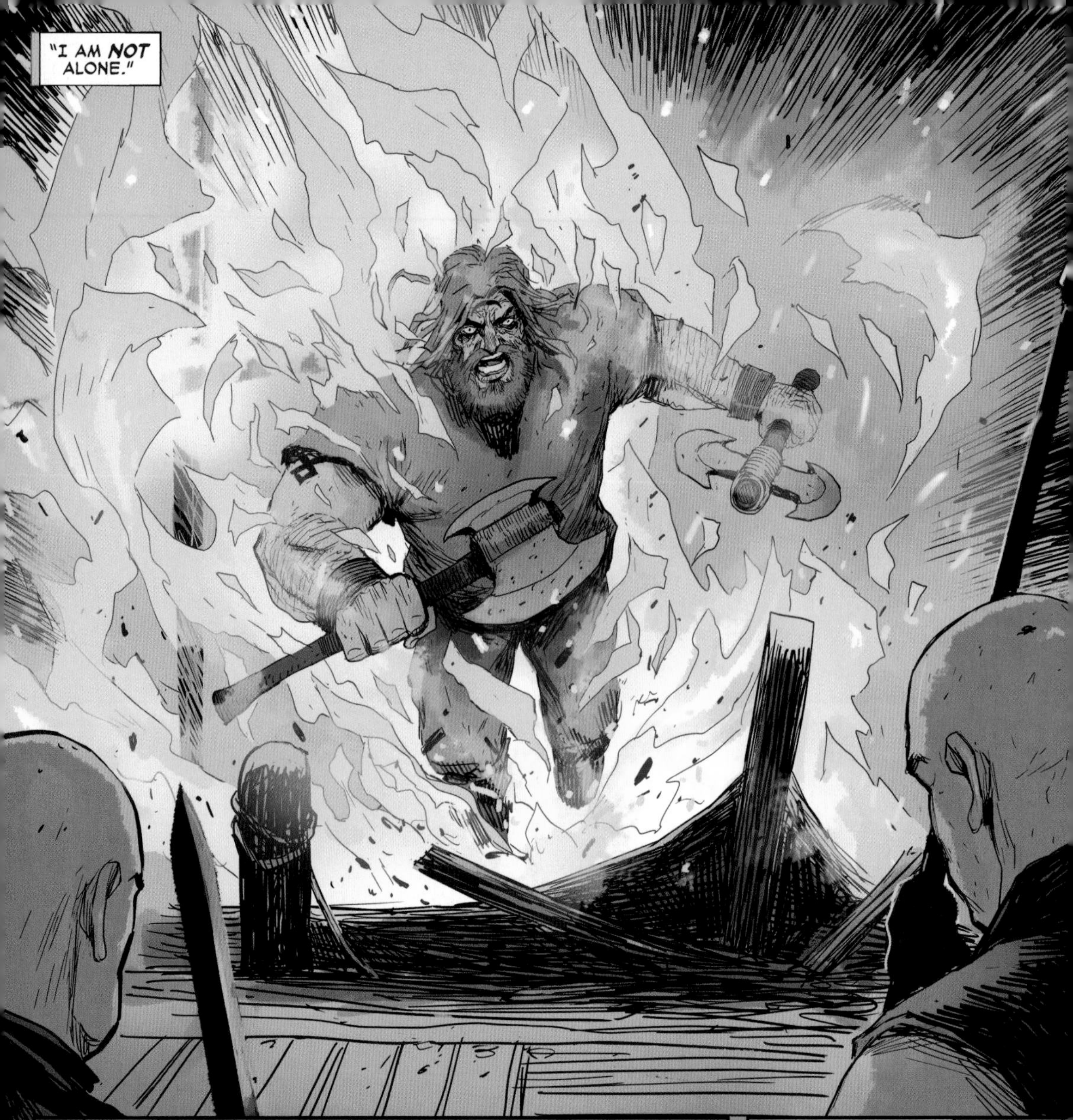
"I AM *NOT* ALONE."

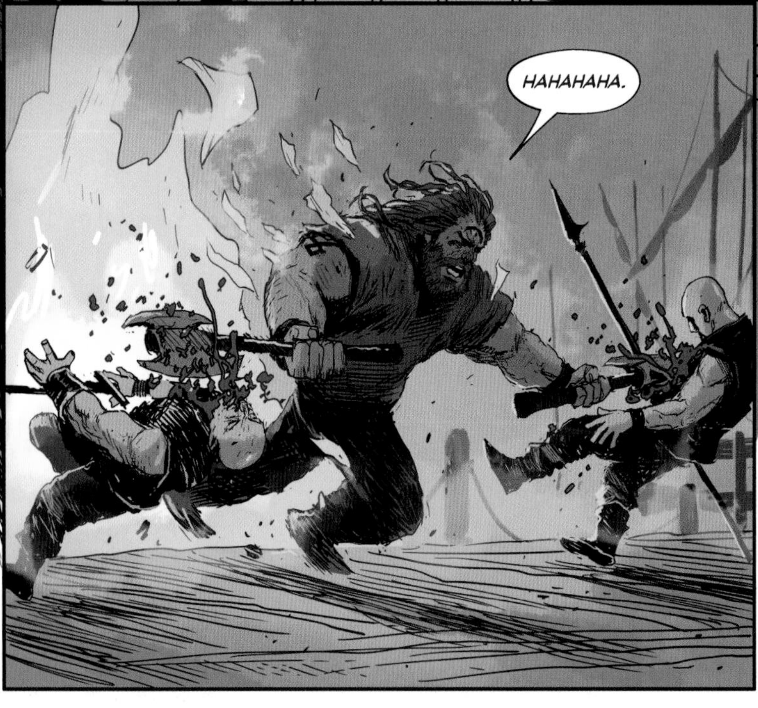
HAHAHAHA.

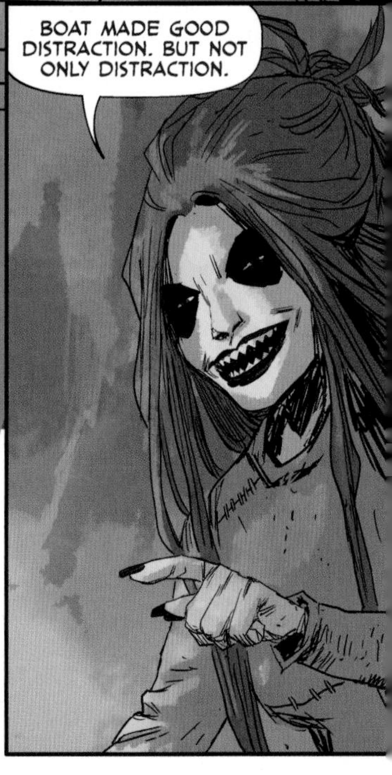
BOAT MADE GOOD DISTRACTION. BUT NOT ONLY DISTRACTION.

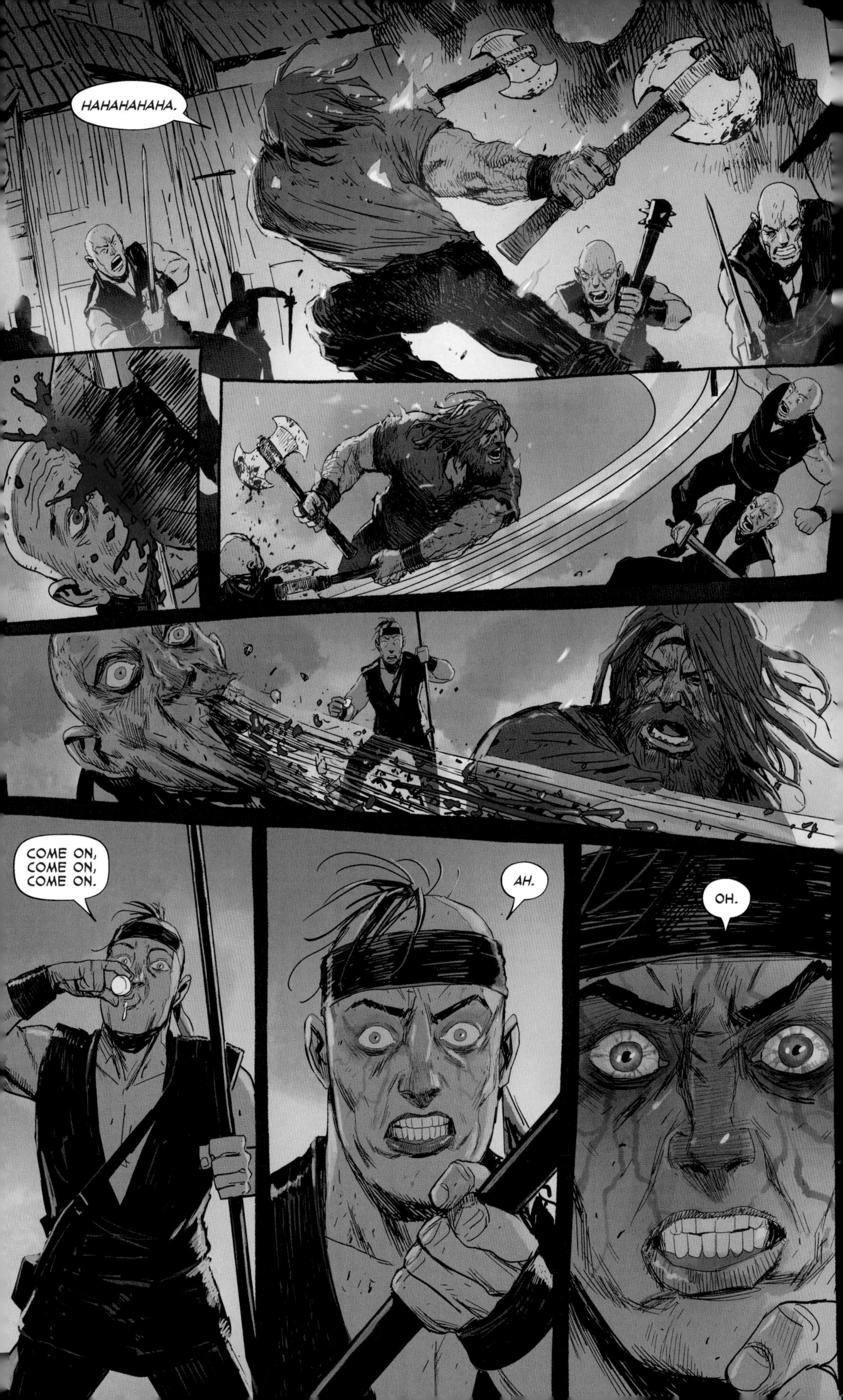
HAHAHAHAHA.
COME ON, COME ON, COME ON.
AH.
OH.

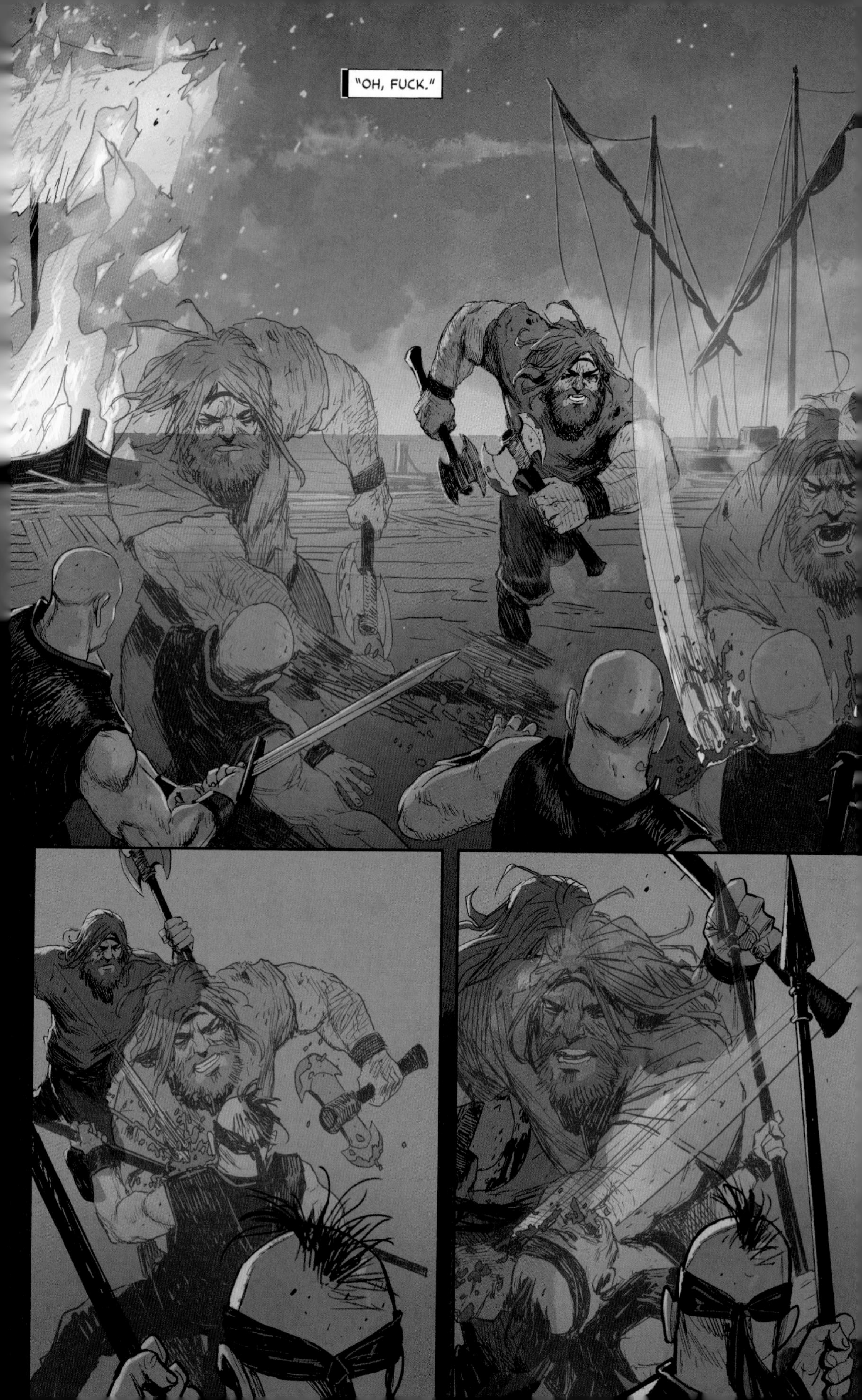
"OH, FUCK."

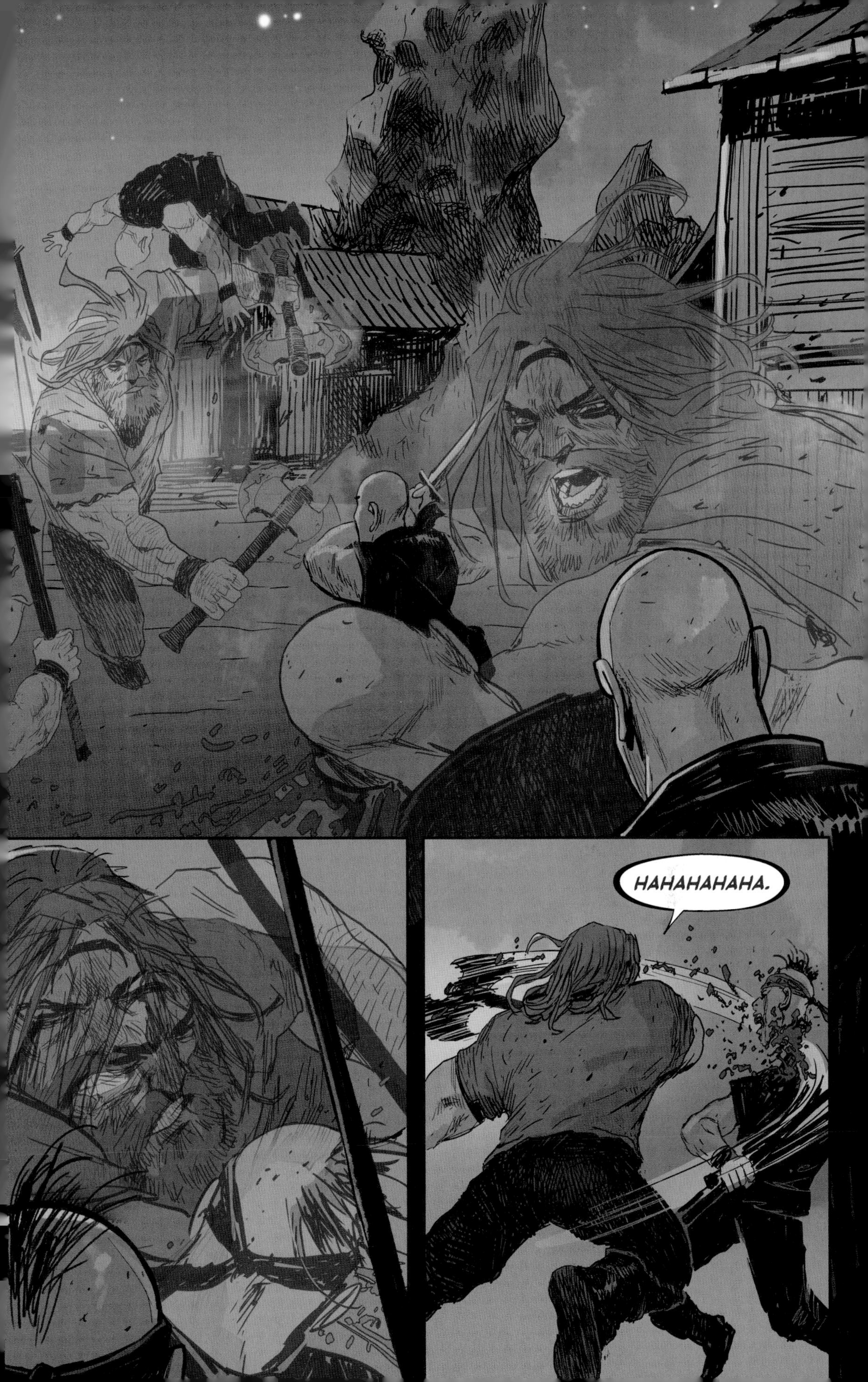
HAHAHAHAHA.

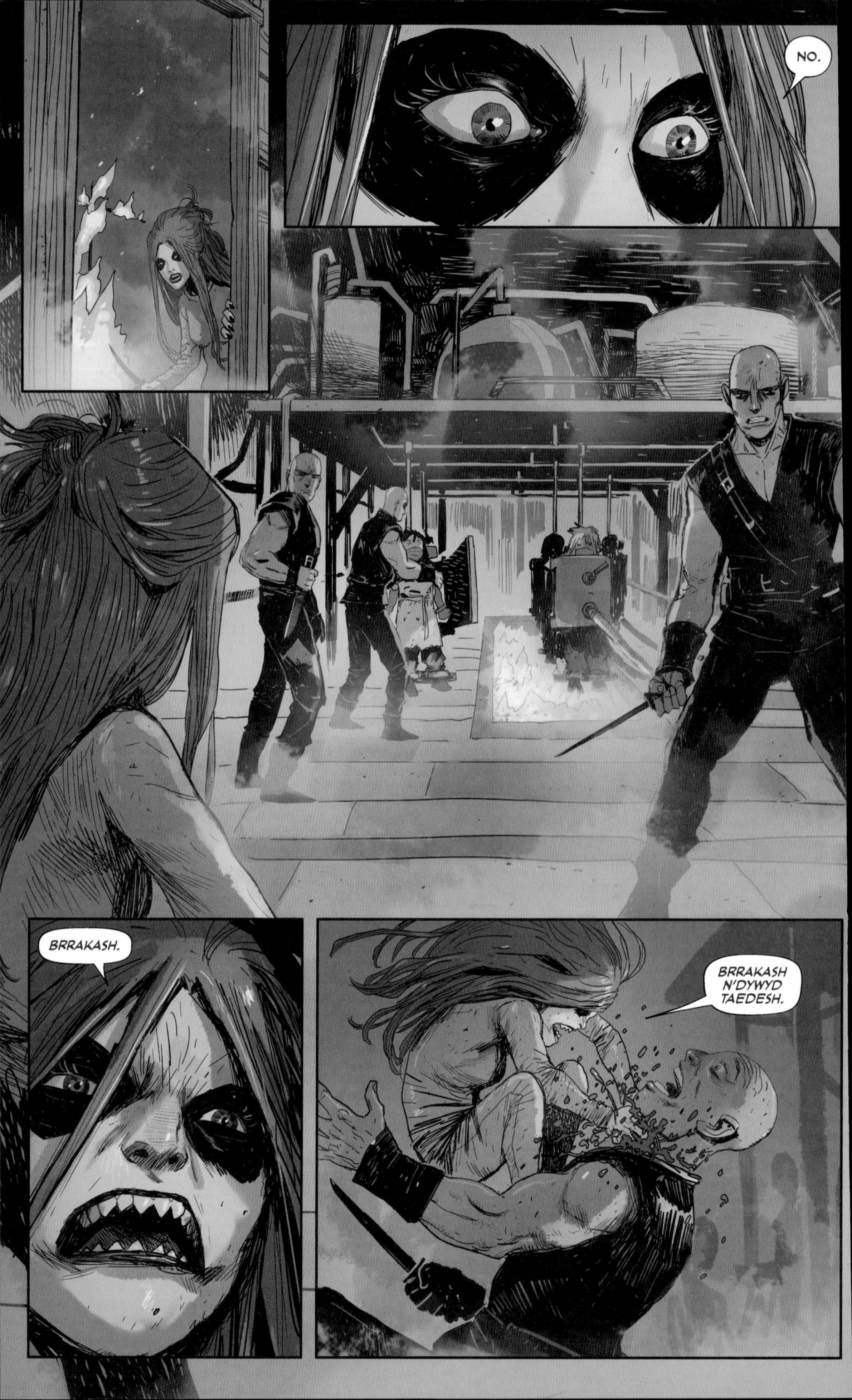
NO.
BRRAKASH.
BRRAKASH N'DYWYD TAEDESH.

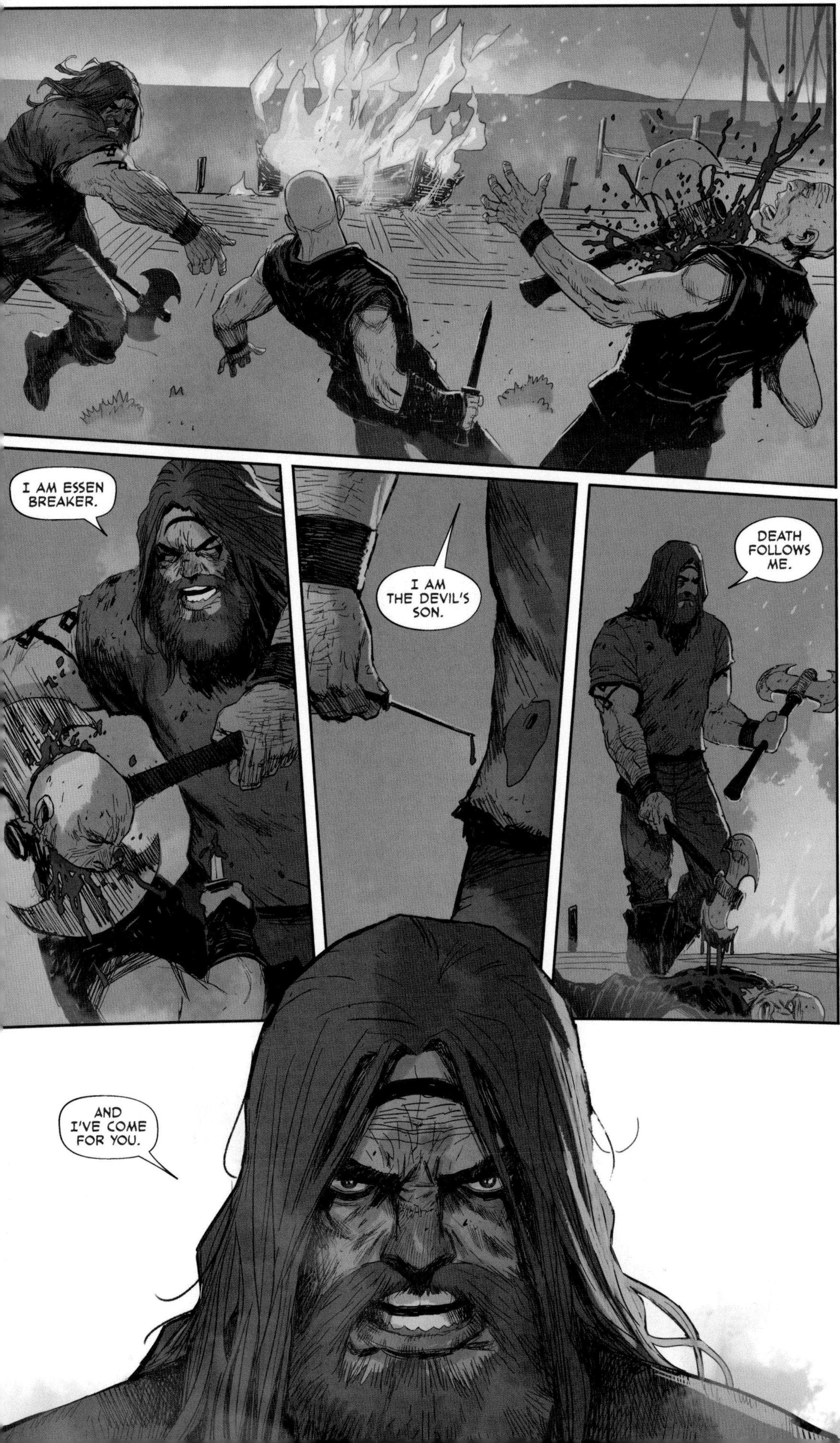
I AM ESSEN BREAKER.
I AM THE DEVIL'S SON.
DEATH FOLLOWS ME.
AND I'VE COME FOR YOU.

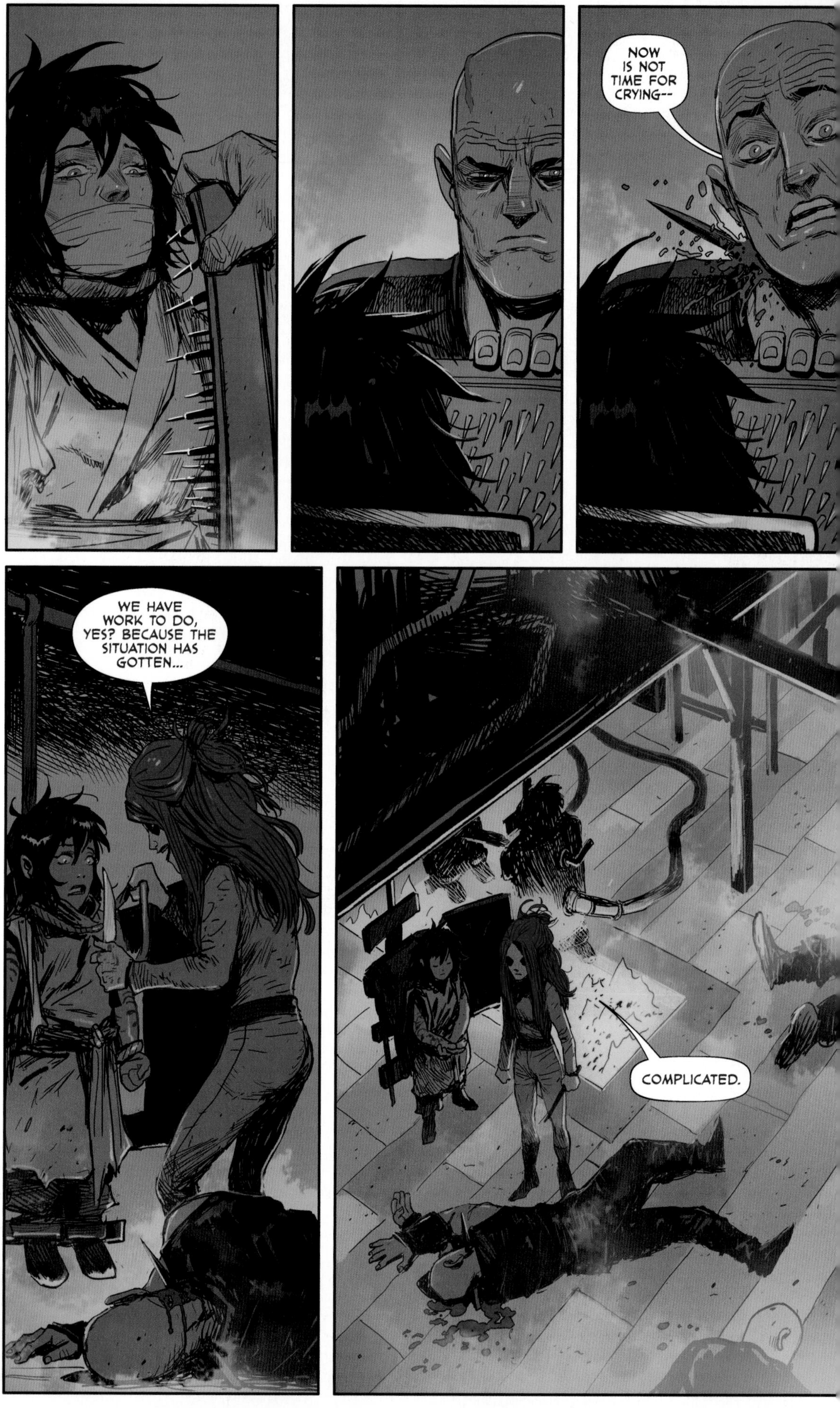
NOW IS NOT TIME FOR CRYING--
WE HAVE WORK TO DO, YES? BECAUSE THE SITUATION HAS GOTTEN...
COMPLICATED.

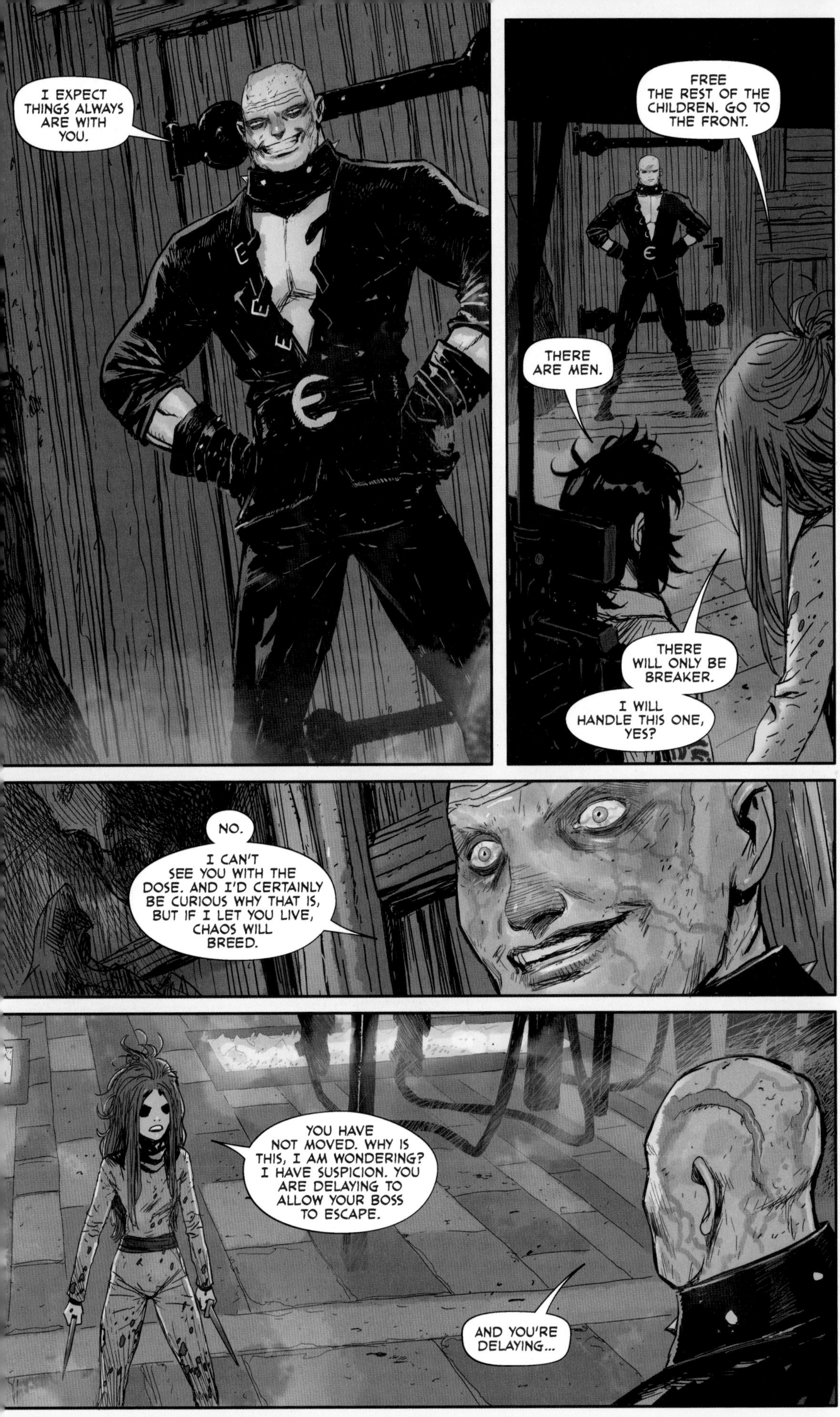

I EXPECT THINGS ALWAYS ARE WITH YOU.
FREE THE REST OF THE CHILDREN. GO TO THE FRONT.
THERE ARE MEN.
THERE WILL ONLY BE BREAKER.
I WILL HANDLE THIS ONE, YES?
NO.
I CAN'T SEE YOU WITH THE DOSE. AND I'D CERTAINLY BE CURIOUS WHY THAT IS, BUT IF I LET YOU LIVE, CHAOS WILL BREED.
YOU HAVE NOT MOVED. WHY IS THIS, I AM WONDERING? I HAVE SUSPICION. YOU ARE DELAYING TO ALLOW YOUR BOSS TO ESCAPE.
AND YOU'RE DELAYING...

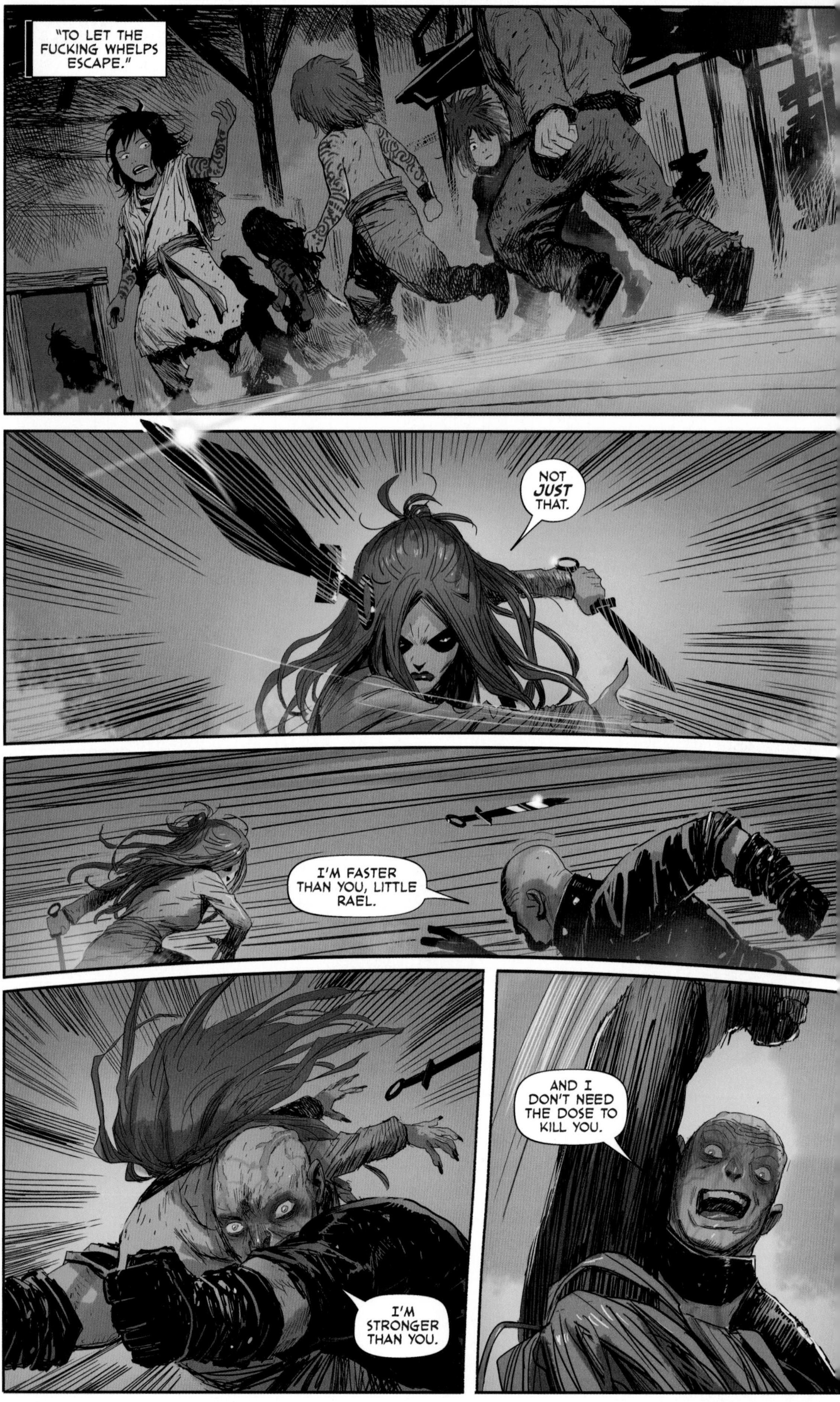
"TO LET THE FUCKING WHELPS ESCAPE."
NOT JUST THAT.
I'M FASTER THAN YOU, LITTLE RAEL.
I'M STRONGER THAN YOU.
AND I DON'T NEED THE DOSE TO KILL YOU.

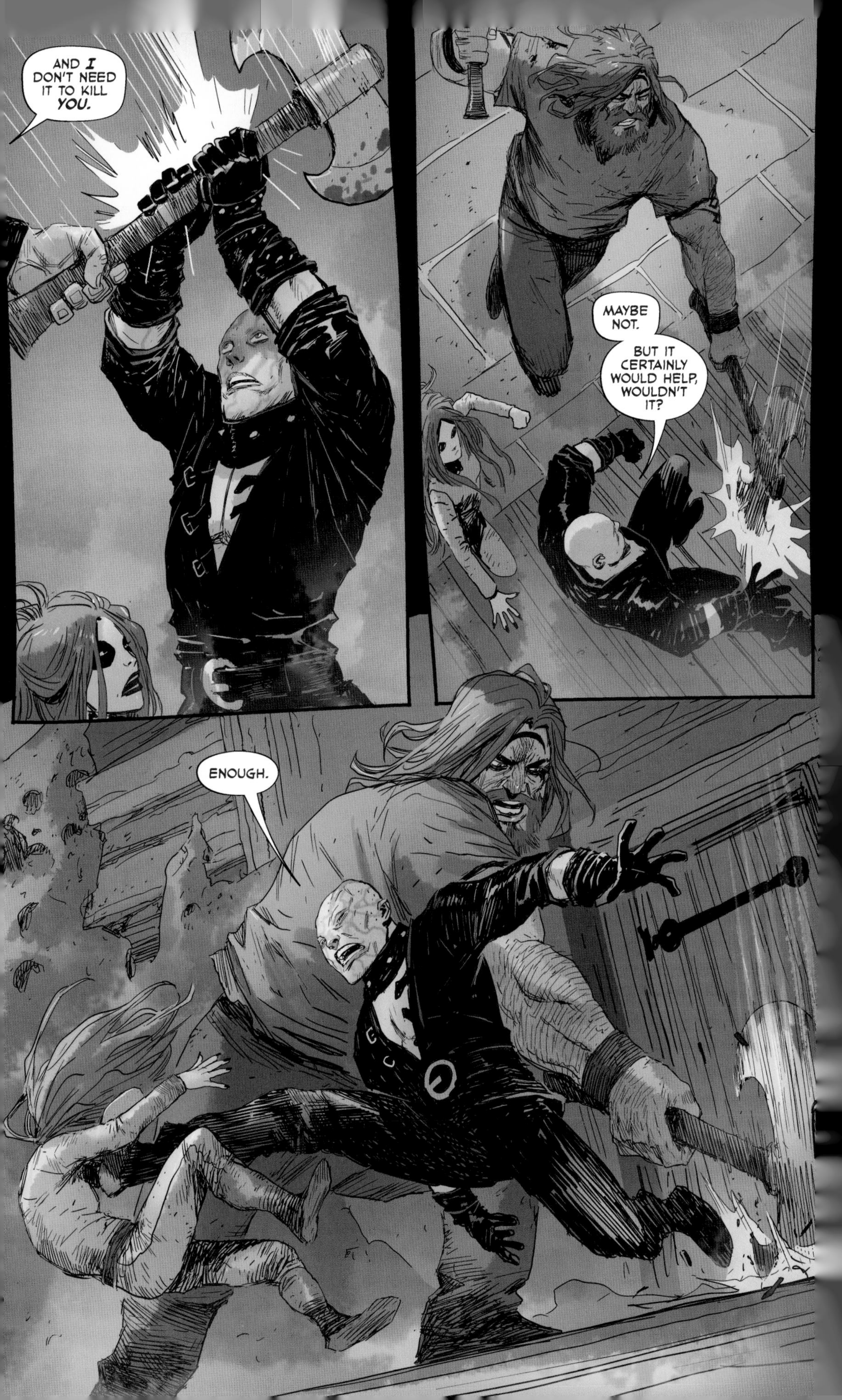
AND I DON'T NEED IT TO KILL YOU.
MAYBE NOT.
BUT IT CERTAINLY WOULD HELP, WOULDN'T IT?
ENOUGH.

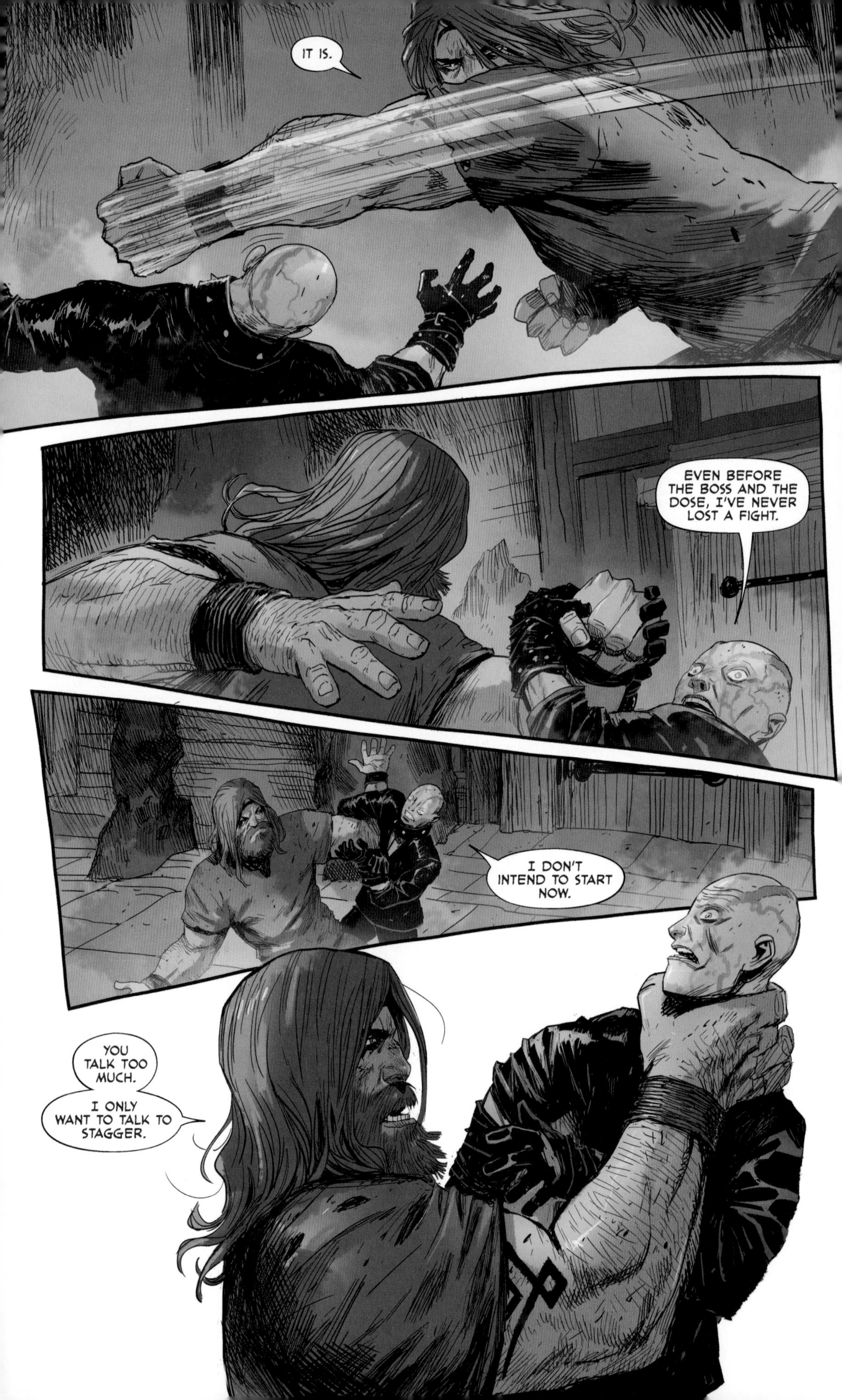
IT IS.
EVEN BEFORE THE BOSS AND THE DOSE, I'VE NEVER LOST A FIGHT.
I DON'T INTEND TO START NOW.
YOU TALK TOO MUCH.
I ONLY WANT TO TALK TO STAGGER.

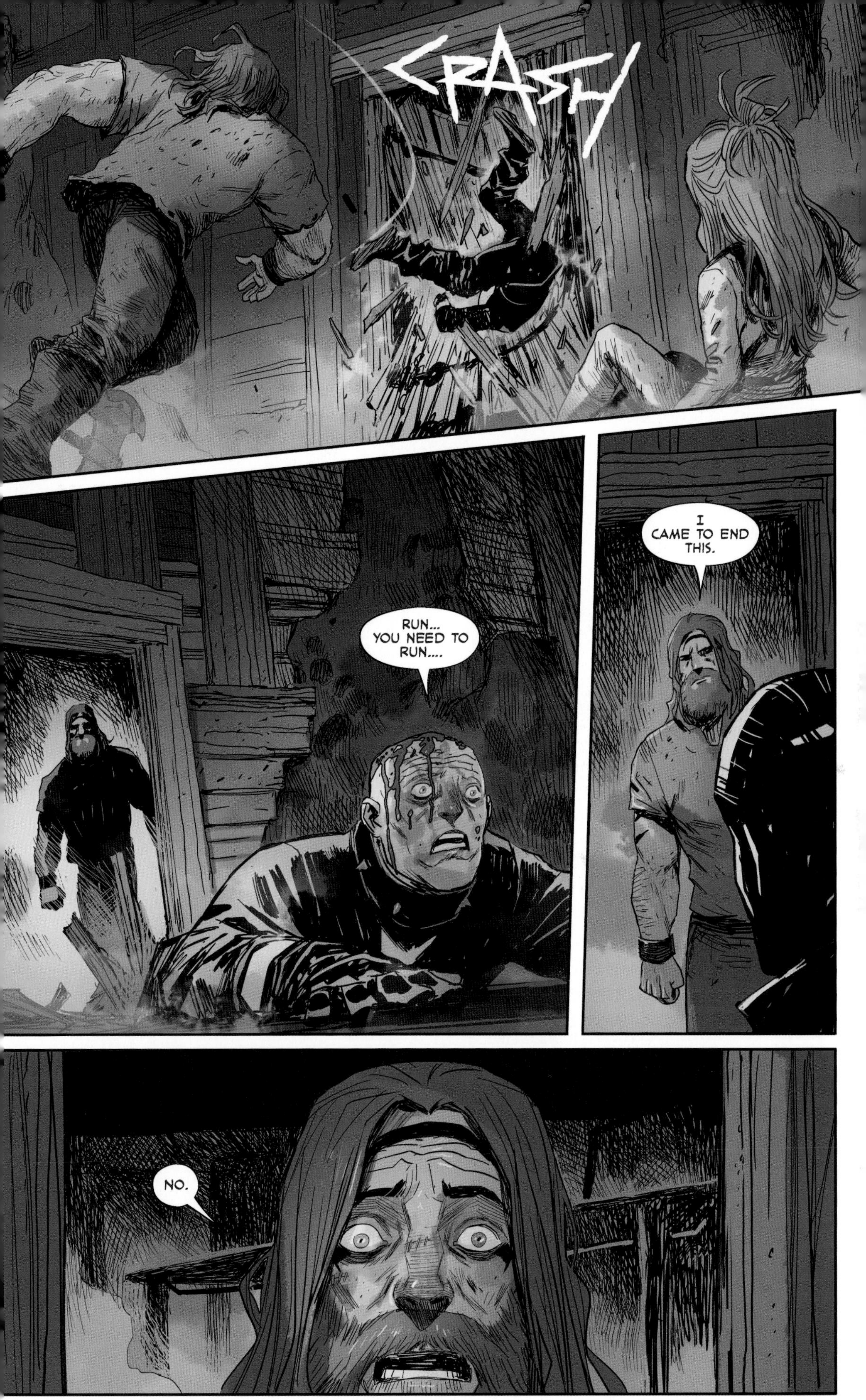
CRASH
RUN... YOU NEED TO RUN....
I CAME TO END THIS.
NO.

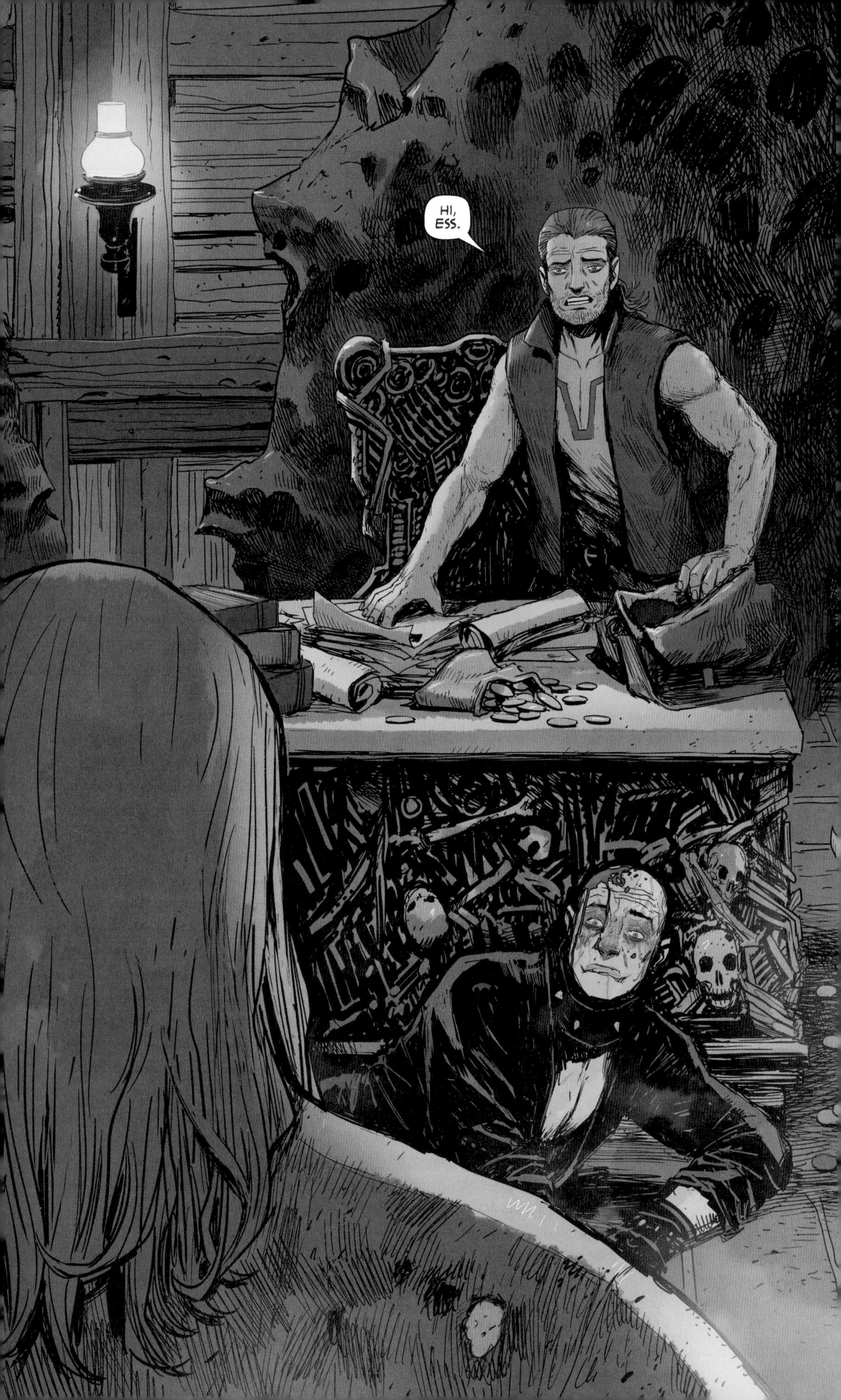
HI, ESS.

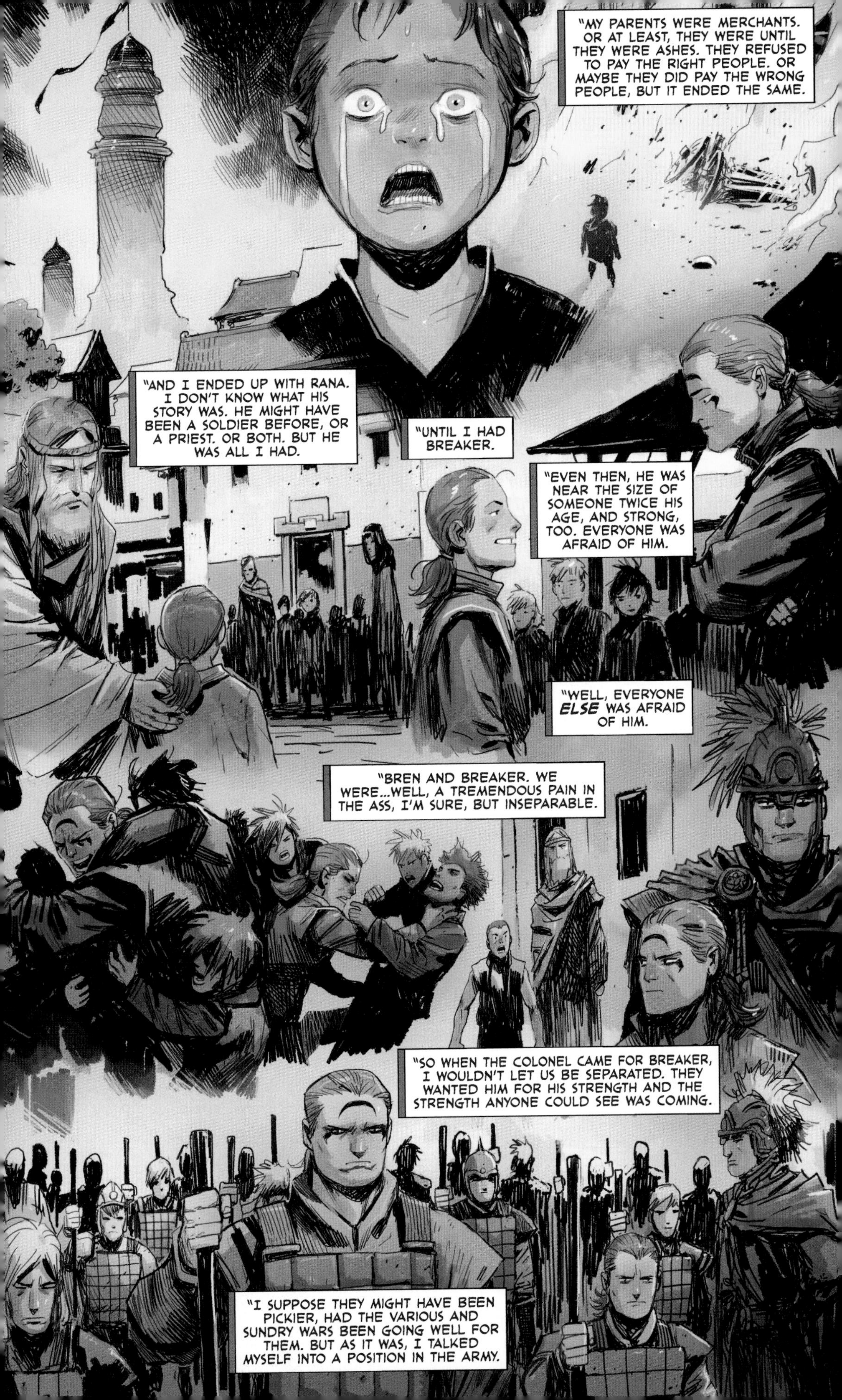
"MY PARENTS WERE MERCHANTS. OR AT LEAST, THEY WERE UNTIL THEY WERE ASHES. THEY REFUSED TO PAY THE RIGHT PEOPLE. OR MAYBE THEY DID PAY THE WRONG PEOPLE, BUT IT ENDED THE SAME.
"AND I ENDED UP WITH RANA. I DON'T KNOW WHAT HIS STORY WAS. HE MIGHT HAVE BEEN A SOLDIER BEFORE, OR A PRIEST. OR BOTH. BUT HE WAS ALL I HAD.
"UNTIL I HAD BREAKER.
"EVEN THEN, HE WAS NEAR THE SIZE OF SOMEONE TWICE HIS AGE, AND STRONG, TOO. EVERYONE WAS AFRAID OF HIM.
"WELL, EVERYONE *ELSE* WAS AFRAID OF HIM.
"BREN AND BREAKER. WE WERE...WELL, A TREMENDOUS PAIN IN THE ASS, I'M SURE, BUT INSEPARABLE.
"SO WHEN THE COLONEL CAME FOR BREAKER, I WOULDN'T LET US BE SEPARATED. THEY WANTED HIM FOR HIS STRENGTH AND THE STRENGTH ANYONE COULD SEE WAS COMING.
"I SUPPOSE THEY MIGHT HAVE BEEN PICKIER, HAD THE VARIOUS AND SUNDRY WARS BEEN GOING WELL FOR THEM. BUT AS IT WAS, I TALKED MYSELF INTO A POSITION IN THE ARMY.

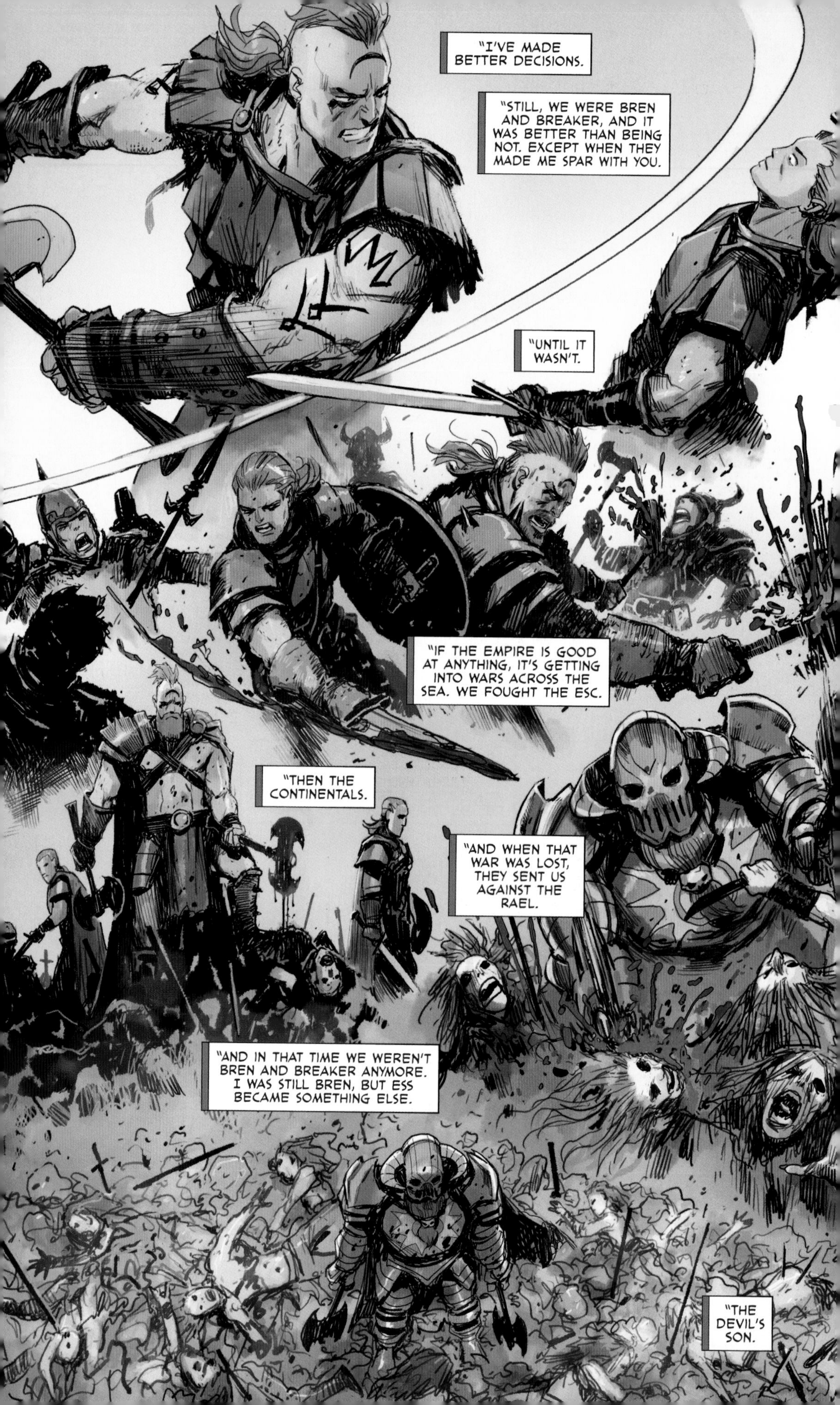
"I'VE MADE BETTER DECISIONS.
"STILL, WE WERE BREN AND BREAKER, AND IT WAS BETTER THAN BEING NOT. EXCEPT WHEN THEY MADE ME SPAR WITH YOU.
"UNTIL IT WASN'T.
"IF THE EMPIRE IS GOOD AT ANYTHING, IT'S GETTING INTO WARS ACROSS THE SEA. WE FOUGHT THE ESC.
"THEN THE CONTINENTALS.
"AND WHEN THAT WAR WAS LOST, THEY SENT US AGAINST THE RAEL.
"AND IN THAT TIME WE WEREN'T BREN AND BREAKER ANYMORE. I WAS STILL BREN, BUT ESS BECAME SOMETHING ELSE.
"THE DEVIL'S SON.

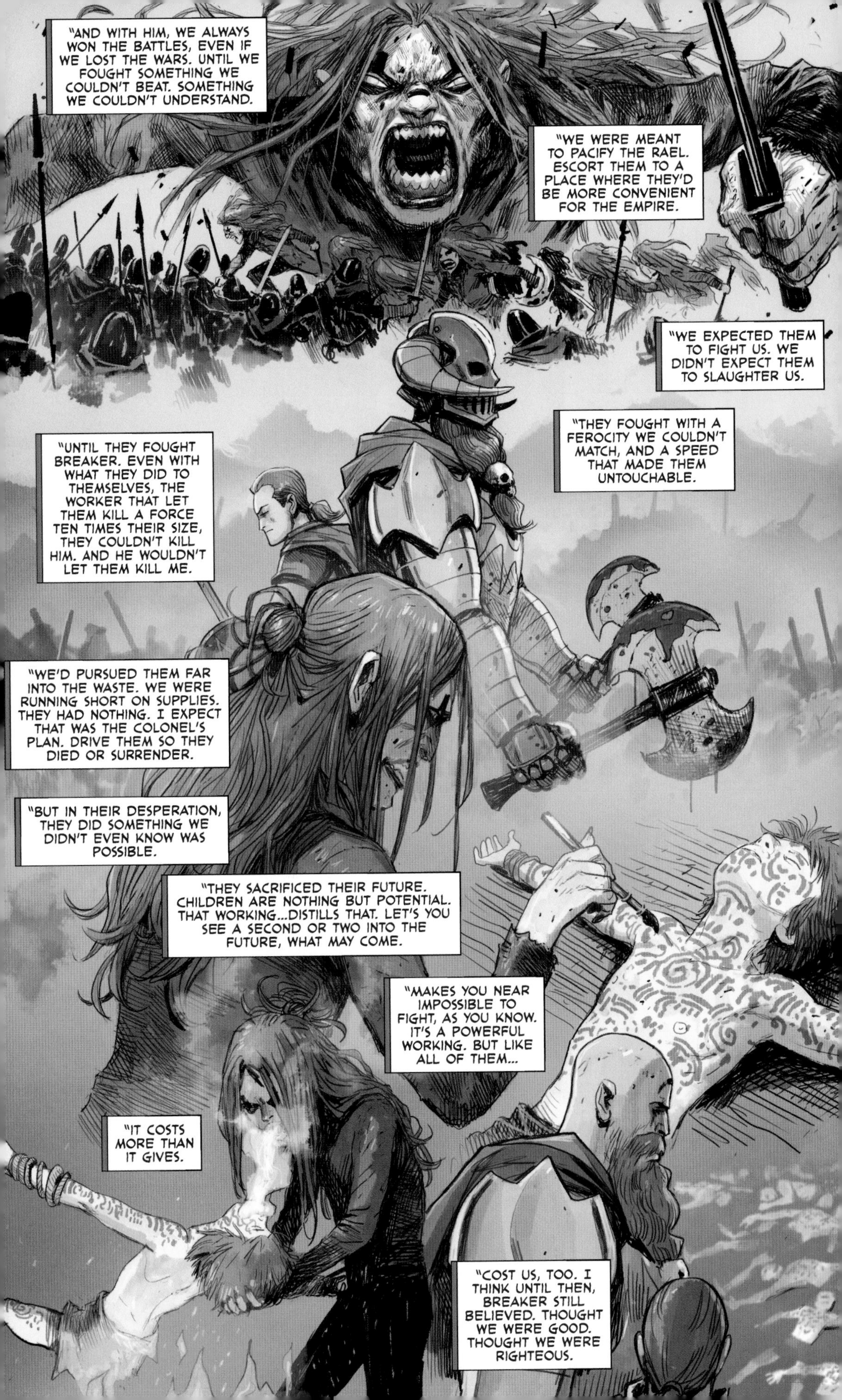
"AND WITH HIM, WE ALWAYS WON THE BATTLES, EVEN IF WE LOST THE WARS. UNTIL WE FOUGHT SOMETHING WE COULDN'T BEAT. SOMETHING WE COULDN'T UNDERSTAND.
"WE WERE MEANT TO PACIFY THE RAEL. ESCORT THEM TO A PLACE WHERE THEY'D BE MORE CONVENIENT FOR THE EMPIRE.
"WE EXPECTED THEM TO FIGHT US. WE DIDN'T EXPECT THEM TO SLAUGHTER US.
"THEY FOUGHT WITH A FEROCITY WE COULDN'T MATCH, AND A SPEED THAT MADE THEM UNTOUCHABLE.
"UNTIL THEY FOUGHT BREAKER. EVEN WITH WHAT THEY DID TO THEMSELVES, THE WORKER THAT LET THEM KILL A FORCE TEN TIMES THEIR SIZE, THEY COULDN'T KILL HIM. AND HE WOULDN'T LET THEM KILL ME.
"WE'D PURSUED THEM FAR INTO THE WASTE. WE WERE RUNNING SHORT ON SUPPLIES. THEY HAD NOTHING. I EXPECT THAT WAS THE COLONEL'S PLAN. DRIVE THEM SO THEY DIED OR SURRENDER.
"BUT IN THEIR DESPERATION, THEY DID SOMETHING WE DIDN'T EVEN KNOW WAS POSSIBLE.
"THEY SACRIFICED THEIR FUTURE. CHILDREN ARE NOTHING BUT POTENTIAL. THAT WORKING...DISTILLS THAT. LET'S YOU SEE A SECOND OR TWO INTO THE FUTURE, WHAT MAY COME.
"MAKES YOU NEAR IMPOSSIBLE TO FIGHT, AS YOU KNOW. IT'S A POWERFUL WORKING. BUT LIKE ALL OF THEM...
"IT COSTS MORE THAN IT GIVES.
"COST US, TOO. I THINK UNTIL THEN, BREAKER STILL BELIEVED. THOUGHT WE WERE GOOD. THOUGHT WE WERE RIGHTEOUS.

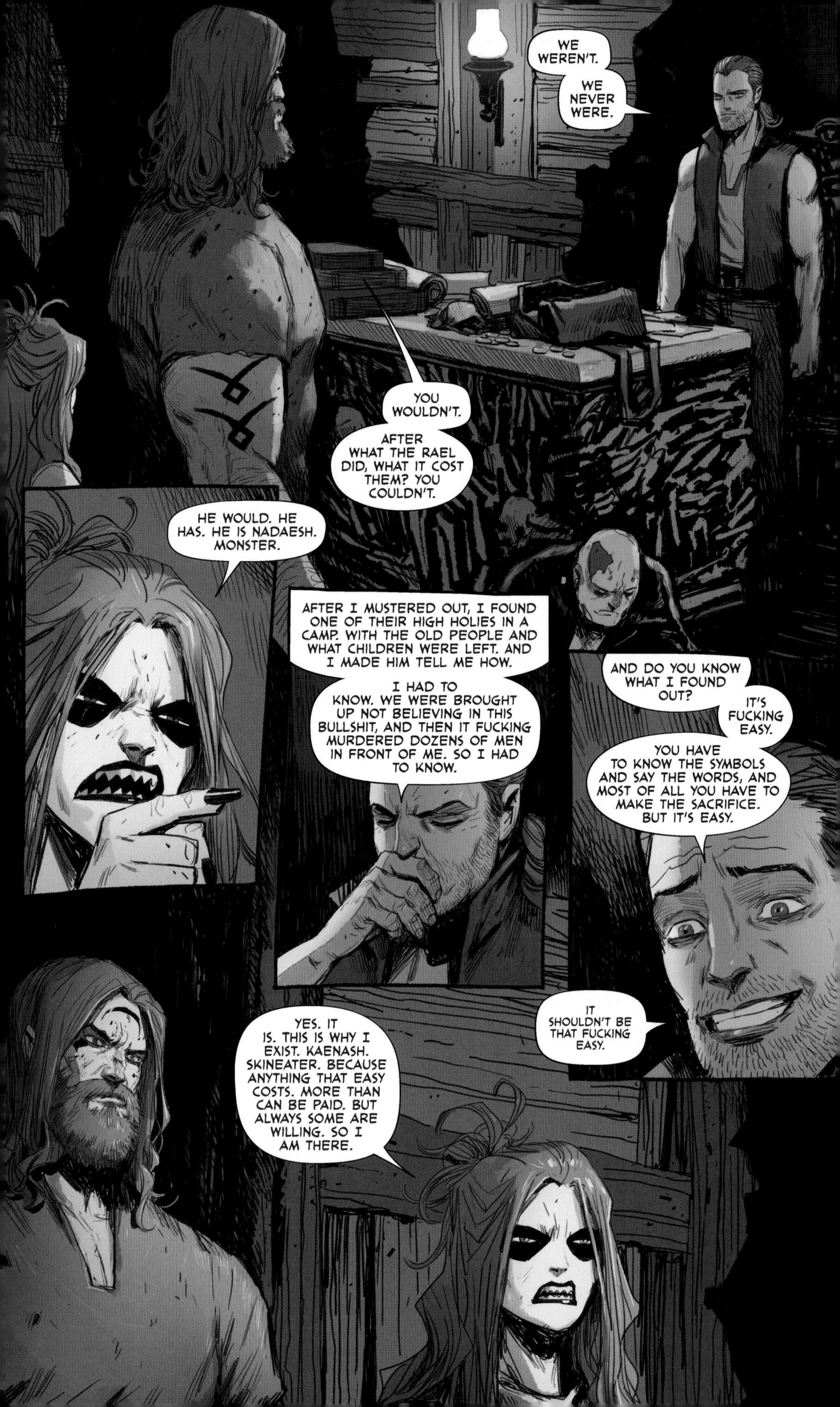
WE WEREN'T.
WE NEVER WERE.
YOU WOULDN'T.
AFTER WHAT THE RAEL DID, WHAT IT COST THEM? YOU COULDN'T.
HE WOULD. HE HAS. HE IS NADAESH. MONSTER.
AFTER I MUSTERED OUT, I FOUND ONE OF THEIR HIGH HOLIES IN A CAMP. WITH THE OLD PEOPLE AND WHAT CHILDREN WERE LEFT. AND I MADE HIM TELL ME HOW.
I HAD TO KNOW. WE WERE BROUGHT UP NOT BELIEVING IN THIS BULLSHIT, AND THEN IT FUCKING MURDERED DOZENS OF MEN IN FRONT OF ME. SO I HAD TO KNOW.
AND DO YOU KNOW WHAT I FOUND OUT?
IT'S FUCKING EASY.
YOU HAVE TO KNOW THE SYMBOLS AND SAY THE WORDS, AND MOST OF ALL YOU HAVE TO MAKE THE SACRIFICE. BUT IT'S EASY.
IT SHOULDN'T BE THAT FUCKING EASY.
YES. IT IS. THIS IS WHY I EXIST. KAENASH. SKINEATER. BECAUSE ANYTHING THAT EASY COSTS. MORE THAN CAN BE PAID. BUT ALWAYS SOME ARE WILLING. SO I AM THERE.

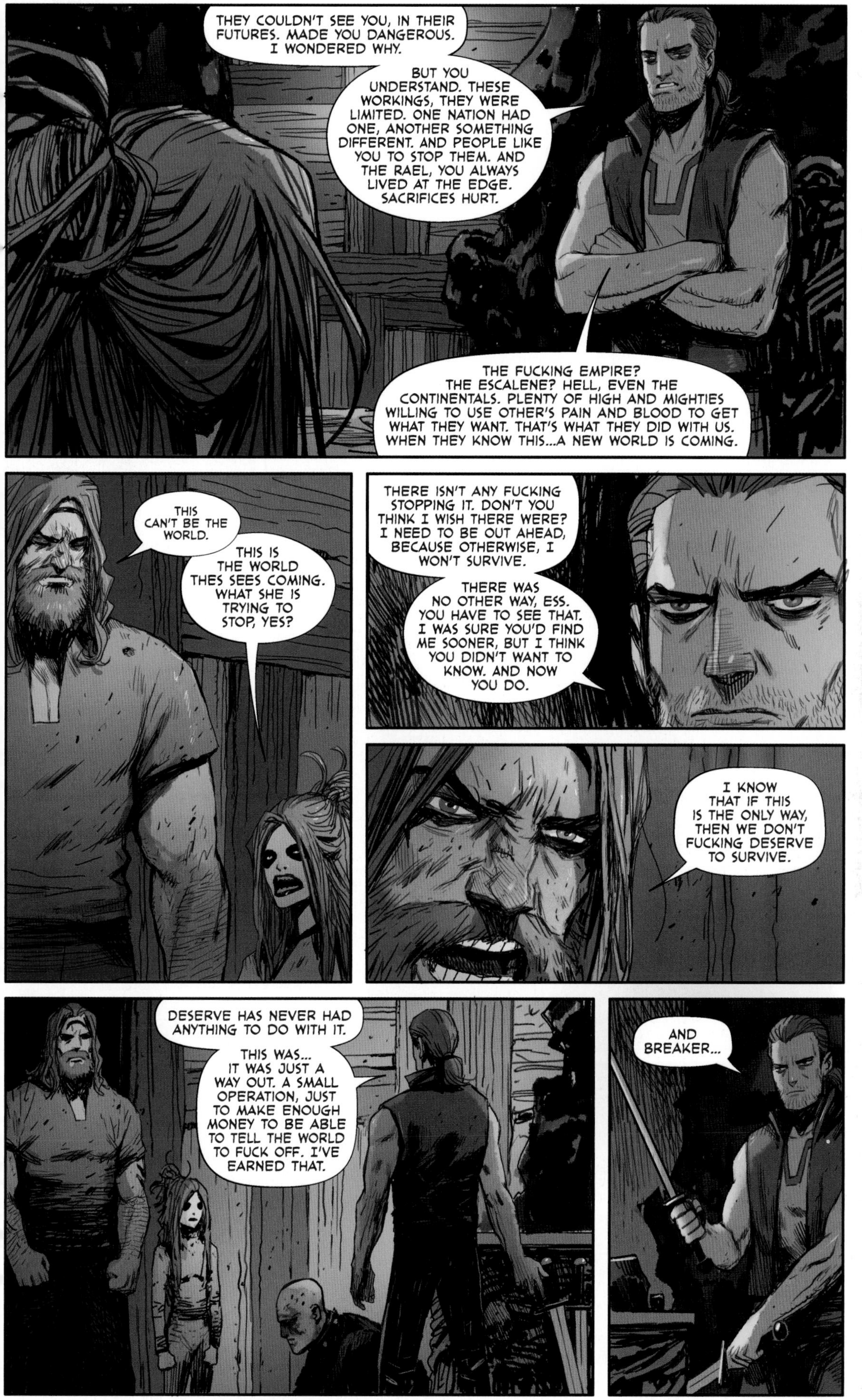
THEY COULDN'T SEE YOU, IN THEIR FUTURES. MADE YOU DANGEROUS. I WONDERED WHY.
BUT YOU UNDERSTAND. THESE WORKINGS, THEY WERE LIMITED. ONE NATION HAD ONE, ANOTHER SOMETHING DIFFERENT. AND PEOPLE LIKE YOU TO STOP THEM. AND THE RAEL, YOU ALWAYS LIVED AT THE EDGE. SACRIFICES HURT.
THE FUCKING EMPIRE? THE ESCALENE? HELL, EVEN THE CONTINENTALS. PLENTY OF HIGH AND MIGHTIES WILLING TO USE OTHER'S PAIN AND BLOOD TO GET WHAT THEY WANT. THAT'S WHAT THEY DID WITH US. WHEN THEY KNOW THIS...A NEW WORLD IS COMING.
THIS CAN'T BE THE WORLD.
THIS IS THE WORLD THES SEES COMING. WHAT SHE IS TRYING TO STOP, YES?
THERE ISN'T ANY FUCKING STOPPING IT. DON'T YOU THINK I WISH THERE WERE? I NEED TO BE OUT AHEAD, BECAUSE OTHERWISE, I WON'T SURVIVE.
THERE WAS NO OTHER WAY, ESS. YOU HAVE TO SEE THAT. I WAS SURE YOU'D FIND ME SOONER, BUT I THINK YOU DIDN'T WANT TO KNOW. AND NOW YOU DO.
I KNOW THAT IF THIS IS THE ONLY WAY, THEN WE DON'T FUCKING DESERVE TO SURVIVE.
DESERVE HAS NEVER HAD ANYTHING TO DO WITH IT.
THIS WAS... IT WAS JUST A WAY OUT. A SMALL OPERATION, JUST TO MAKE ENOUGH MONEY TO BE ABLE TO TELL THE WORLD TO FUCK OFF. I'VE EARNED THAT.
AND BREAKER...

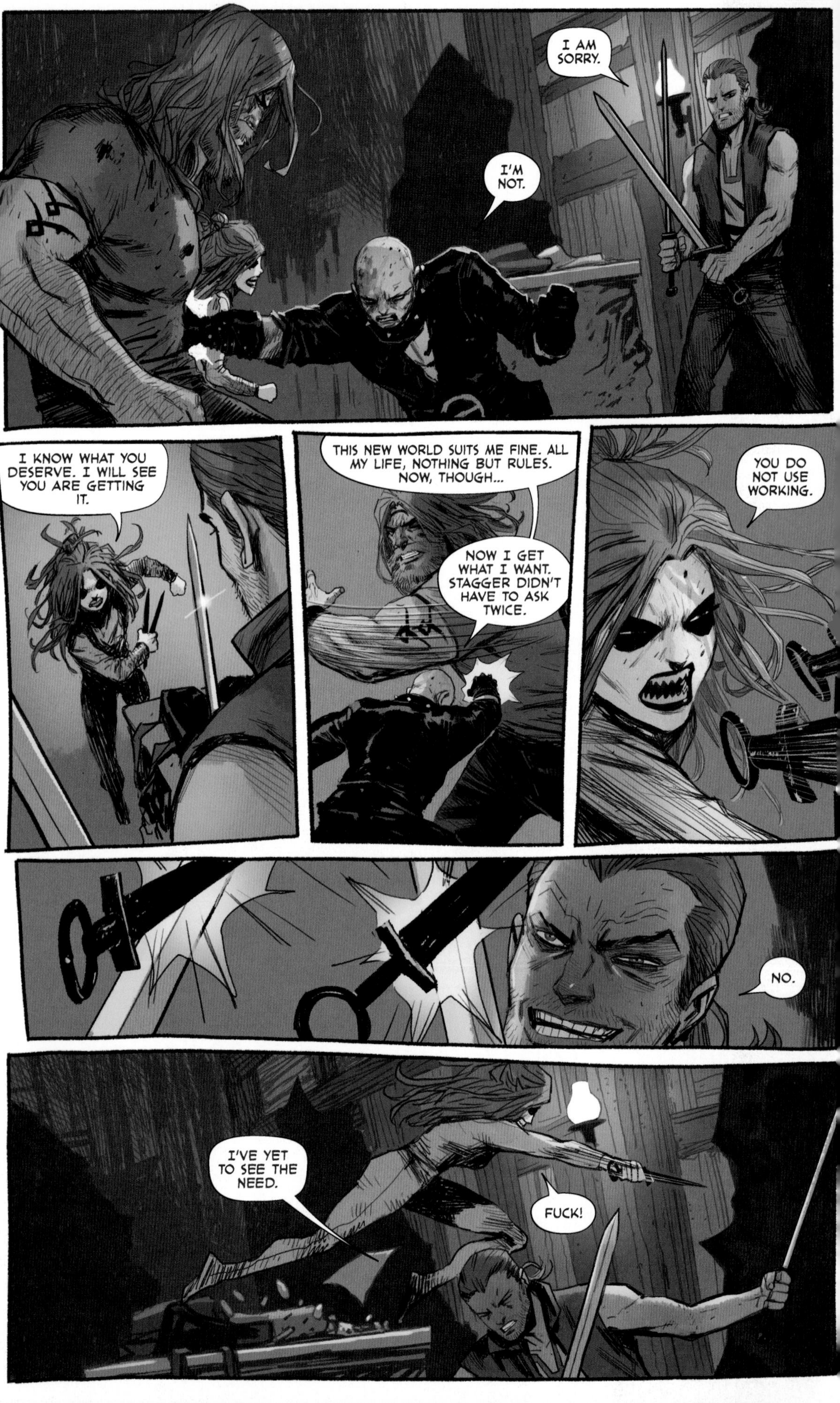
I AM SORRY.
I'M NOT.
I KNOW WHAT YOU DESERVE. I WILL SEE YOU ARE GETTING IT.
THIS NEW WORLD SUITS ME FINE. ALL MY LIFE, NOTHING BUT RULES. NOW, THOUGH...
NOW I GET WHAT I WANT. STAGGER DIDN'T HAVE TO ASK TWICE.
YOU DO NOT USE WORKING.
NO.
I'VE YET TO SEE THE NEED.
FUCK!

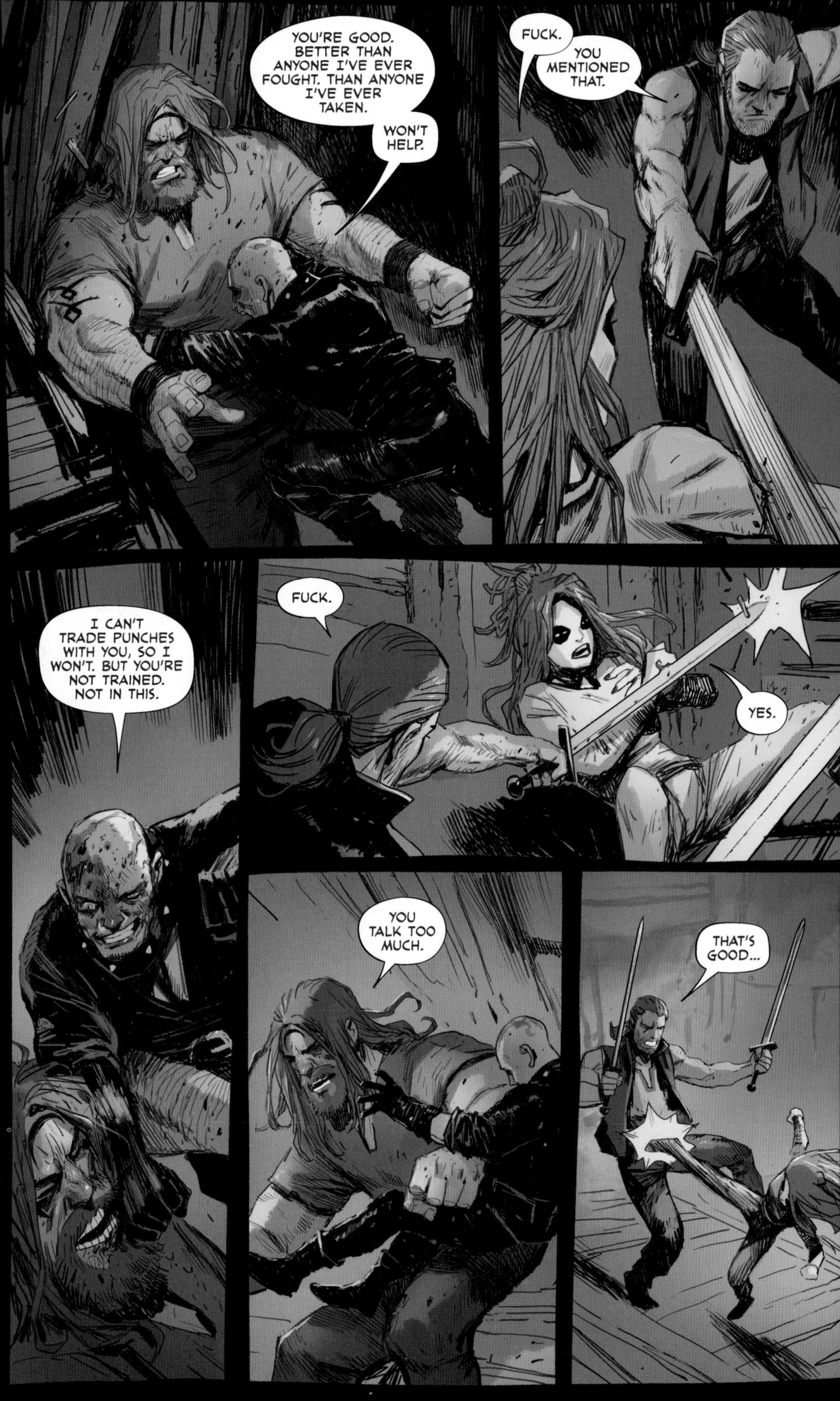
YOU'RE GOOD. BETTER THAN ANYONE I'VE EVER FOUGHT. THAN ANYONE I'VE EVER TAKEN.
WON'T HELP.
FUCK.
YOU MENTIONED THAT.
I CAN'T TRADE PUNCHES WITH YOU, SO I WON'T. BUT YOU'RE NOT TRAINED. NOT IN THIS.
FUCK.
YES.
YOU TALK TOO MUCH.
THAT'S GOOD...

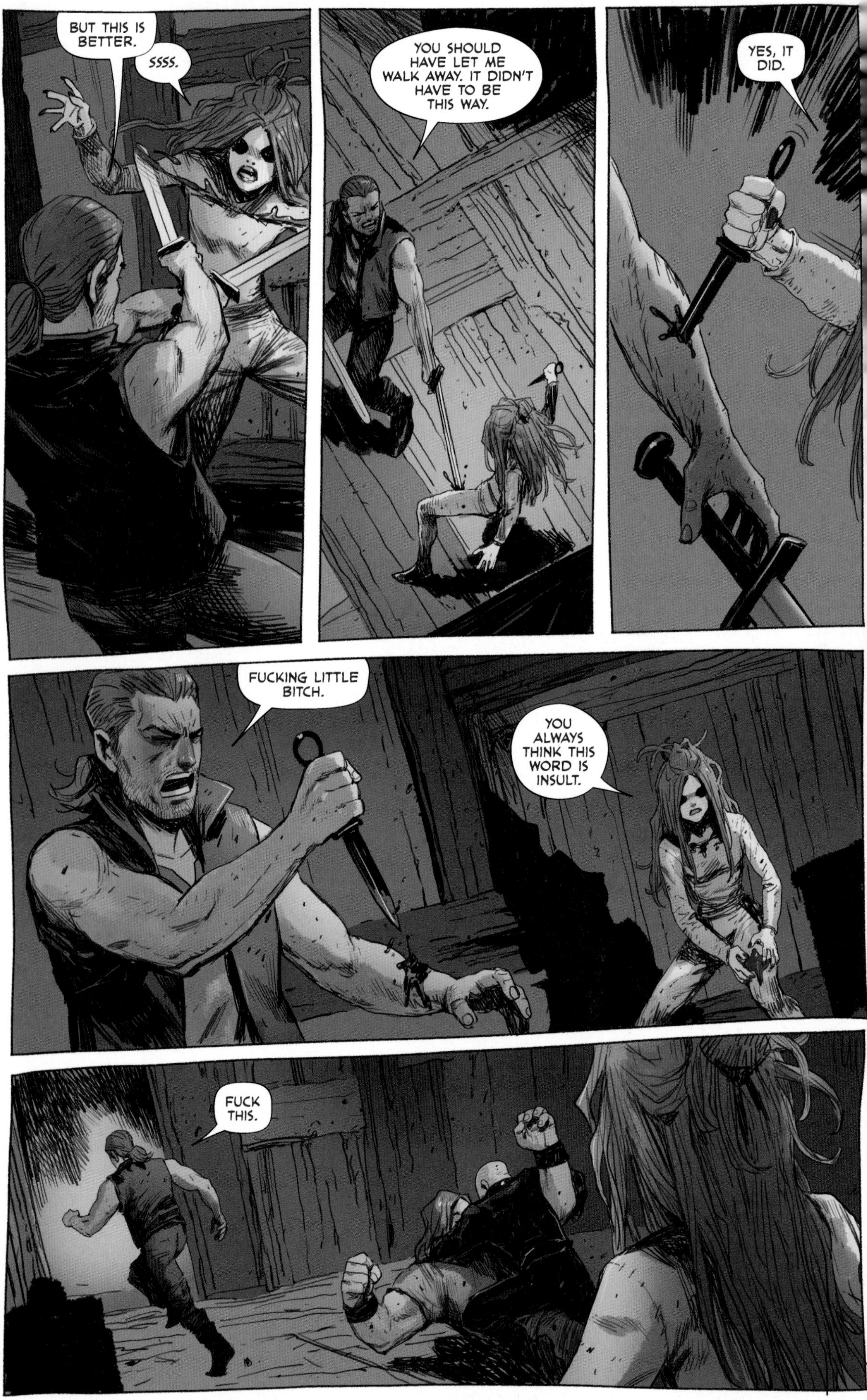

BUT THIS IS BETTER.
SSSS.
YOU SHOULD HAVE LET ME WALK AWAY. IT DIDN'T HAVE TO BE THIS WAY.
YES, IT DID.
FUCKING LITTLE BITCH.
YOU ALWAYS THINK THIS WORD IS INSULT.
FUCK THIS.

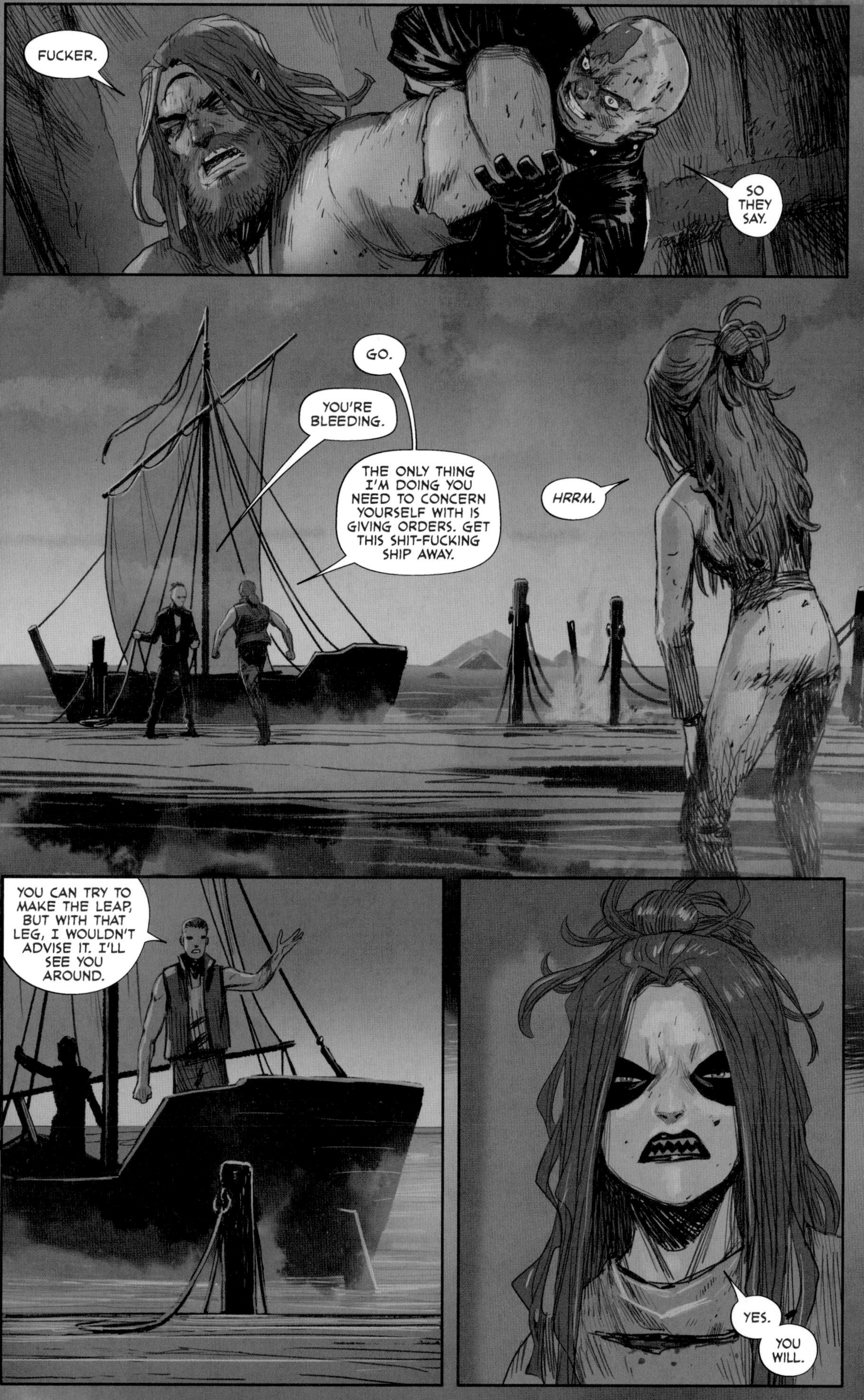
FUCKER.
SO THEY SAY.
GO.
YOU'RE BLEEDING.
THE ONLY THING I'M DOING YOU NEED TO CONCERN YOURSELF WITH IS GIVING ORDERS. GET THIS SHIT-FUCKING SHIP AWAY.
HRRM.
YOU CAN TRY TO MAKE THE LEAP, BUT WITH THAT LEG, I WOULDN'T ADVISE IT. I'LL SEE YOU AROUND.
YES.
YOU WILL.

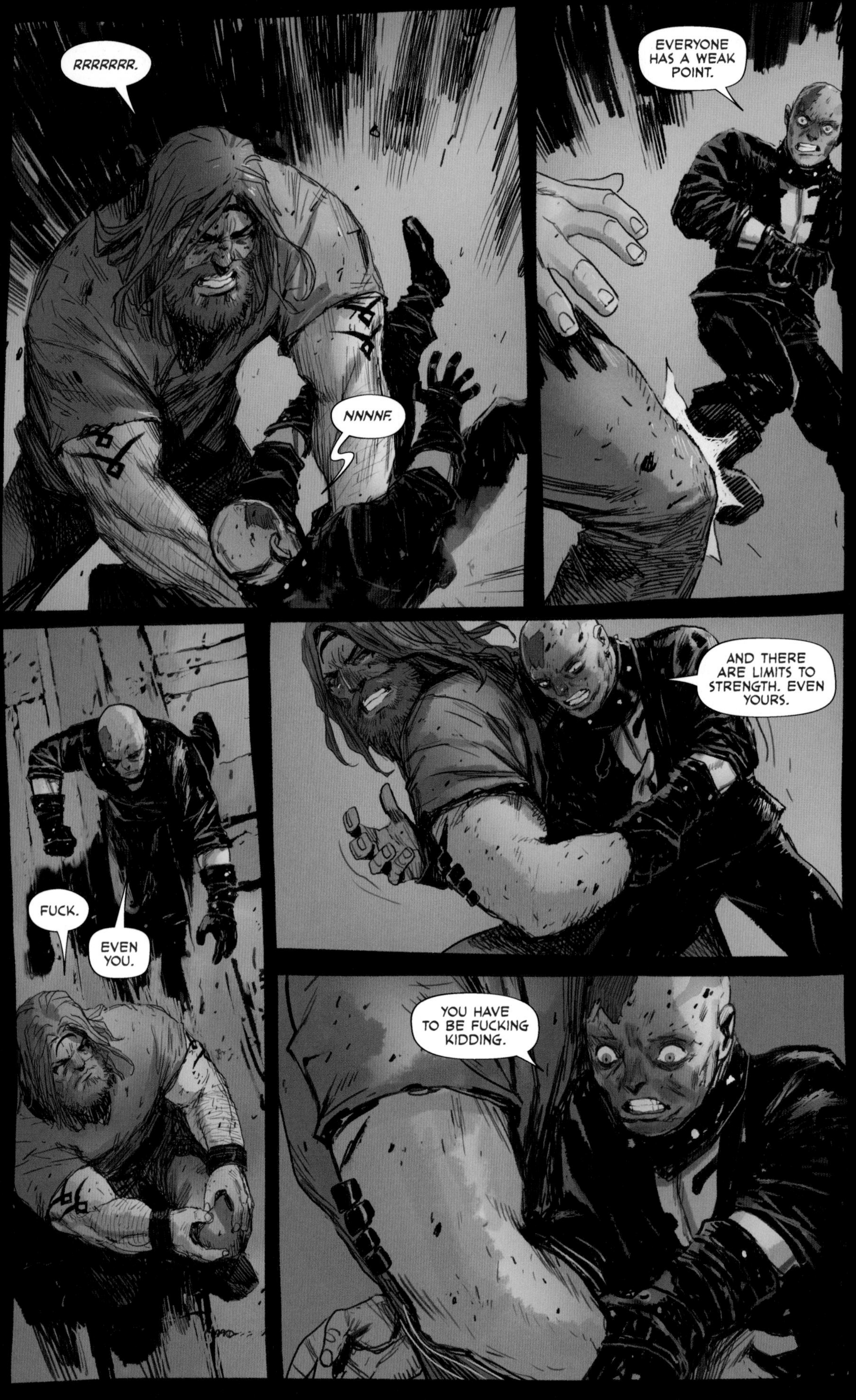
RRRRRRR.
NNNNF.
EVERYONE HAS A WEAK POINT.
FUCK.
EVEN YOU.
AND THERE ARE LIMITS TO STRENGTH. EVEN YOURS.
YOU HAVE TO BE FUCKING KIDDING.

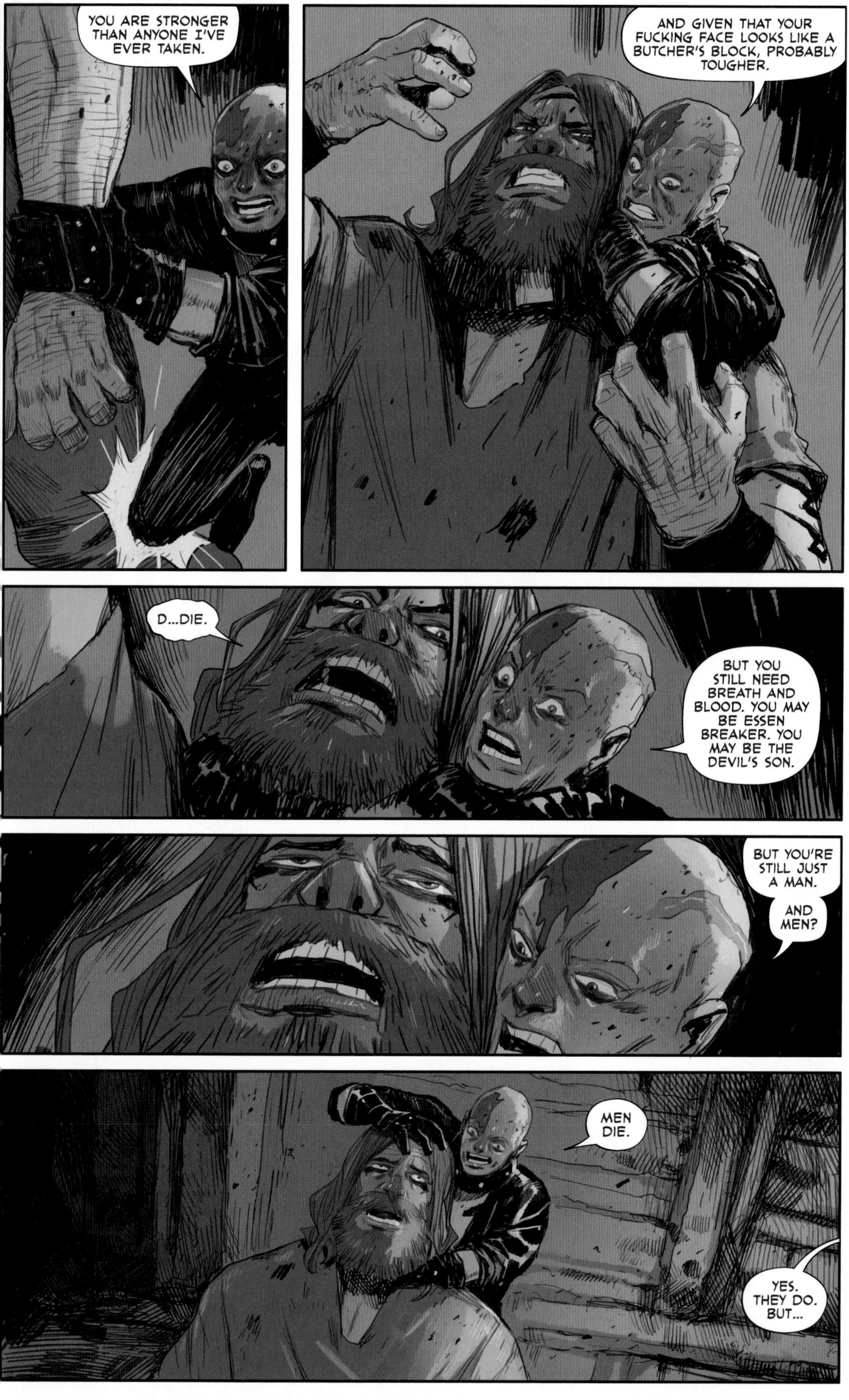
YOU ARE STRONGER THAN ANYONE I'VE EVER TAKEN.
AND GIVEN THAT YOUR FUCKING FACE LOOKS LIKE A BUTCHER'S BLOCK, PROBABLY TOUGHER.
D...DIE.
BUT YOU STILL NEED BREATH AND BLOOD. YOU MAY BE ESSEN BREAKER. YOU MAY BE THE DEVIL'S SON.
BUT YOU'RE STILL JUST A MAN.
AND MEN?
MEN DIE.
YES. THEY DO. BUT...

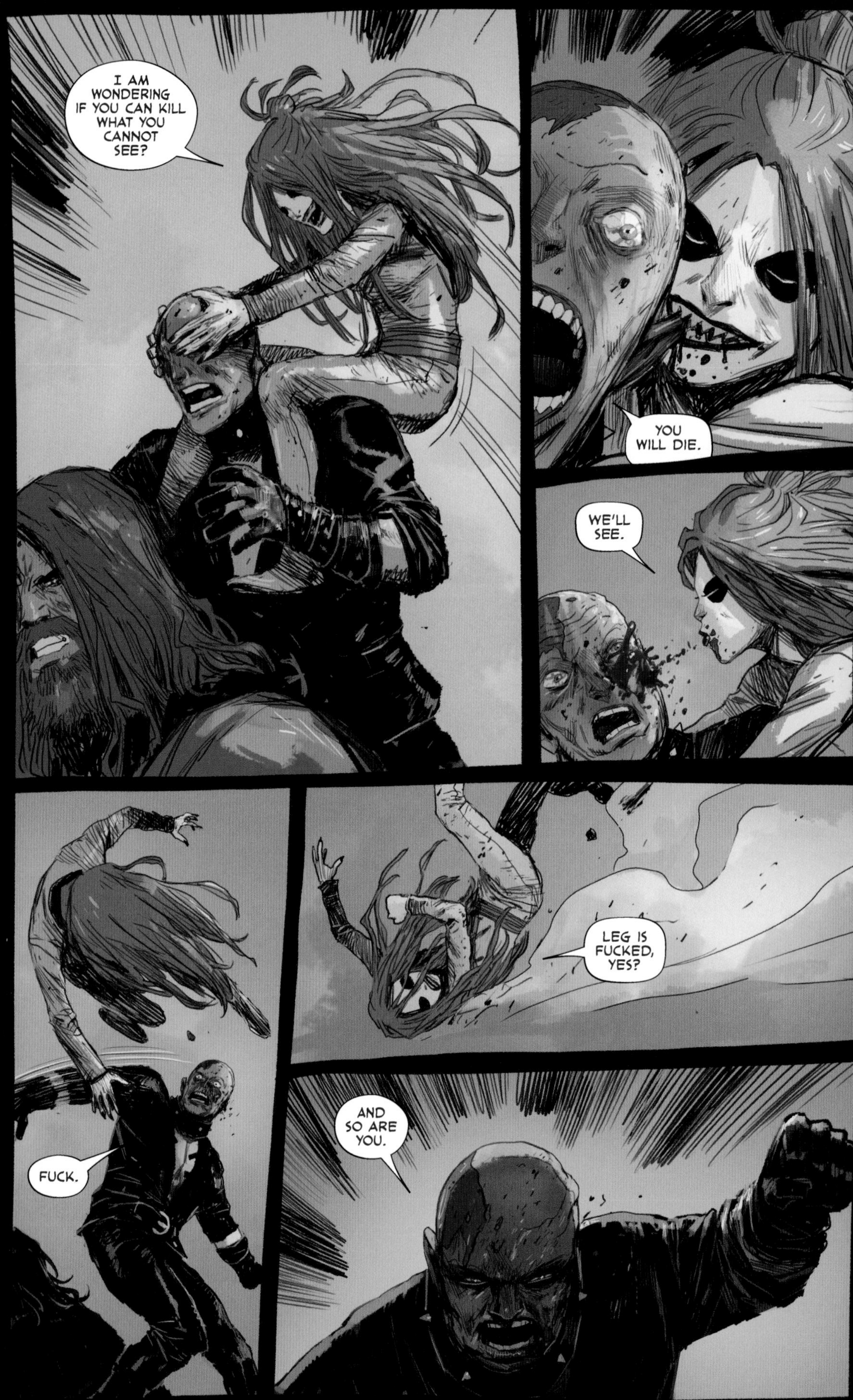
I AM WONDERING IF YOU CAN KILL WHAT YOU CANNOT SEE?
YOU WILL DIE.
WE'LL SEE.
FUCK.
LEG IS FUCKED, YES?
AND SO ARE YOU.

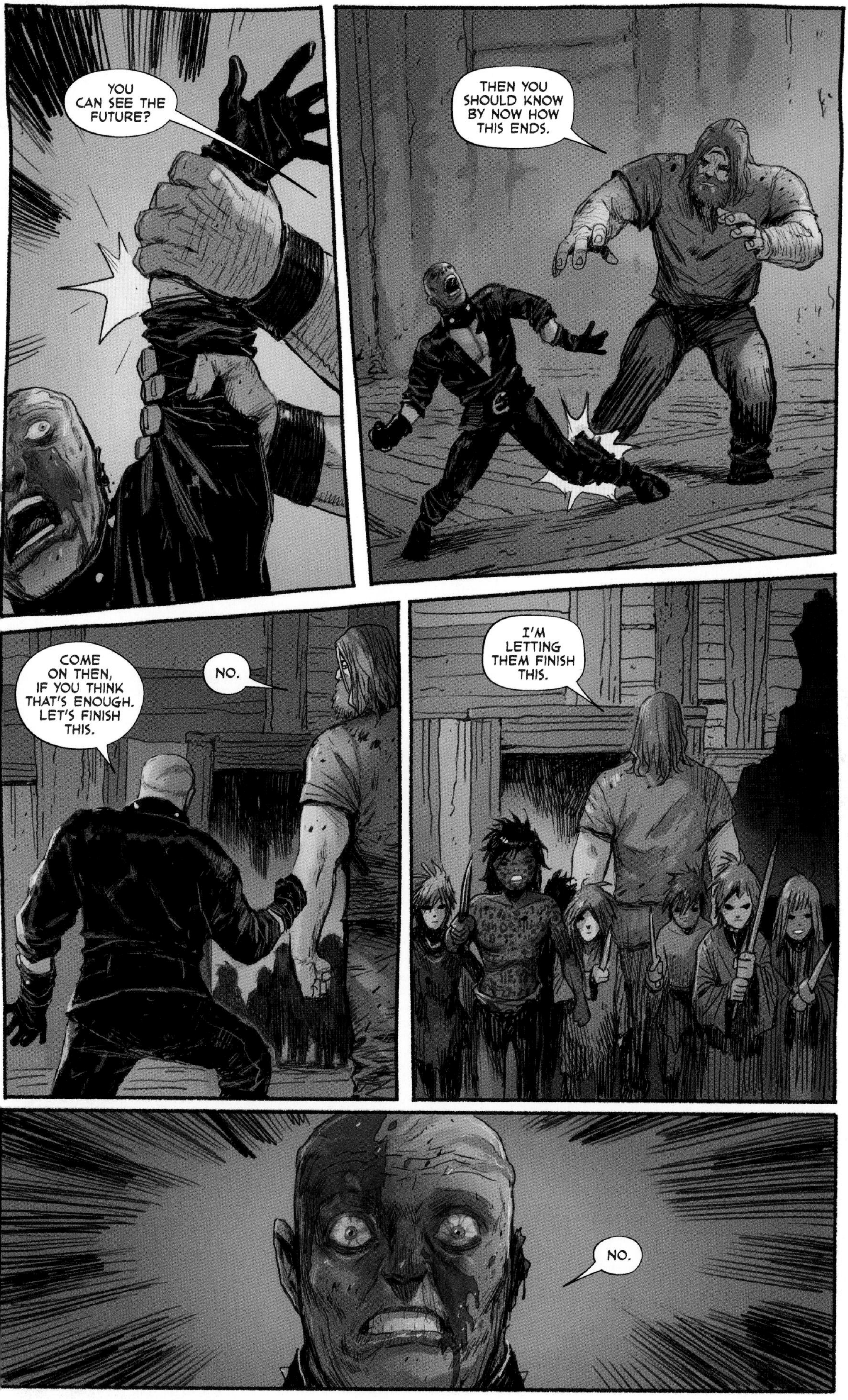
YOU CAN SEE THE FUTURE?
THEN YOU SHOULD KNOW BY NOW HOW THIS ENDS.
COME ON THEN, IF YOU THINK THAT'S ENOUGH. LET'S FINISH THIS.
NO.
I'M LETTING THEM FINISH THIS.
NO.

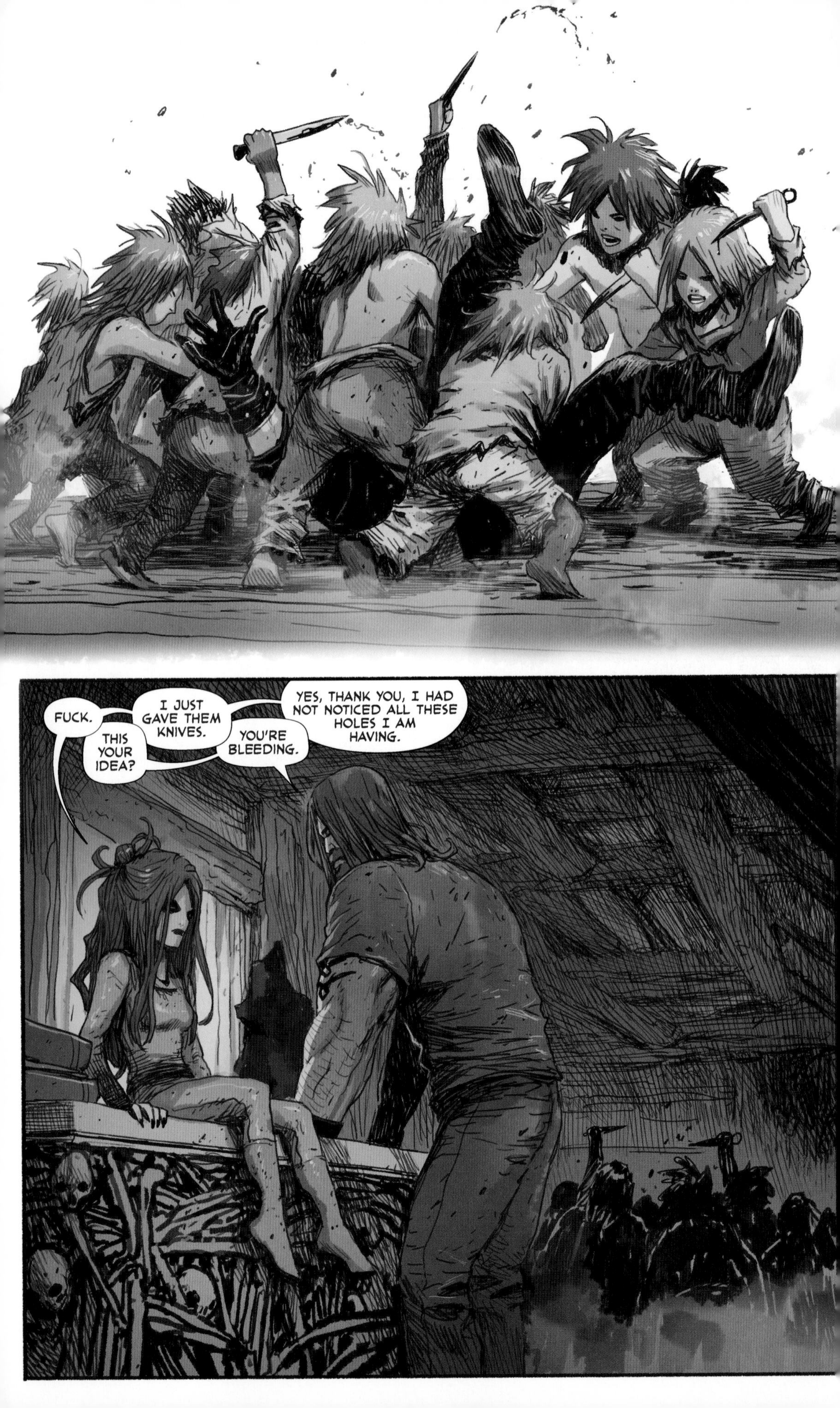
FUCK.
THIS YOUR IDEA?
I JUST GAVE THEM KNIVES.
YOU'RE BLEEDING.
YES, THANK YOU, I HAD NOT NOTICED ALL THESE HOLES I AM HAVING.

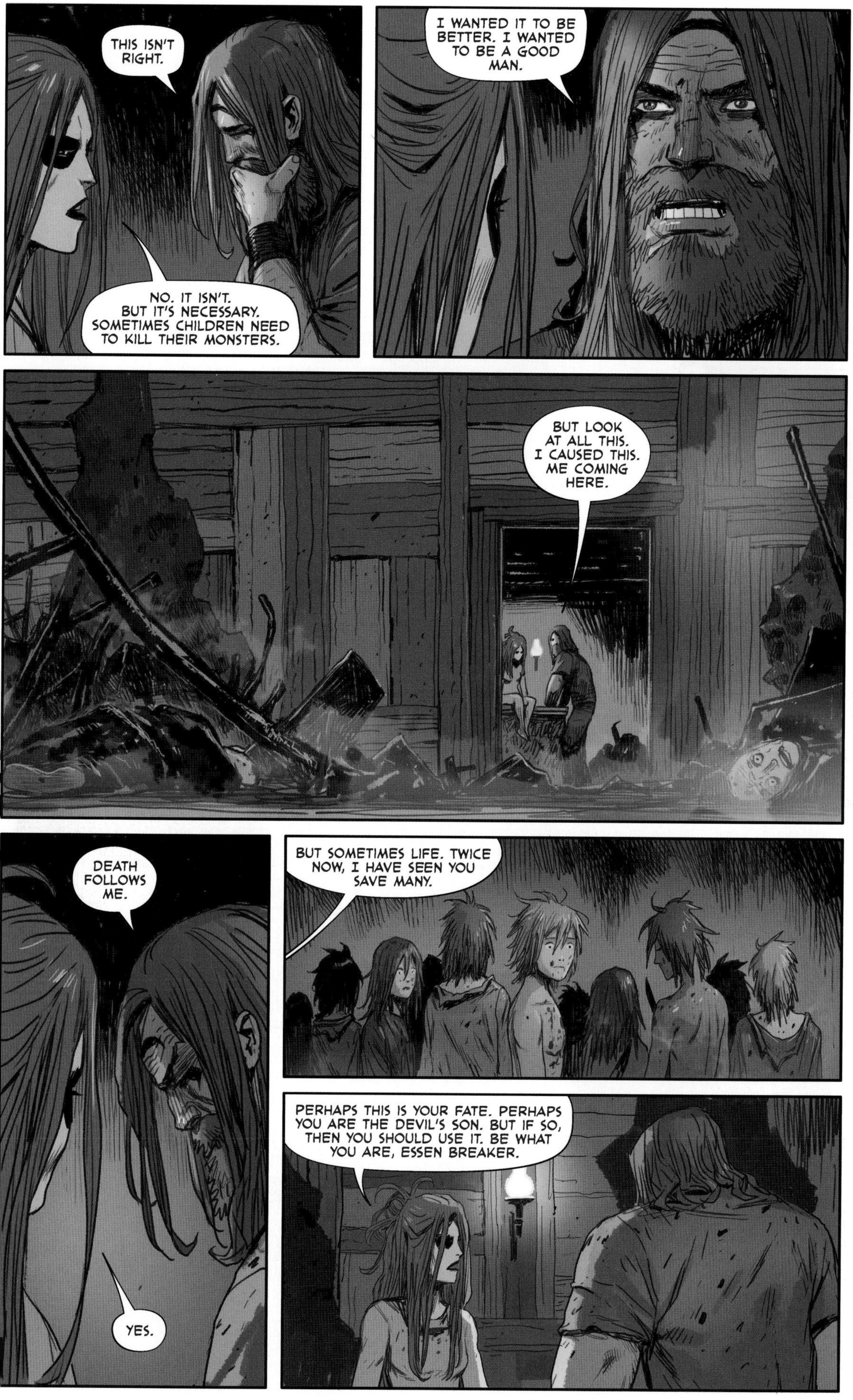
THIS ISN'T RIGHT.
NO. IT ISN'T. BUT IT'S NECESSARY. SOMETIMES CHILDREN NEED TO KILL THEIR MONSTERS.
I WANTED IT TO BE BETTER. I WANTED TO BE A GOOD MAN.
BUT LOOK AT ALL THIS. I CAUSED THIS. ME COMING HERE.
DEATH FOLLOWS ME.
YES.
BUT SOMETIMES LIFE. TWICE NOW, I HAVE SEEN YOU SAVE MANY.
PERHAPS THIS IS YOUR FATE. PERHAPS YOU ARE THE DEVIL'S SON. BUT IF SO, THEN YOU SHOULD USE IT. BE WHAT YOU ARE, ESSEN BREAKER.

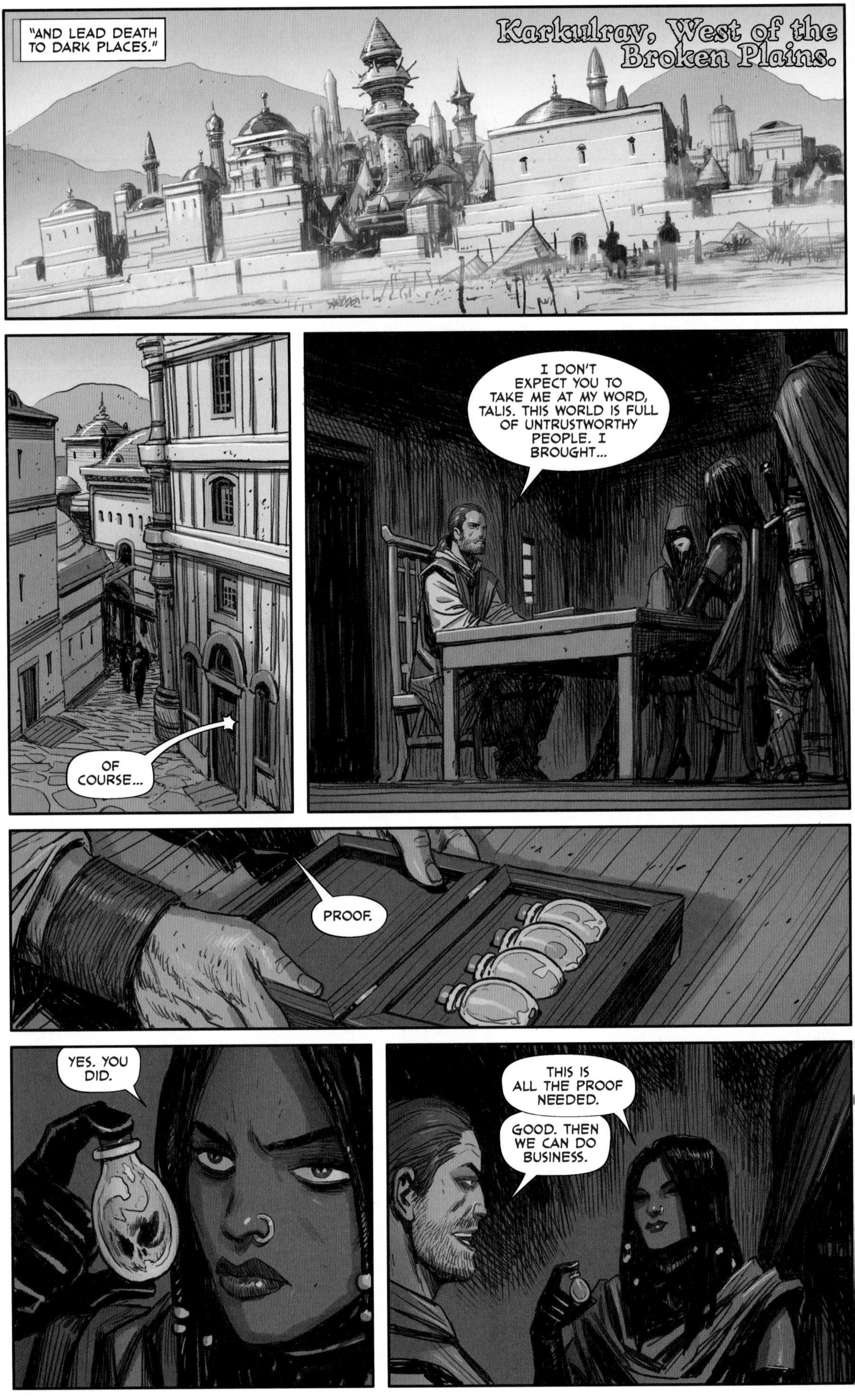
"AND LEAD DEATH TO DARK PLACES."
Karkulrav, West of the Broken Plains.
OF COURSE...
I DON'T EXPECT YOU TO TAKE ME AT MY WORD, TALIS. THIS WORLD IS FULL OF UNTRUSTWORTHY PEOPLE. I BROUGHT...
PROOF.
YES. YOU DID.
THIS IS ALL THE PROOF NEEDED.
GOOD. THEN WE CAN DO BUSINESS.

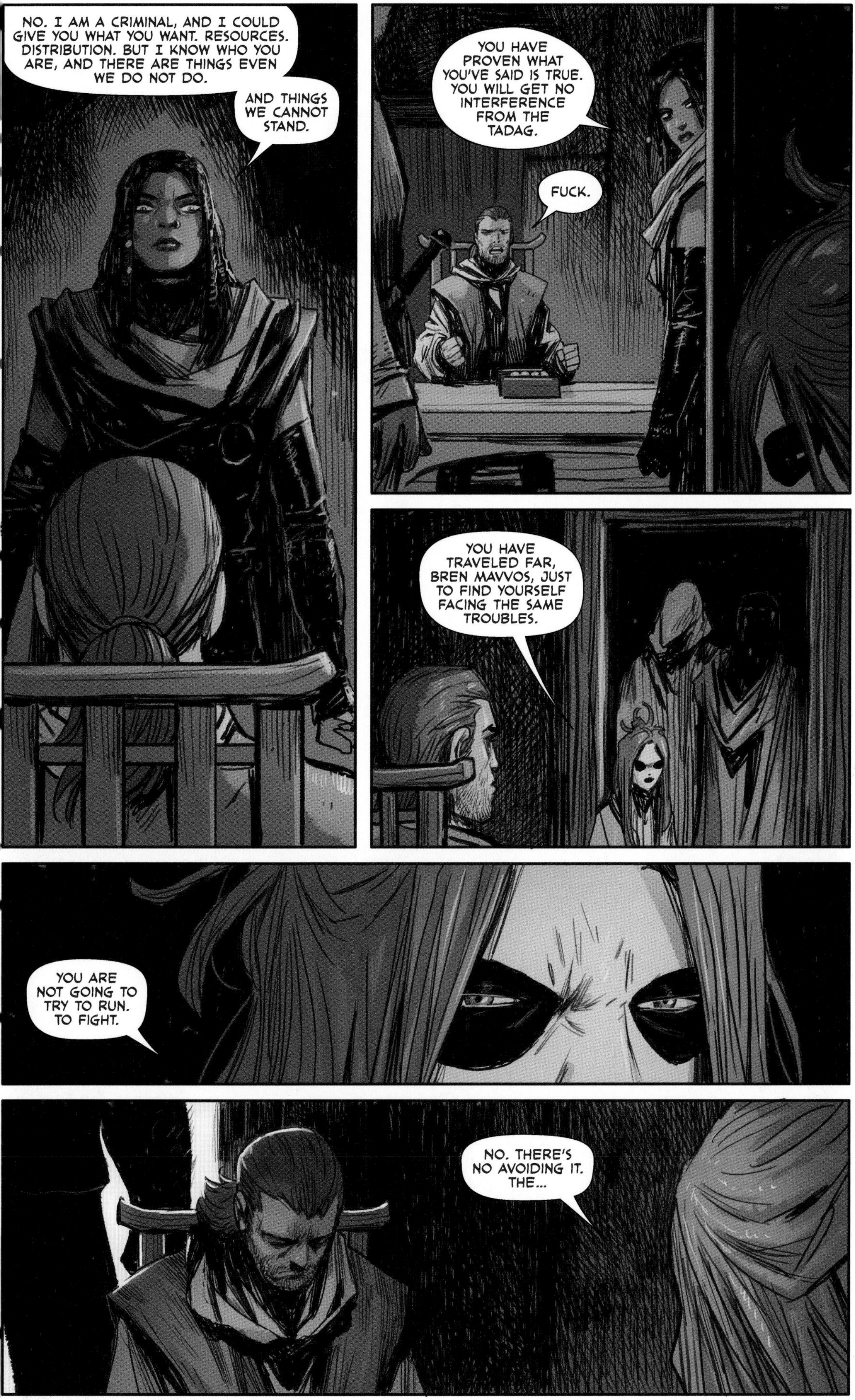
NO. I AM A CRIMINAL, AND I COULD GIVE YOU WHAT YOU WANT. RESOURCES. DISTRIBUTION. BUT I KNOW WHO YOU ARE, AND THERE ARE THINGS EVEN WE DO NOT DO.
AND THINGS WE CANNOT STAND.
YOU HAVE PROVEN WHAT YOU'VE SAID IS TRUE. YOU WILL GET NO INTERFERENCE FROM THE TADAG.
FUCK.
YOU HAVE TRAVELED FAR, BREN MAVVOS, JUST TO FIND YOURSELF FACING THE SAME TROUBLES.
YOU ARE NOT GOING TO TRY TO RUN. TO FIGHT.
NO. THERE'S NO AVOIDING IT. THE...

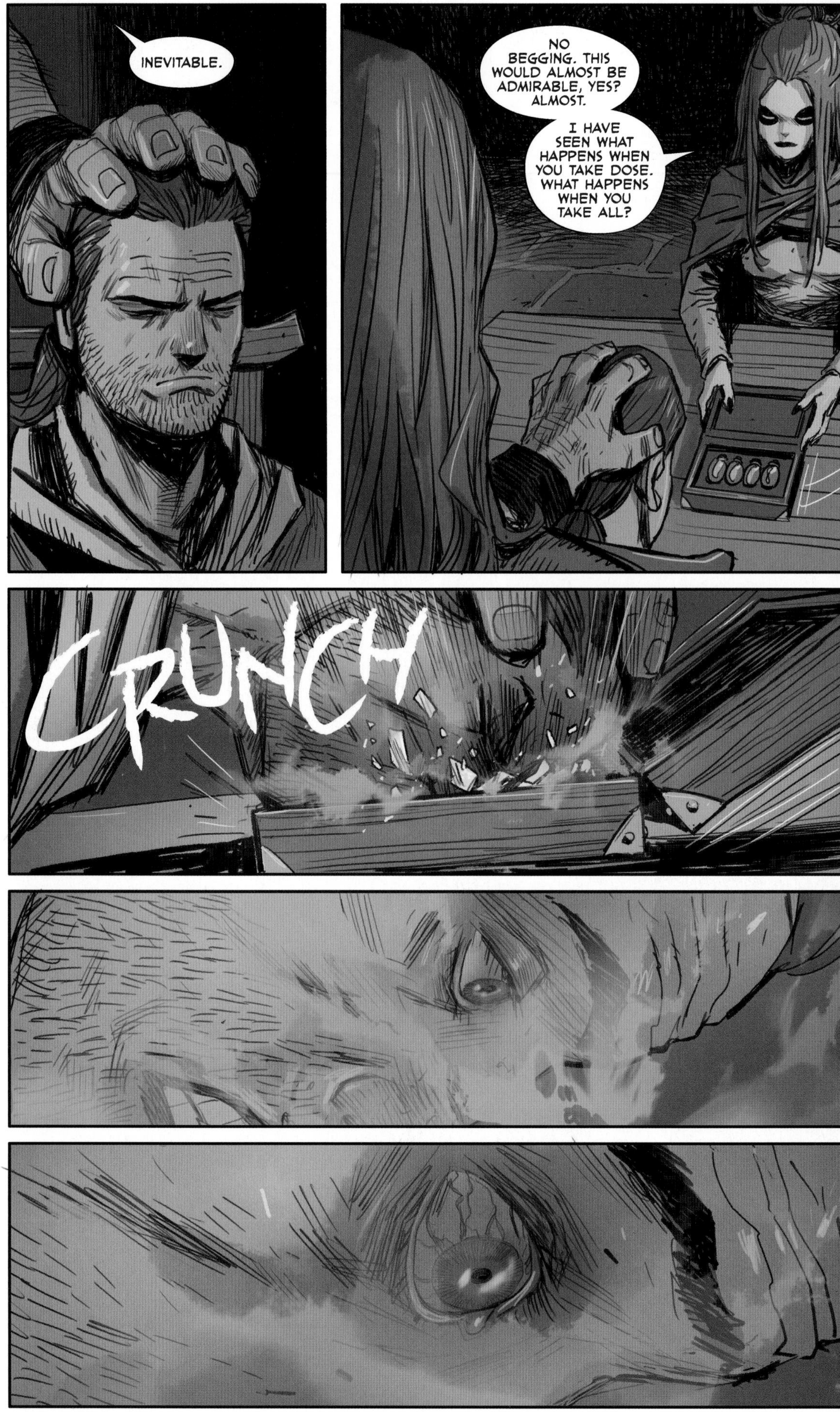
INEVITABLE.
NO BEGGING. THIS WOULD ALMOST BE ADMIRABLE, YES? ALMOST.
I HAVE SEEN WHAT HAPPENS WHEN YOU TAKE DOSE. WHAT HAPPENS WHEN YOU TAKE ALL?
CRUNCH

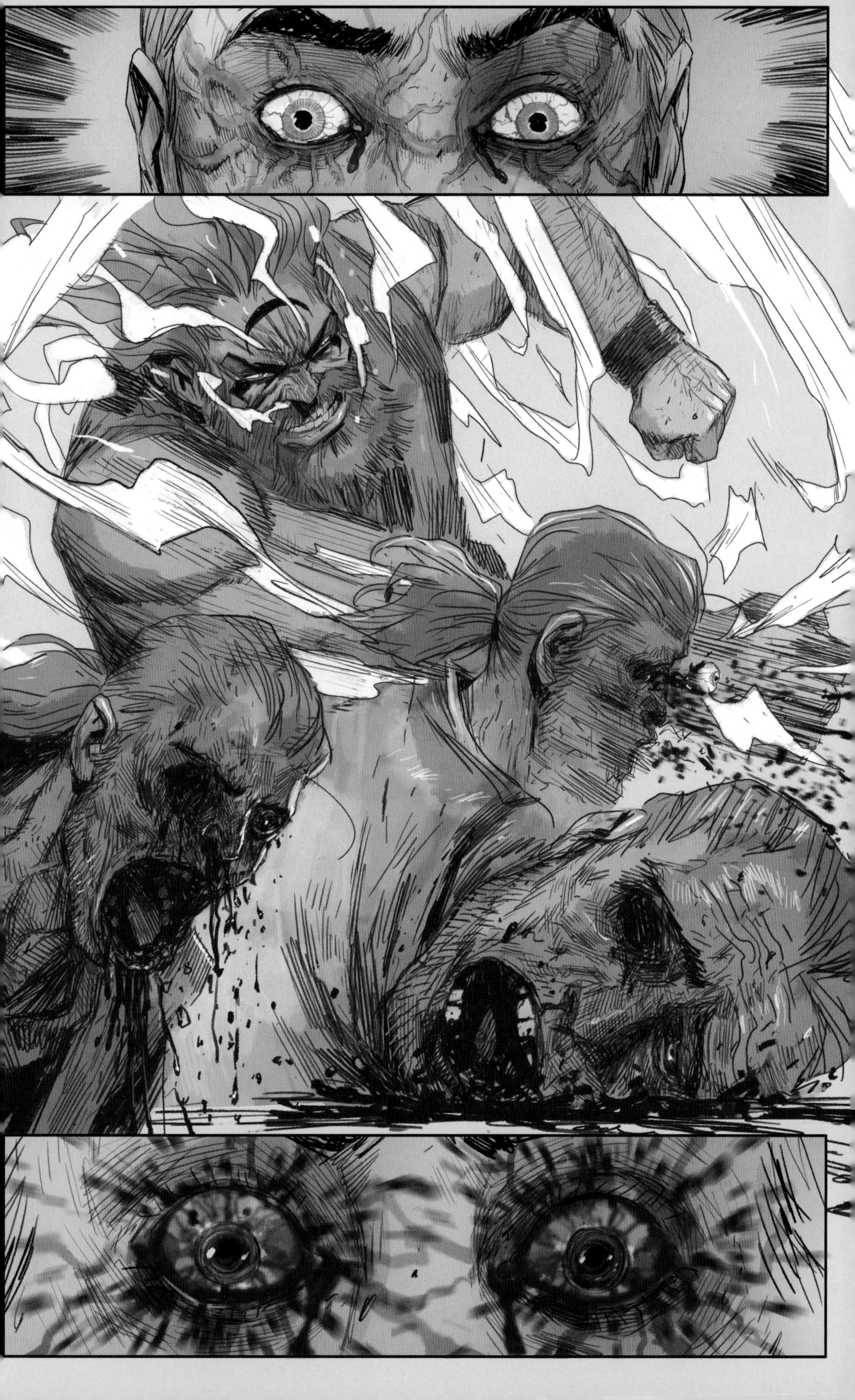

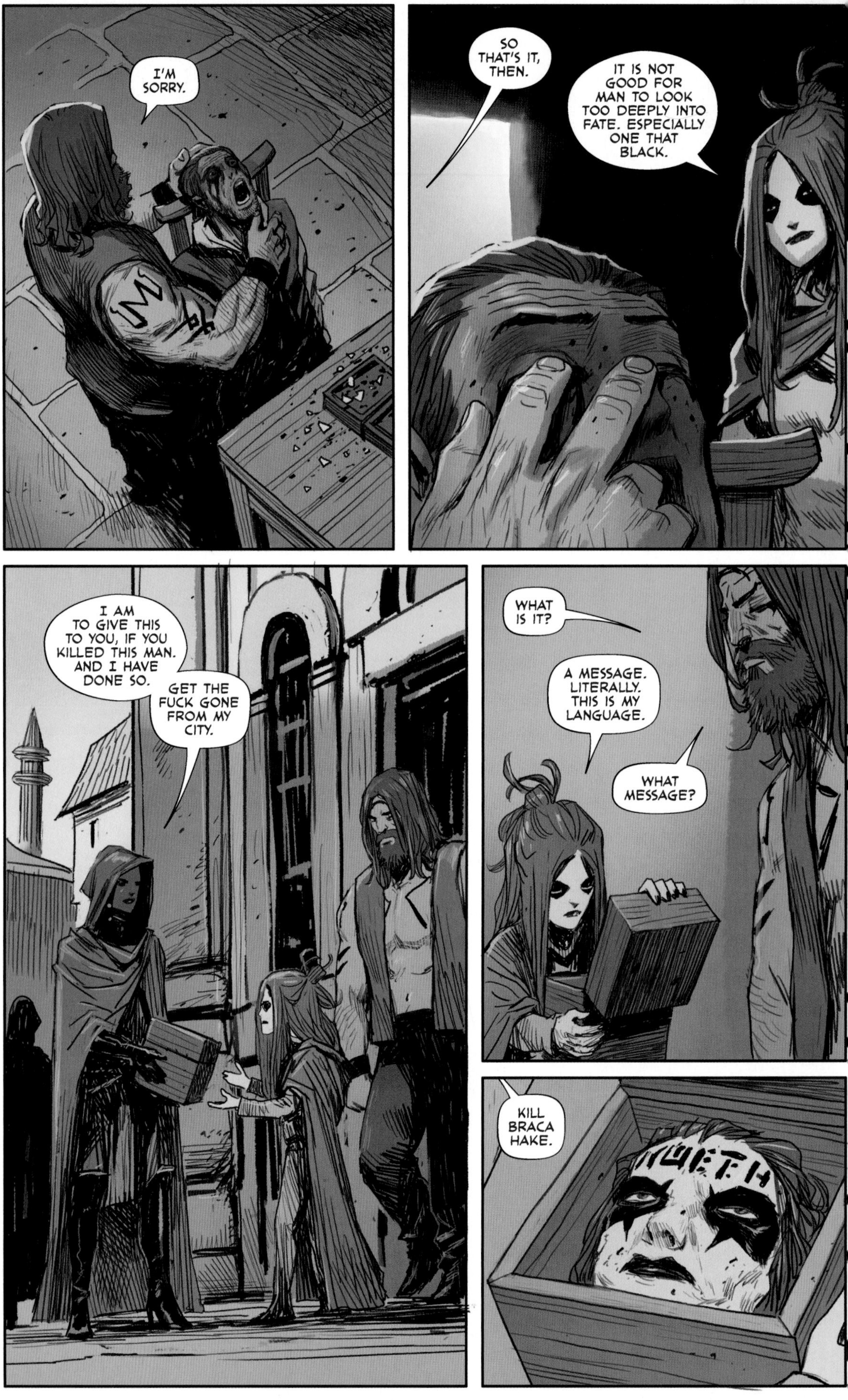
I'M SORRY.
SO THAT'S IT, THEN.
IT IS NOT GOOD FOR MAN TO LOOK TOO DEEPLY INTO FATE. ESPECIALLY ONE THAT BLACK.
I AM TO GIVE THIS TO YOU, IF YOU KILLED THIS MAN. AND I HAVE DONE SO.
GET THE FUCK GONE FROM MY CITY.
WHAT IS IT?
A MESSAGE. LITERALLY. THIS IS MY LANGUAGE.
WHAT MESSAGE?
KILL BRACA HAKE.

TO BE CONTINUED

"I RAN FROM FATE...

...BUT IT FOUND ME ANYWAY."

For more tales from **ROBERT KIRKMAN** and **SKYBOUND**

VOL. 1: KILL THE PAST
ISBN: 978-1-5343-11362-0
$16.99

VOL. 1: PRELUDE
ISBN: 978-1-5343-1655-3
$9.99

VOL. 1: HOMECOMING TP
ISBN: 978-1-63215-231-2
$9.99

VOL. 2: CALL TO ADVENTURE TP
ISBN: 978-1-63215-446-0
$12.99

VOL. 3: ALLIES AND ENEMIES TP
ISBN: 978-1-63215-683-9
$12.99

VOL. 4: FAMILY HISTORY TP
ISBN: 978-1-63215-871-0
$12.99

VOL. 5: BELLY OF THE BEAST TP
ISBN: 978-1-5343-0218-1
$12.99

VOL. 6: FATHERHOOD TP
ISBN: 978-1-53430-498-7
$14.99

VOL. 7: BLOOD BROTHERS TP
ISBN: 978-1-5343-1053-7
$14.99

VOL. 8: LIVE BY THE SWORD TP
ISBN: 978-1-5343-1368-2
$14.99

VOL. 9: WAR OF THE WORLDS TP
ISBN: 978-1-5343-1601-0
$14.99

VOL. 1: FLORA & FAUNA TP
ISBN: 978-1-60706-982-9
$9.99

VOL. 2: AMPHIBIA & INSECTA TP
ISBN: 978-1-63215-052-3
$14.99

**VOL. 3: CHIROPTERA &
CARNIFORMAVES TP**
ISBN: 978-1-63215-397-5
$14.99

VOL. 4: SASQUATCH TP
ISBN: 978-1-63215-890-1
$14.99

**VOL. 5: MNEMOPHOBIA &
CHRONOPHOBIA TP**
ISBN: 978-1-5343-0230-3
$16.99

VOL. 6: FORTIS & INVISIBILIA TP
ISBN: 978-1-5343-0513-7
$16.99

VOL. 7: TALPA LUMBRICUS & LEPUS TP
ISBN: 978-1-5343-1589-1
$16.99

CHAPTER 1
ISBN: 978-1-5343-0642-4
$9.99

CHAPTER 2
ISBN: 978-1-5343-1057-5
$16.99

CHAPTER 3
ISBN: 978-1-5343-1326-2
$16.99

CHAPTER 4
ISBN: 978-1-5343-1517-4
$14.99

VOL. 1: DEEP IN THE HEART
ISBN: 978-1-5343-0331-7
$16.99

VOL. 2: EYES UPON YOU
ISBN: 978-1-5343-0665-3
$16.99

VOL. 3: LONGHORNS
ISBN: 978-1-5343-1050-6
$16.99

VOL. 4: LONE STAR
ISBN: 978-1-5343-1367-5
$16.99